TIME STOPPERS

Also by Carrie Jones

Need
Captivate
Entice
Endure

★

With Steven E. Wedel
After Obsession

TIME STOPPERS

CARRIE JONES

BLOOMSBURY

NEW YORK LONDON OXFORD NEW DELHI SYDNEY

First published in the United States of America in May 2016
by Bloomsbury Children's Books
www.bloomsbury.com

Bloomsbury is a registered trademark of Bloomsbury Publishing Plc

For information about permission to reproduce selections from this book, write to
Permissions, Bloomsbury Children's Books, 1385 Broadway, New York, New York 10018
Bloomsbury books may be purchased for business or promotional use. For information on bulk
purchases please contact Macmillan Corporate and Premium Sales Department at
specialmarkets@macmillan.com

Library of Congress Cataloging-in-Publication Data
Names: Jones, Carrie, author.
Title: Time stoppers / by Carrie Jones.
Description: New York : Bloomsbury Children's Books, 2016.
Summary: Foster child Annie Nobody discovers a new world of magic, power, and scary creatures
in a hidden, magical town, Aurora, where she and her new best friend, Jamie Hephaistion
Alexander, learn it is up to them to protect their new home from those who want to misuse the
great power, even if it means diving headfirst into magical danger.
Identifiers: LCCN 2015022933
ISBN 978-1-61963-861-7 (hardcover) • ISBN 978-1-61963-862-4 (e-book)
Subjects: | CYAC: Fantasy. | Magic—Fiction. | BISAC: JUVENILE FICTION/Fantasy & Magic. |
JUVENILE FICTION/Action & Adventure/General. | JUVENILE FICTION/Humorous Stories. |
Classification: LCC PZ7.J6817 Tim 2016 | DDC [Fic]—dc23
LC record available at http://lccn.loc.gov/2015022933

Book design by John Candell
Typeset by RefineCatch Limited, Bungay, Suffolk
Printed and bound in USA by Berryville Graphics Inc., Berryville, Virginia
2 4 6 8 10 9 7 5 3 1

All papers used by Bloomsbury Publishing, Inc., are natural, recyclable products
made from wood grown in well-managed forests. The manufacturing processes
conform to the environmental regulations of the country of origin.

*For Emily Ciciotte, who believed in magic and
became a warrior, and for Shaun Farrar, who
was a warrior and became magic*

1

The Wiegles

Remember, you're not special, Annie," Mrs. Betsey told the small girl next to her as they stood on the rickety wooden step of the trailer. "Not special at all. So don't go in there putting on airs, pretending you are above these people."

Shivering in the Maine winter air, Annie Nobody wrapped her arms around her skinny body and her bright-yellow polka-dot parka that was a hand-me-up from her last foster home and was far too large around her middle but short in the sleeves. The last person to wear the jacket was nine years old. Annie was twelve; she seemed younger only if you didn't peer closely enough at her to notice the sadness around her eyes. She cleared her throat and tried to sound patient. "I know, ma'am. You already told me that in the car."

"What did you say?" From an oversize pink purse, Mrs. Betsey pulled out her identification card and official papers that proclaimed she worked for the state, placing young people without parents into homes. She clutched the papers so tightly her knuckles turned white. "Speak loudly enough so I can hear you."

"I said 'I know.' I know I'm not special." Annie spoke a little louder even though she didn't want to say the words herself. It made them truer somehow.

"Good. So once again, may I reiterate that this is *the last* time I'll be bringing you to a new family? I mean, really, dear. Is this your twelfth placement?"

Annie didn't want to admit it, but it was. The first family had been the Farrars, who only wanted babies, and the mom refused to ever leave the house. Then when she'd turned two, she'd been sent to the Kerns family, who said that she was too pale and that Mr. Kerns's boss wouldn't promote him if his children weren't good-looking. The Days moved to another state. The Wharffs didn't like how dogs would follow her everywhere. Mr. O'Neill was sent to jail for assaulting a bartender. The Tierneys' house burned down after their daughter cut Annie's hair and left boxing gloves on the stove. The Pinkhams' house burned down, too, after the rabbits started showing up in the heating vents. And so it went.

For as long as Annie could remember, she had been shuffled from one unloving foster home to another. The only constants in her life, for better or for worse, were the equally unloving Mrs. Betsey and Hancock County, Maine, which is where all her foster homes had been. Now, here she still was, this time in Mount Desert, a town with a split personality. In the summer, it was full of wealthy people from faraway places like Connecticut and New York, people with last names on plaques in front of libraries and museums. In the winter, those people went back to their real homes, leaving a town of a thousand or so laborers, lobstermen, teachers, artists, and scientists who worked at Jackson Lab in Bar Harbor. And, apparently, her newest foster family, Mrs. Wiegle and her son, Walden.

Annie couldn't help staring at the Wiegles' lopsided trailer with its dirty white paint and sky-blue trim. She shivered even more. Loud TV noises shook the entire structure. Dogs started yipping inside. Dogs! She loved dogs. Dogs licked you and wagged their tails and let you hug them. They never yelled at you or told you how un-special you were.

"It'll be fine." Annie's voice turned cheerful and even a tiny bit louder. "I'm sure it will be great here. I think they have dogs."

She stood there for a moment hoping she was right, but above her small frame, the evening sky turned a somewhat menacing color. Crows cackled in the distance. The trees that encircled the property drooped from the weight of the dirt and dust and snow. It seemed as if a good wind might topple the trailer down any second.

"Did you see the sky?" Mrs. Betsey ignored Annie's answer. "It's purple. How strange. There must be a storm coming."

Something howled in the woods behind them. Annie scooted closer to Mrs. Betsey, who quickly shirked away, as if Annie's touch would contaminate her immaculate clothes.

Something balled up inside Annie's stomach and ached. It would be good to get this over with. "Did you ring the bell?"

"Of course, I rang the bell!" Mrs. Betsey lied and pressed the button for the doorbell. Her small eyes squinted at the sky. "What a strange sky . . . absolutely strange."

Annie hopped from one foot to the other. Her duffel bag bopped against her shoulders. She glanced nervously into the woods. "Are you *sure* it's the right place?"

"Yes, it's the right place. Would I have walked you to the door if it was the wrong place? I've been here before. Mrs. Wiegle and her son are lovely. They seem perfect for you." Mrs. Betsey shook her head. "If such a thing is possible. Now stop bouncing. You're acting like a nervous rabbit."

A nervous rabbit . . . Annie loved to draw animals—and rabbits especially—but she never thought she actually resembled one. Plus, the problem was that whenever she drew rabbits, or any animal for that matter, they seemed to randomly show up, which was always difficult to explain to foster parents. She eventually gave up trying.

That very morning (when Annie's life began a whole new course and nothing could ever go back to the way it was again), Annie had packed her duffel bag one last time. Inside were the usual boring things: underwear, three pairs of socks, and two pairs of jeans. Also in it were her treasures. There was a journal, not of words but of pictures that she'd drawn when bored, plus several pencils she'd used so much they were merely stubs. There were also some pastel crayons a nice babysitter gave her once after a cranky foster sister at the Blands' slammed a two-by-four on top of her skull. The headache was worth it for the special crayons. They made it feel like magic when she drew, like she was drawing with fairies. She'd rolled those crayons up in a pair of socks that she always kept dirty. That way no one ever found them to steal. No matter how bad the place was, no matter how bad the people were, no one wanted to touch dirty socks.

The people here wouldn't, either, right? She pulled her bag a little closer to her, hugging it against her body.

"We've been waiting forever!" Mrs. Betsey announced, tapping the back of her heel against the step.

"Maybe they aren't home," Annie said. Sadness tightened her throat. "We could come back late—"

The door flew open, revealing a large woman wearing an incredibly tight T-shirt. An ugly boy's face was screen-printed across the cotton/polyester blend. Annie's mouth dropped open.

The woman gushed in a fake cheery voice, "Well, there's our new girl. Oh, she's pretty puny, isn't she? Well, I hope she's quieter than she looks." She plucked the fabric of her T-shirt away from her chest so that they could see the face plastered across it better. "This here is my son, Walden. Isn't he handsome?"

Mrs. Betsey poked Annie in the side with a long gel fingernail, urging her to remember her manners.

"Yes," Annie blurted. "He is."

"No falling in love with him. Only the most special girl can win my Walden's heart." Walden's mother scrutinized Annie, her voice becoming much more stern. "You work hard and listen to your elders?"

Annie's body shook. "Yes, ma'am."

"Good. You're not a whiner or the complaining type, are you? Not a chatterbox?"

"Um . . . I . . ." Annie hopped off the step and tiptoed backward toward Mrs. Betsey's car. But Mrs. Betsey noticed and grabbed Annie's elbow, pushing her up the stairs toward the trailer door.

A ghastly smile mortared itself to Mrs. Betsey's face. "Mrs. Wiegle, so good to see you again. Here's your Annie and your first check. I'm going to run. It appears as if it might storm. I'm sure you two will get along like hens to butter."

Annie turned around, terrified, reaching out to grab the hem of Mrs. Betsey's skirt, but the social worker had already scurried away, hopping into her car, shutting the door, and roaring off.

The taillights flickered as the car rushed over the bumps

in the dirt driveway, and then she was gone. Annie was abandoned. Again.

Mrs. Wiegle hustled Annie into the kitchen and hopped around in a happy dance, holding the check from Mrs. Betsey in front of her like it was a waltzing partner. "Walden! Your new sister is here! And so is the first check!"

Walden heaved himself off the couch and plodded into the kitchen. He rubbed his hands together. "New gold mine, you mean. I can't believe we're getting paid for taking in this nothing, nobody of a girl. It's almost too easy."

He eyeballed Annie up and down as she stood by a crooked stove with a big scorch mark on the front. Six small dogs stopped yapping and all cuddled in next to her shins, like they were trying to protect her from Walden's gaze. She bent down and picked up a poodle. He licked her face. She laughed and hugged him closer.

"The dogs like her," Walden muttered. "The dogs don't like nobody."

"They're nice dogs," Annie said, voice shaking, as she studied the poop-strewn floor and the piles of trash in the corner. Doritos bags and candy wrappers clumped together into little litter mountains. Flies buzzed around everywhere. She shuddered, and the poodle licked her again consolingly. "What's his name?"

"Little Mister Number One," Mrs. Wiegle answered. "That

one sniffing your shoe is Little Mister Number Two. Then the one pawing your pants is Little Mister Number Four. The others are Little Mister Numbers Five, Six, and Seven. We lost Little Mister Number Three to a couch-squishing incident a couple of weeks back."

"Oh. That's horrible. I'm sorry. Um . . . hi, Little Mister Number One," Annie crooned, rubbing her nose against the dog's nose. Little Mister wagged his tail.

"What kind of loser *are* you, kissing dogs?" Walden's voice was disdainful, and he gawked at his mother. "What good is she? Shouldn't they have given us someone better? Her voice is so light and fluffy and annoying."

Mrs. Wiegle pinched Annie's arm. "Tender."

Annie yelped. Her skin already began to bruise.

Walden chomped on a Cheese Doodle–type snack. "I think we should send her back."

"Who are you kidding? We finally actually got someone. It's the dregs for us, and she's the dregs," Mrs. Wiegle said with a gleam in her eye. "This kid is no good, not special at all, and that means she's *perfect* for us."

Annie stared forlornly between the grimy slats of the trailer's cheap vinyl blinds as the first few flakes of snow started to fall. *Home sweet home*, she thought. *Again.*

2

When a Grandmother
Is a Monster

The snow fell hard that night. It fell hard and fast and quiet, as if it were trying to hide not just everything that was happening, but everything that was about to happen. It didn't need to bother. On this particular cold December evening, Annie, the Wiegles, and most everyone else in the little village of Mount Desert was fast asleep. No cars zipped through the tiny mountain range that surrounded most of the town. The shops waiting for winter's end were boarded up—all except for Gut's, the tiny grocery, and First National, the bank. Even the local police station positioned at the bottom level of the Mount Desert Town Office Building was quiet and motionless.

One of the few Mount Desertans still awake that night

was twelve-year-old Jamie Alexander. He lived with his father, Hercules, who scowled a lot, smelled like hate, and was currently working the night shift as a police dispatcher, and Jamie's odd-acting grandmother, Alma. Jamie didn't like to think about his grandmother, because thinking about her made him shudder all the way down to his bones. It was her teeth, maybe, and the way they seemed five sizes too large for her wide mouth. Or maybe it was just her voice and how it cackled and barked, more like an angry dog's than a person's.

None of Jamie's friends, and not even Jamie himself sometimes, could quite understand how the three were related. Jamie didn't resemble his father or his grandmother. He had much darker skin, a much shorter nose, and his bones weren't the kind made for lifting heavy things. He figured he resembled the mom he'd never met and that she was probably African American. His family had only ever said one thing about his mother: she was dead, end of story. Jamie had always hoped there was more to the story, but he wasn't sure. He wasn't sure about much of anything except about how mean the Alexanders were and how worthless his life was, always doing chores, never having enough food, always being yelled at.

Most days, Jamie tried desperately to avoid both of them. But as everyone knows, it's hard to keep away from the people you live with.

Though it was hours past his official bedtime, Jamie crept on his hands and knees across the icy floorboards of his house, making sure to sidestep all the creaky places. He had intended to sneak down to the kitchen to steal some food. He was always hungry, since his father and grandmother rationed his meals, only allowing him to eat canned meat—usually two cans of Vienna sausages per day. But a noise drew him to the bedroom window. He pressed his nose against the pane. As he stared down at the snowy lawn, his breath left him in a quick, excited puff and fogged up the window. He wiped a circle clean so he could see better. It appeared that he didn't need to worry about sneaking around the bedroom. His grandmother wasn't in the house at all. Instead, she was standing out on the side lawn. The wind whipped at her thin, gray hair, yanking it up in straggly strands, and her huge, misshapen bare feet were firmly planted in the icy snow. Jamie had never seen her feet before. She always wore hideous pink running shoes that he thought must be ten sizes too large.

"Why isn't she wearing shoes?" he murmured. He shivered, partly from the thought of it and partly from the cold in his room. His father had duct-taped the radiators shut because he thought heat made boys' bones weak. Jamie's room was so cold he could see his breath make clouds in the air. He was too afraid to take the duct tape off. He was too afraid to do much of anything, usually.

Outside, his grandmother began stomping, which Jamie knew from personal experience was never a good sign. She seemed to be talking to herself. Against his better judgment, Jamie leaned an ear against the window. The cold snapped at him, sending splinters of pain through his skin. He couldn't quite hear what his grandmother was mumbling. But he felt the tremor of something, many things, rattle up from the floor through the walls and window of his bedroom. The thudding vibrations of heavy objects in motion shook the house. And they were coming closer. His pulse rammed hard and fast against his skin as his grandmother clapped impatiently.

Jamie watched silently as fear froze his fingers against the windowpane. Twenty large, ugly people with bulbous noses emerged from the woods at the edge of the yard. They each stood about seven feet tall. They thundered across the property directly toward his grandmother. Jamie almost shouted out a warning, but something inside him, some tiny little nugget of common sense, stopped him.

His grandmother waved them along, and they rushed toward her, green skinned and so much larger than regular people. Their ears stuck out from their heads, and their hands were as large as tigers' paws, with thick fingers that appeared as if they could smash rocks.

They weren't people at all, Jamie realized, forgetting to breathe. They were monsters.

His grandmother jumped with excitement. The creatures caught up to her, and for a moment Jamie couldn't find her among all the greenish-gray skin. Then he spotted her at the end of the line, even taller than normal, her skin tinted both greener and grayer. Her ears and nose had broadened, but it was her. He recognized her fluorescent-orange flowered housecoat and her cackling laugh as she ran off with the rest of the beast things into the dark night.

For a moment, Jamie knelt by the window in shock. His grandmother—his own grandmother—was one of those horrible, awful, scary-looking creatures. He wondered if it was a genetic condition or some sort of werewolf/vampire–style curse. That's what happened in the horror movies his father loved. Vampires and werewolves bit people and turned them into monsters. He hoped that it was the latter because he had no desire to wake up one day supersized and greenish and howling.

"But she would have bitten me already if she wanted to, wouldn't she?" he asked the quiet room, trying to reassure himself.

His stomach growled and Jamie stood up, suddenly realizing that he was alone in the house. *He was alone in the house!* He could go downstairs and eat something without being caught and punished. He rushed across the room, hauling open the door and racing into the hallway. He only wanted some crackers or cheese or something to stave off the hunger pains. Finally, *finally*, he could eat!

He ran past the walls crowded with pictures of his father and his grandmother with their pale-gray skin and large noses with the super-huge nostrils. There were no pictures of his mother. The one time he had mentioned that, he was knocked in the ear and told that his mother, like Jamie, had been far too ugly to pose for the camera. He rushed down the hall and onto the stairs that were crammed with batteries and lightbulbs and radios and flashlights, all totally different sizes and thrown into their respective boxes.

Never can have too many of these babies, his father always said, *just in case of the end of the world.*

Jamie thudded down the rest of the stairs, thinking about his grandmother.

"If she had to be something magical, why couldn't she be something nice like a pixie?" he mumbled. "Cute little wings . . . glitter dust . . ."

He was alone. The quiet whispered against Jamie's skin, a warning not to take too long. His grandmother—his awful, green, too-tall grandmother—could come back at any time. He whooshed into the kitchen and opened the fridge only to see moldy chicken carcass leftovers and half-empty ketchup bottles. He slammed the fridge shut, gagging. His hands shook from anger as he jumped up onto the sticky counter.

Pulling open the cupboards, he grew more determined.

Jamie peered around the all-too-familiar cans of corned beef hash, Spam, and other meat products. He swore he could almost smell the sugar calling to him. Finally, hidden behind canned pork loaf and potted luncheon meat, he found a box of cookies and yanked out as many as he could. His stomach grumbled.

Jamie sighed as he jammed a cookie into his mouth and carefully put the box back, hoping nobody would notice that it was lighter. His pajama bottoms stuck to the countertop, so he pushed off and stood upright in the middle of the dark kitchen. He chomped down on the cookie, savoring it. He'd had sugary treats before; his friend Kekla was always sharing her lunch with him, pretending like he was doing her a favor by helping her eat her food. He whirled back against the wall, moaning happily.

"This is the best cookie ever," Jamie whispered, shoving another one in his mouth.

Something skittered in the walls.

"Mice," he reassured himself, but still he retreated to his bedroom hoping against hope that he would spend the rest of the night alone and that his grandmother wouldn't ever return.

3

Trying to Be Good and Failing

Annie woke the next morning stiff and tired. The night before, Mrs. Wiegle had plopped a dirty mattress on the kitchen floor near the garbage can for her and all the little dogs to sleep on. Even with them cuddled up next to her, she felt horribly alone when she woke.

The television in the living room blared out the local news.

"Strange reports keep filtering in from throughout the entire state, Jim." A woman's voice pulsed from the television speakers, shaking the entire trailer. Annie rubbed at the sleep in her eyes. "Scientists say it might be linked to global warming. The governor thinks it could be a Canadian plot. Citizens of Ellsworth have reported seeing bright little lights flitting around their houses. A resident of Bar Harbor insists that a horde of bats swooped into his house, searched all the rooms, and then exited through the front door."

"Strange," droned a male newscaster's voice.

"ENOUGH WITH THIS! I WANT TO WATCH PUPPY FIGHTS!" Walden roared.

Annie rolled over, itching to peek at the television screen. Mrs. Wiegle was standing over her, hands on her hips. "There's no school on account of the snow."

"Oh," Annie said, sitting up. "Thank you for letting me know."

"That means you are going to have to be here all day with us, and we aren't one bit excited about that, so I think we should set some ground rules so you know what's what around here," Mrs. Wiegle demanded as Annie's heart sank a little deeper into her chest.

"Okay." She wanted to behave well so that the Wiegles would love her, but she was having a hard time even *liking* the Wiegles.

"'Okay' is not good enough," Mrs. Wiegle explained. "It's actions that matter. You want people to love you? You want to be worth something? Then you got to do what we say and be quiet about it. And when I say 'we,' that means me and my darling Walden."

Annie tried to understand. She rubbed her eyes again as

one of the dogs licked her ankle. "Right . . . do what you say and be quiet . . ."

Mrs. Wiegle triumphantly pulled a list out from the deep pocket of her bathrobe. "Here you go."

Annie's hand trembled, but she took the piece of paper. It was smudged with orange fingerprints—remnants of the processed cheese chips, she guessed. Mrs. Wiegle had written in large, curving letters:

RULES OF THE HOUSE

1. Don't talk to us.
2. Don't bother us.
3. Don't make any noise.
4. Be invisible.
5. Above all else, stay out of our way!

Annie had read the house rules, but surely if she did something nice for her new foster family, maybe they'd like her just a little bit? So while Mrs. Wiegle and Walden spent the morning watching TV, Annie tiptoed into the kitchen and did her best to cook the quietest breakfast possible. At her other foster homes the parents usually liked eggs for breakfast. She'd gotten really good at making scrambled eggs. The Wiegles' refrigerator was stocked with eggs, cheese, milk, herring, sardines, Twinkies, peanut-butter cups . . . you name it. She'd never seen such a full refrigerator. After taking out the eggs, milk, and cheddar, she quietly shut the refrigerator door.

"What was that?" Walden yelled from the living room.

"The girl."

"What's she doing?"

Annie froze.

"Making noise," Mrs. Wiegle yelled back.

"Obviously." Walden snorted. "She better be worth the money."

Mrs. Wiegle yelled, "Keep it down in there!"

Annie didn't answer. Answering would be making noise. She was supposed to be silent. She tiptoed to the stove and turned it on. She opened the egg carton in slow motion. But the eggs . . . How would she crack the eggs silently? The little dogs sensed food was happening, and they all came in, yapping. The sound was the perfect cover. She cracked six eggs into the pan in ten seconds. She breathed again. She hadn't even realized she'd been holding her breath. The Wiegles probably thought she breathed too loudly, too.

She dropped some shredded cheddar into the eggs and poured a tiny bit of milk into the mixture. One of the dogs scratched at her shins, trying to get picked up. She wanted to talk to it, but talking made noise. Everything made noise, even stirring the eggs with the spatula, even the eggs simmering. Everything.

How could she be silent?

It was impossible. The Wiegles were never going to love her. Ever. And they would decide that she was definitely not worth the money and that would be it. She'd be rejected again. She gave up, squatted down, and captured the gray dog in a hug. It kissed her cheek. She kissed its nose and went back to cooking.

Once it was done, Annie brought the Wiegles' breakfast into the living room. They were planted on the couch, shaking their fists and ranting as they watched two puppies fight on their wide-screen television.

"Kill him! Kill that prancing poodle!" Walden yelled as Annie placed his heaping plate on the television tray.

She peeked up at the screen and quickly glanced away again, sickened by the sight of the fight. "They won't, will they?"

"Of course they will."

Annie gasped. She crouched down and hugged the Wiegles' own small dogs, worrying. "Isn't that illegal?"

"Not in the country of Hukador, which is where this is broadcast from," Walden said, shoveling food into his mouth.

Mrs. Wiegle pounded her fist on her television tray. "And what the heck is this? Did I tell you to waste my food? No, I did not. I told you to leave us alone. What good are you? I'll tell you what. You're no good at all!"

"Sorry, Mrs. Wiegle. I was trying to help out. I just wanted to do something nice," Annie said quickly.

Right then the puppy fight switched to a commercial break, followed by the alarming jingle of the hourly local-news update. A blond woman with a lot of blue mascara and bright-red lips blathered on the screen.

"Hi, this is Amber Casey with your Channel Five news update. A one-car accident on Route Eleven took the life of an Eddington woman this morning."

The screen flashed to a shot of a station wagon flipped over and in a ditch.

"Cool," Walden murmured.

Annie gawped at him. He didn't notice.

The anchorwoman came back on. "In other news, the Bar Harbor man who claimed that vampire bats stormed through his house has been taken for psychiatric evaluation at Mount Desert Island Hospital. He was treated and released. That's it for now from your First News every hour, on the hour, Channel Five. Enjoy the rest of your show."

"About freaking time," Walden grumped. He noticed Annie. "What are you doing?"

Annie tried to stutter out a "good girl" answer, but she was distracted by the scrambled egg globbed on Walden's chin.

Mrs. Wiegle's eyes narrowed. "Don't you have a doll or something you can play with by yourself? Alone? In silence?"

Annie backed up, shaking her head. "Um, I guess I could—"

"Well, what you waiting for? An invitation?" Mrs. Wiegle laughed. Walden joined in as if it was the funniest joke in the world.

Annie stumbled out of the room, the sounds of the Wiegles' evil laughter pounding in her ears.

After spending the morning on her grungy mattress silently counting the rust stains on the trailer ceiling, Annie thought back to her previous foster homes. That's what Mrs. McLaughlin, a foster mom, once said to do if she felt angry: imagine beauty. The McLaughlins' house was so nice, full of stuffed-animal owls made of felt, and happy yellow walls. She'd really liked it there until Mr. McLaughlin fell in love with the fry girl at Burger King. After that she went to the Cakes', where the mom hit her because she'd used their cross-country skis without asking. Their house burned down right after that. Then it was the Blands. Their house burned down, too, right after Mr. Bland locked her in the basement because thirty bunnies suddenly appeared in her bedroom one morning. She still wondered what happened to those bunnies.

Thinking about all the awful families from before, Annie found it harder and harder to want to stay with the Wiegles, but Mrs. Betsey had insisted that this was her last chance at a home, ever. Now, as she watched Walden shovel what barely passed as a tuna fish sandwich into his mouth, Annie wondered if living in a group home or a jail or anywhere else might not be so bad.

Mrs. Wiegle had made lunch for herself and Walden and said that Annie could make her own after they were finished eating. Walden's sandwich was a drippy mile-high stack that practically defied gravity. Lima beans and pickles were layered between sardines, which sprawled beneath head-cheese, which was squashed beneath gummy worms, which seemed to almost wiggle beneath a thick layer of tuna fish and black licorice. The tuna fish itself was doused in mayon-naise, because Mrs. Wiegle was concerned that Walden wasn't getting enough calcium to make his bones strong. The result was more like mayonnaise soup with tuna flakes.

Annie's stomach flip-flopped. Great globbing glops of tuna snuck between Walden's fingers and puddled on the floor. She stared at the walls of the kitchen, at the black velvet posters of the old rock star Elvis riding a unicorn, at the framed photo of the long-dead actress Marilyn Monroe standing on one foot atop a Siberian tiger—anywhere but at Walden.

In a small, small voice, Annie asked, "Walden, after you're done with lunch, do you want to do something with me? We could go play outside . . . maybe? Maybe build a snowman? Go sledding? Do you like sledding?"

Walden cleared his throat. "Listen, you heard the rules. You're supposed to leave us alone. I don't want to be your brother, and I definitely don't want to be your friend. I don't want to go anywhere with you. If you're needing something to do, go outside to the wolf pen. Teach 'em to do backflips."

"What?" Annie peeped at him, and before she could help herself, said, "Uck."

Pickle juice and mayonnaise were smeared all over Walden's face. Annie's stomach heaved. She quickly focused on Walden's mother instead. A wide smile exposed the woman's gums. She hadn't put her teeth in yet that morning. They were sitting on the counter, on top of a loaf of squishy white bread. Annie made a mental note: *DO NOT EAT THE BREAD.*

Mrs. Wiegle cackled like a witch. She shot Walden an adoring glance. "Isn't it a great idea? Walden thought of it. My boy's a genius, ya know. He is. Brilliant."

She smacked him on the back. He belched.

The odor almost knocked Annie over. She sputtered and waved the fumes away from her face. She spoke as if she were explaining calculus to a two-year-old: "Dogs can't *do* backflips."

"So talky! They ain't dogs. They're wolf hybrids. Big Mister Number Seven and Big Mister Number Nine. Ain't the same thing at all. What kind of stupid are you, not knowing something like that?" Mrs. Wiegle pulled on the lapels of her bathrobe as if she were a supermodel.

"Ma, we are supposed to stay on point. You . . ." He jabbed a finger toward Annie. "Out!"

"But . . . I don't . . . I . . . I can't do that . . . ," Annie said, hopelessly confused and worried. She took a step toward Mrs. Wiegle.

The woman's face turned purple with rage. So did her son's.

"No talking! Be invisible! Do NOT exist!" Crumbs fell off Walden's shirt and onto the floor, but all the dogs ignored them and stood between Annie and Walden, as though each of their six pounds of doggy muscle could suddenly protect her against the Wiegles. The dogs growled at Walden.

"No," Annie whispered, urging them backward. "Don't bite him. He could kick you. You could get hurt."

She backed up toward the refrigerator, bracing herself for the explosion.

But it wasn't Walden who exploded. It was Mrs. Wiegle.

"Why, you ungrateful little turd!" she yelled. "You WILL do as we tell you, you puny little scarecrow!" Mrs. Wiegle's eyes nearly burst out of her face as she continued yelling. "You will be invisible and quiet and nothing, a nothing girl. You WILL go outside. You WILL do what we say. You WILL teach those wolf-dogs tricks. And don't come back until you do! That'll keep you out of our hair for a good long while."

"No, you don't mean that . . . ," Annie started. It was so unfair. Annie clenched her fists, powerless. She was always so powerless. She couldn't choose where to live. She couldn't leave. She had nowhere to go. No one ever listened to her.

Nobody ever loved her, not even the people who were supposed to be her family. She couldn't stand it. She bit the inside of her cheek. "You can't really want me to—"

Mrs. Wiegle shoved her out the door. "No more talking from you, or I'll get my paddle and use it on that tiny little heinie of yours! Out with the wolves with you. Best get started. Out. Out. Out!"

4

Gnome Is in the House

Jamie slept late, after a night of tossing and turning and worrying and fearing. He was curled up in a ball with his one blanket wound tightly around him like a cocoon. His mouth pressed into a tight line. The snow had mostly stopped.

A crow landed on his windowsill, then tapped against it with her beak. One moment later, a huge roar echoed through the house, rattling the windows and causing the crow to hastily fly off, black wings flapping against the wind.

"JAMES HEPHAISTION ALEXANDER!"

Jamie flew out of bed. His feet tangled in his blanket, and he fell to the hardwood floor with an *oomph*, catching himself with the palm of his hand.

"GET YOUR SKINNY BUTT DOWN HERE RIGHT

NOW, OR THERE'S NO TELLING WHAT I MIGHT DO!"

Everything that had happened the night before suddenly came rushing back, and Jamie wondered if he had been dreaming. But deep down, he knew it had all been real, and his grandmother was not just the kind of human who seemed monstrous because she was so mean, but another sort of monster altogether. One more thought crossed his mind: *my grandmother has definitely come back.*

He had really hoped that she would stay gone.

"Crud." Jamie untangled himself from the blanket. His right palm pulsed red and hot where it had hit the wood floor. A splinter had thrust into the skin right below his thumb, but he had no time to deal with that now. He never had time to deal with anything.

"JAMES HEPHAISTION ALEXANDER, I AM WARNING YOU!"

He swallowed hard, mouth dry, and stood up, throwing open his bedroom door and hustling down the hallway and to the stairs. His heart beat wickedly quick, each beat a warning and a memory of the night before.

"I will pretend she is not a monster," he whispered as he hurried past the pictures of her and his father out hunting on Schoodic Mountain, past the piles of batteries mounded on the floor. He tried hard to convince himself. "I will pretend she's not—"

Two huge hands took him by the neck of his T-shirt, lifting him off the stairs. His head almost touched the ceiling. He glanced down, cringing. Several pieces of twigs had stuck in his grandmother's thin, gray hair. Dirt smudged her right cheek. The smell of chickens wafted off her clothes, her hair, and her breath. Jamie did his best not to gag as she glared up at him, her light-blue eyes fixed upon him.

"What kind of slug are you, boy?" she whispered, and her whisper was much scarier than her roar. Jamie gagged as she asked, "What took you so long?"

"I—I—I'm so sorry. I was sleeping," he managed to croak as his feet waved about in midair.

"Sleeping?!?" Her nostrils flared.

Jamie nodded. It was all he dared to do. A dust bunny rolled on the floor past his grandmother's feet, blown by a draft from the front door. She stomped on it, still clutching Jamie's T-shirt. The fabric began to tear from the strain.

"You are such a stupid thing," she finally said, dropping him to the floor. "A very stupid, wimpy thing. You're afraid of everything, aren't you? Even your own family. Even your own shadow, aren't you?"

He crashed with a thud at her sneakered feet. The moldy smell of foot fungus caused him to skitter backward on his butt until he hit the bottom stair and couldn't go any farther. He didn't even think of telling her that his best friend, Kekla, said that "stupid" was a hate word and he agreed.

He certainly felt pretty hated when his grandmother called him that.

"Stupid, stupid, worthless boy," she said, making the word "boy" seem like some sort of insult. "Grab the toothbrush you used to clean the dinner dishes and go clean the toilets till they shine. Don't let me catch you wasting a good sponge when that toothbrush has plenty of clean left in it! No school today, so you should have plenty of time to do that and clean the shower, too. Use my old underwear, the ones with the gold stars on the back. The toothbrush is too small for the shower."

Jamie's hands flattened against the hard, cold floor. His mouth dropped open. "No school?"

If there was no school then he'd be stuck with her for the entire day.

"Nope. Too much snow, they said." She stretched up to her full height and stared completely away from him. "I ate a lot last night, and something about eating a lot makes me terribly hungry. It's an endless cycle. Eat. Get hungry. Eat more. Get more hungry. Eat. Eat. Eat! So go about your cleaning right now. You best skedaddle."

She callowly cackled. Her hands went to her hips, and she leaned over until her face was right in front of Jamie's small, scared eyes and her large, hungry mouth was just inches away from Jamie's own quivering lips.

A wicked glint shimmered in her blue eyes.

"Or," she said, stomach growling like a lion on the hunt, "would you prefer I just eat you?"

She stood up again, cackling even more loudly, turning back upstairs, and Jamie rushed off toward the front door. He was not giving her the chance to eat him. No way. *Not that she would*, he thought. *Right? Right?!? No, never. Grandmothers didn't eat their grandsons. That was ridiculous.*

As he started pulling on his boots, he peeked behind his shoulder. His grandmother was nowhere in sight. The television blared the day's news from the other room.

"Twenty-five chickens were found without heads in the little town of Mount Desert this morning," the newscaster said. "Police have no leads."

Jamie's stomach flip-flopped. Those poor chickens. Headless. Dead.

"Also, a local townsperson reported the theft of a treasured lawn gnome from her front yard," the male reporter continued.

The newscast switched to a woman's voice: "That gnome has been in my family for over one hundred years. My grandmother said it brought us good fortune."

The speaker sounded kind, older, and intelligent, as if she thought through each word before saying it, sort of like the school nurse.

"And now it's just gone," the voice concluded.

"Ha!" his grandmother shouted. "Sissy woman. You had

it long enough. Snivelers don't deserve lawn gnomes—don't deserve nothing, I say. You hear me, Jamie? Snivelers don't deserve nothing!"

Jamie knew well enough to respond, and he did. "I hear you."

"Hurry up and get to work before I eat you!"

Jamie's grandmother had said things like this his entire life. It always freaked him out, but he never thought she was actually serious. Now? He wasn't so sure. He didn't think about it long because he noticed a splotch by the door. There was some sort of feather stuck to the floor and . . . Yes, there it was. A deep-red splotch like . . . like . . .

"Blood," Jamie whispered, jerking backward and hitting his hip on the umbrella stand.

"Son?" His father, Hercules Alexander, appeared at the door, still in his dark-blue Mount Desert Police Department work shirt. Coffee stained part of it an even darker blue. Mr. Alexander loomed there for a moment, his rugged body taking up the entire frame of the doorway.

The Alexanders, aside from Jamie, were a large kind of pale people that seemed to suck the air out of the room the moment they entered it. They demanded to be noticed. And *would* be noticed even if they weren't so large and loud and smelled so much like fried pork products mixed with locker room toilets. And they liked it that way, too. But Jamie? He knew it was safer to be invisible. Nobody could eat you that way.

Jamie stared hard at the floor, deliberately not catching his father's eye. Sometimes that provoked him.

"What is going on in here?" his father asked in a voice that was both deceptively quiet and calm.

"Grandmother wanted me to go out," Jamie lied, quickly shoving on his coat. He'd get in trouble for sure, but the toilets and shower would still be there to clean later. And so would the filthy toothbrush and his grandmother's underwear.

His father rubbed the stubble on his chin. "Did she now?"

Jamie couldn't remember how to speak. Fear robbed him of his voice.

"Well, you best go do that. Double time, boy. Double time," he said as Jamie shoved on the paper bag he used for a hat and moved toward the door.

But something caught his eye, something that had never, ever been there before. A miniature ceramic man was perched against the door, dried blood on its red hat and a sad, sad look in its eye. Its blue clothing was smudged with dirt. A little tear smeared its cheek.

"He looks how I feel, poor guy," Jamie murmured.

A beefy hand whacked him on the back of the head. Jamie stumbled forward from the blow, barely managing to avoid hitting his head against the wall.

His father's voice roared into his ear so loudly that Jamie was sure his eardrum would tear apart and explode from the force of it. "WHAT ARE YOU DOING, YOU HORRIBLE,

POINTLESS BOY? GAWKING AT THE DOOR? GET OUT!"

"Oh, um, yes . . . yes, sir," Jamie stuttered and hurried out the front door and past the sad-looking lawn ornament.

The snow had given way to blue skies by the time Jamie left the house. It was frigid out, an icy cold that freezes your nose hairs together and makes air feel like shards of broken crystals. Of course, Jamie didn't have a knitted scarf or gloves.

"Waste of money," his grandmother would say. "So what if you lose an ear or a nose. It'll build character. Plus, yarn isn't good for my digestion."

His grandmother and his father hated spending money on Jamie. If it wasn't illegal to go to school naked, he wouldn't have any clothes at all. It didn't matter, Jamie decided. Nothing mattered. Just getting out of the house and away from them was good enough.

He stopped at the end of the driveway and stared up and down the road. There weren't any cars tumbling about. Mount Desert was like that after a storm. Only the snowplows moved, rumbling around like giants, shoving snow onto sidewalks.

He had few options. He could roam around aimlessly, or he could walk to the library and try to figure out what those creatures were last night. Or, more specifically, what his grandmother might be. Libraries kept books about everything, and if he was lucky, maybe Mr. Nate, the librarian, would let him stay there awhile among the dusty volumes and dog-eared newspapers and pet iguana. Jamie often hid out in the library after school, and, though he never really talked to Mr. Nate, he saw how kind and gentle he was with everyone. *That's exactly what I could use today*, Jamie thought. *Some kindness.*

Something howled in the distance, and Jamie's shudder grew so big that it threatened to take over his entire body.

Jamie chose the library.

The Mount Desert Library perched on top of a hill above town, directly across from Jamie's school. A former sea captain's home, its white clapboard walls reached up for three stories. A widow's walk sat at the top so that people could stare out to sea, hoping for ships to come safely back to the harbor. Nobody was allowed up there anymore, not that Jamie knew of at least. *It seems safe there, though*, he thought, *like a good vantage point in case monsters are coming.*

Monsters.

Monsters like his grandmother.

The thought stopped him dead still. A normal kid would be able to tell his dad what he saw his grandmother do, but Jamie guessed he'd never actually been a normal kid. A normal kid didn't *have* a grandmother who became a monster. A normal kid would have a loving dad. Now that he knew how un-normal he was, there was nothing to do but deal with it.

Jamie's eyes closed for the briefest of seconds, and he wished with all his might that the world could be just the tiniest bit less freaky. He opened his eyes again and bounded the last few yards to the library. Mr. Nate would help him sort this all out. He had to.

Jamie was running so hard that he couldn't stop quickly enough on the snow-covered porch. He slammed into the white wooden door of the library. With a painful *oomph*, he fell backward. A piece of fluorescent-orange paper fluttered off the door onto his shirt.

LIBRARY CLOSED TODAY DUE TO STORM.

What? No. It couldn't be. Desperation sank in. Jamie stood up and pounded his fist against the door.

"Hello?" he called. "Hello!"

Something like panic filled his voice. Thoughts of headless chickens seemed to flood his brain.

"Please!"

The door swung open. Mr. Nate stood, tall and lean, wearing a dark shirt with a wool suit jacket over it and what appeared to be suspenders underneath. There was also a bow tie involved. His face was folded into lines of concern, and Jamie worried that the concern was about having to talk to a child. His grandmother and father hated having to do that. They said it was dull.

"Come in! Come in! Jamie Alexander, is it? Paper-bag hat? No mittens? How horrible." Mr. Nate ushered Jamie inside the library and out of the cold. "Although, I suspect you'd rather wear gloves than mittens. More manly, right?"

Jamie nodded, too confused to really know how to respond. He cleared his throat, feeling a new sense of urgency. He had to tell someone about last night and who better than a librarian, a person who dealt with stories and facts, who had access to old knowledge as well as new. "Mr. Nate . . . I have something to tell you. It's . . . it's important."

"Of course! What is it about? Let me guess . . . girls? . . . dogs? . . . parental relations? . . . school bullies?" Mr. Nate chattered as he brought Jamie past the stacks of new books by the front door, and then past the children's room with its reading dinghy and giant papier-mâché giraffe. The lights weren't on, and the building was lit from the white sun coming in through the windows. "Are you hungry? I expect you're hungry. I can hear your stomach growling through your clothes. No worries. I have sandwiches in my office, which is in through here."

There was nobody at the broad, shiny circulation desk. A clock clicked. The windows behind it showed the woods. Nothing seemed to move out there. Nothing at all.

Mr. Nate led Jamie into a small room crowded with books.

Tools and mops hung on shelves and in corners. A wooden cuckoo clock was suspended on the wall, ticking loudly. The room smelled of sawdust and pickles. An old-fashioned radio was disassembled. Pieces of electrical equipment were scattered along a wooden table marred by graffiti. In carved letters, BETTY proclaimed her true love always to LEW, and others decided that SCHOOL SUX. The result of it all was a jumbled, homey mess.

With a giant sweeping motion of his arm, Mr. Nate moved most of the electronics off the table to make room. While Jamie watched, the thin man opened up the door to a tiny refrigerator and began pulling out food.

"Deviled eggs . . . hummus . . . carrot sticks . . . Let's see . . . grilled cheese, pre-grilled and still warm despite the refrigeration . . ." He quickly set the items down on the table.

Something seemed to murmur from within the fridge.

"What was that?" Jamie asked as Mr. Nate slammed the refrigerator door shut.

"Oh . . . that? Just a radio." Mr. Nate's eyes opened a little too widely. Jamie could tell he was lying.

"It seemed like it said, 'Eat me!' and 'Nobody likes sprouts.'" Jamie blushed. It sounded ridiculous when he said it aloud. He imagined his story about his grandmother might sound even more ridiculous, actually, and he had momentary second thoughts about telling Mr. Nate what had happened. But, no . . . He had to tell someone.

Mr. Nate handed Jamie a sandwich and plopped into a rickety chair painted bright yellow and covered with glittery sticker stars. He enthusiastically bit into his own sandwich. "Really? How odd."

Jamie was about to say that it was odd to have a radio in the refrigerator in the first place but realized that would be kind of rude. Plus, he was incredibly hungry and the grilled cheeses smelled so good. He grabbed one. It was warm in his hand. "Thank you."

"No problem!" Mr. Nate sprang out of his chair, reached into the fridge to pull out a jar, and quickly slammed the door shut again. "Pickles! I forgot the pickles. You can't have a meal without pickles. Even breakfast. I love pickles and pancakes. How about you?"

"I've never had them," Jamie confessed, biting into his sandwich.

"Which? Pickles or pancakes?"

"Neither." Jamie had already finished his sandwich. It was so good.

Mr. Nate slammed his hand on the table. It made a huge noise, startling them both. "Why, that is just incalculably wrong!"

Jamie had no idea what to say. He offered, "It's okay. Do you mind if I have some carrots?"

"It is not okay! No!" He quickly corrected himself as Jamie snatched his hand away from the food. "You can have carrots, of course! It *is* wrong that you've never had pickles! Pickles are the elixir of the gods! And you may have whatever food you like, young Jamie Alexander. Do you like baked goods? My Helena is the best baker in existence. Better than Gramma Doris, but you can't tell Doris that. Someday you will have to sample her pies."

Jamie grabbed some carrot sticks and chomped. They tasted fresh, like spring. He couldn't believe how good they were. He wasn't 100 percent sure what Mr. Nate was going on about, so he tried to get back on track. "So, um . . . I was hoping I could maybe tell you about what happened to me last night . . . Well, not *to* me . . . More like what I saw happen."

"Of course," said Mr. Nate, making up another plate of carrots, "I would love to hear it."

"It might sound a bit unbelievable." His splinter throbbed in his hand.

"Nothing is unbelievable."

"Well, you haven't heard this," Jamie said and then cleared his throat dramatically. The sound startled him, and he coughed in an awkward way before finally beginning. "I woke up in the middle of the night . . . Well, it wasn't the exact middle . . . and there were noises outside . . ."

Mr. Nate leaned forward, elbows on the table. "What kind of noises?"

"Like giants running," Jamie said, studying Mr. Nate's expression. He didn't seem shocked. "So, I snuck out of bed and to my window. My grandmother was standing in the snow. She had no shoes on."

He paused as his mouth dried out. What if Mr. Nate didn't believe him?

"Go on." Mr. Nate petted Jamie's hand.

"She was excited . . . like she was waiting for something to happen, and then these huge things . . . these . . ." Jamie coughed. He closed his eyes and said, ". . . these monster things came out of the woods and they surrounded her and then she was one . . . She was a monster."

The room was silent. Jamie peeked open one eye.

Mr. Nate had both hands in his own hair and was scratching it furiously, the same way he did when he was trying to think of the perfect spy book for a fourth-grade book report or when he was trying to find a good early reader that wasn't about misbehaving pets or dinosaurs on the loose. "I see."

Jamie gulped, opened both eyes, and blurted out the rest of the story—about his grandmother running off with them, about the chicken feathers and blood, about how she always talked about eating him, and that's when Mr. Nate stood up, yelled "Aha!" and stopped the story in search of a book.

"Do you believe me?" Jamie whispered as Mr. Nate scavenged through a couple of rolling bookshelves.

"Of course!" Mr. Nate scoffed. "What kind of person would I be if I didn't believe the story of a starving boy in mortal danger? But more importantly, what kind of librarian would I be?"

"Does the book you're trying to find have something to do with what happened last night?" Jamie asked as Mr. Nate abandoned the bookshelves and moved toward the kitchen area again.

"Yes . . . yes . . . You could say that it does . . ." Mr. Nate pulled a large, ancient-looking book out from underneath a toaster oven. The cover was a cracked leather that seemed maroon. Gold framed the binding. The room suddenly smelled of knowledge and dust and campfires.

Mr. Nate flipped open the book and pointed to a picture. A fairy with a very sneaky face was slipping through the window of a house. She held a baby in her arms. He tapped the drawing. "See this? These are changelings. There are millions of stories about them. Fairies would trade human babies for their own sickly children, abscond with the humans, and nobody would know any better."

Jamie swallowed carrot bits and processed this information for a moment, trying to figure out what the word "abscond" meant. Steal? Why was Mr. Nate telling him this? "Um . . ."

Mr. Nate went terribly still and stared him in the eye. "This is about you, Jamie Alexander."

"Are you saying that I'm a fairy changeling?" Jamie tried to reason this out. It was kind of unbelievable. "No offense,

Mr. Nate, but my dad and grandmother don't really seem like the fairy type."

"True." Mr. Nate flipped through the pages of the book, obviously searching for something important. "But there are other creatures that they do resemble, other creatures that have been known to steal human children," he said while his fingers moved through the thick, yellowing pages.

"Why?" Jamie's voice shook. His fingers clutched a carrot, but he'd forgotten he was even holding it.

Mr. Nate's glasses dangled from the tip of his nose. He stopped flipping the pages. The wooden clock on the wall sang out a cuckoo, and a tiny bird appeared from a little hinged door. "Why what?"

"Why do they steal human children?"

Jamie's free hand balled into a fist on his lap, but he leaned forward, waiting for an answer.

"Oh . . . well . . . it's never good, of course . . . never good to steal in the first place, but to steal children . . . that's the lowest of the low . . . Some towns have a history of . . . Yes . . . right." Seeming to recover from the question a bit, Mr. Nate flipped through the book again and found what he was searching for. "Aha!"

He tapped the page with an enthusiastic finger, and turned the book around so that Jamie could see it right side up. "Look familiar?"

Gasping, Jamie could only motion that it was. The creature

in the center of the illustration appeared to be exactly like the beasts he'd seen the night before, grayish green and ugly, larger than basketball players. The creature held the severed body of a child in its meaty hands, and its mouth dripped drool or blood. Jamie couldn't tell quite which.

"Thought so," Mr. Nate whispered in a terribly serious tone. "How many years have they been there? Right under my nose. And did I see them? No. No. What a fool! An ignorant fool, and with you, poor thing, right there with them."

"Wh-what is it?" Jamie asked.

"It's a troll."

Jamie's mouth moved but no words came out. He rubbed at his forehead, forgetting he was holding a carrot. It broke in half and fell to the floor, rolling into a radio. He picked it up, and then he finally managed to say, "A . . . a . . . troll . . . A troll?"

Mr. Nate nodded.

Jamie slammed up out of the chair and began pacing furiously, back and forth and back and forth. "You're telling me that my grandmother is a troll?"

The side of Mr. Nate's lips pressed together, and once again he gave only the slightest of nods.

"That's unbelievable!" Jamie protested, but even as he said it, he knew that it truly wasn't all that unbelievable.

"All that makes something unbelievable is the unwillingness to believe," Mr. Nate admonished.

"Okay . . ." Sometimes Jamie felt like he had no idea what Mr. Nate was talking about. It didn't matter anyway. What mattered was that Jamie *had* seen trolls last night on the snow. He *had* lived with his grandmother his whole entire life, and he knew she was mean and beastly and not at all like other grandmothers. And the apple didn't fall far from the tree, because his dad was . . . Jamie swallowed hard and met Mr. Nate's eyes. "My father? Is he . . . ?"

"Most likely."

Jamie slouched back into the chair, utterly defeated. His useless, horrible life made sudden sense. He finally dropped the remaining pieces of the carrot back on the plate. Images from his whole life shuffled in front of his brain: all the times they'd made fun of him for being puny, the way they'd lock him in his room, the way they'd pinch his arms or even slap him in the head, and the way they never loved him. Jamie always thought it was his fault, that it was ridiculous to even dream of a different life because he didn't deserve one, but maybe that wasn't it at all. Maybe it wasn't that he was unlovable. It was just that trolls weren't capable of love.

Mr. Nate's face loomed right in front of him. "I think you will have to leave that house."

Jamie's head jerked up. "What?"

"Just what I said. I think you need to leave that house. And soon." Mr. Nate's big hand clamped down on Jamie's shoulder. "There is danger there."

"There is danger everywhere," Jamie said slowly.

"True," Mr. Nate said, tapping his fingers against the wall. "But most of the time danger doesn't pretend to be your relatives."

5

Into the Wolf Pen

Annie toppled out of the trailer and into the backyard-turned-dog-kennel, yelping. The Wiegles' two gray wolf-dogs backed away from her, momentarily too surprised to do much else. Everything in the dog run was muddy from the wolves' pacing back and forth all day and night. Paws trampled any plant life that might have grown. A tall fence encased the entire area. The only way in or out was through the trailer door.

She stood up. Snowy mud caked her jeans and feet. Mrs. Wiegle had thrown her outside before she'd gotten a chance to put her sneakers back on. Some dirt scraped across her socks. She shivered and pulled her shirtsleeves down so that they would cover her hands. Panic found an empty room inside her heart.

She knocked on the door. No one came.

She pounded on the door. No one came.

She smashed her head against the door, denting it. Walden came.

"What?" One beady eye and half a nose peeked through the crack in the door. "You are annoying me, girl. Remember? You aren't supposed to exist. You are a nothing girl. Be quiet and act like a good nothing."

"I need my shoes." She put her shaking hand on the metal door handle so that he couldn't shut it again. Her head killed. "Walden, I really need my shoes."

"Too bad." Walden smirked.

Something inside Annie hardened up. Being good and following the rules was definitely not working out for her here. "My feet are freezing, Walden. Let me get my shoes. Please."

"Tough tigers, twit," he muttered. "You're interrupting my TV viewing. You're as annoying as all those boring news alerts about bats and wolves howling and crud."

Annie stared at him. *It can't be easy being so ugly,* she figured, *but he'd be okay-looking if he didn't squint his eyes so much, or spit at people.* Still, he was so awful inside, all filled up with venom like some sort of nasty snake. She asked the question before she thought better of it. "Walden, why are you so mean?"

He glared at her. Then for a second he sighed and his face

softened, making him seem like a regular boy . . . almost. It only lasted for a second.

"It's more fun than being nice," he roughed out. "Maybe you'll figure that out someday. See where *nice* has gotten you?"

She almost thought he had a point, but she shook the thought away as he yanked the door shut, wrenching her arm. She let out an irritated roar.

Groaning, she sank down on the step with her back to the door. At least the sun was shining. And then, of course, as if on cue, a cloud came from behind the trees and covered the sun up. It grew instantly colder.

"Great," she muttered. "Great. Great. Great."

The two gray half wolves turned and growled. They slunk toward her, tails out straight, heads down. They bared their teeth.

Annie froze. Then her heart began beating again. Then her brain started working again.

"Oh," she said, jumping up. "Sit, doggies. Sit. Sit! Sit?"

The two wolves did not sit. The two wolves came closer.

Annie pivoted to the trailer door and pummeled it with her fists.

"Walden! Mrs. Wiegle! Help me! I think the dogs are going to eat me! Please, please, please come to the door!" she screamed. "Please, come to the door!"

But, of course, no one came.

A massive snarling noise drew the wolves' attention to the edge of the kennel, just beyond the enormous metal fence. A large white dog flew through the air. He launched beautifully over the enclosure and landed in front of Annie, protecting her. He growled a warning rumble that made the wolf-dogs' fur stand up on end.

The wolf-dogs leaped. The white dog met them in the air. A snarling mass of white and gray fur snapped and tore at one another.

"NO!" Annie screamed. "Don't hurt him."

There was a great fury of limbs and teeth. Tufts of fur flew up into the air, and Annie hurled herself forward, trying to tug at fur, trying to pull them apart.

"Stop fighting!" she ordered. Her voice came out powerful, focused and strong, so loud that the Wiegles would definitely hear her. "I said, 'No fighting!'"

Miraculously, they stopped. All three canines flopped on the ground, panting. The two gray wolves had patches of fur torn from their haunches. Blood crept down the white dog's shoulder.

Annie yanked in her breath. Worry plunged forward into her heart. "Oh."

She stood a foot away from the white dog and reached out her hand toward his injured shoulder. "Oh, you got hurt."

Something rumbled in the forest. As they all held their breath, the wind thrust the tops of the trees into one another.

Annie swayed, too, then steadied herself and closed the gap between her and the big white dog. "I'm hoping you're nice, right? Good doggy. Good, good doggy."

She glanced at the other two that remained almost frozen in place. Embarrassment and anger contorted their jowly faces.

"You two better not move," she commanded.

One of the big wolves whimpered.

"I mean it. I totally hate fighting. And you forced him into it, making like you were going to attack me. That was just plain evil mean."

The midday sun cast a glow, illuminating the savior dog as a bright, white, glowing mass. Even his ears gleamed as Annie approached. His deep fur moved in perfect, long strands as the wind smashed against him, but he ignored it. Standing motionless in the middle of the pen, chest sticking out proud, head up high and eyes opened wide, he stared right at Annie. And he kept watching as she crept slowly forward. Her feet had gone numb from the cold. Tears dripped from the dog's eyes, but he was smiling. She was sure of it.

"What are you?" Annie breathed out. Her hand wiggled for the dog to smell. The dog came forward, gazed into her eyes with its own, brown and mysterious and still. He licked her hand, and Annie remembered what it was to be warm. She buried her other hand inside his fur. He licked her face and wagged his tail so hard that his whole body wriggled.

She searched for a collar. None. She wanted to yodel. He could be hers. They could be a team. He could keep her safe. She could hug him and play with him, and he could be her friend. She'd never been in one place long enough to make friends, but now . . .

"Come," she said, leaping up and tapping her leg to make the dog understand. "You can come with me. We'll go together, okay? I don't actually have a place to go, really, not a home or anything." She gestured unhappily behind her toward the trailer.

Walden's voice echoed through the window. "I AM SO SICK OF NEWS FLASHES! I DO NOT CARE! YOU HEAR ME, NEWS LADY? I DO NOT CARE!"

Annie swallowed and turned away from the trailer. "I thought that this would be home."

The dog nuzzled her side with his big black nose, and Annie plunked her hand on his warm back. Her heart cartwheeled inside her chest.

"You're hurt." She shot a glance at the hybrids and then parted the white dog's fur, searching for the source of the blood, a long gash, probably from one of the wolves' claws. "That's horrible."

She shook her finger at the other canines. "You should be ashamed of yourselves."

The wolf-dogs whined but didn't move.

She whipped off her sweater and pressed the white dog's wound. "That should stop the bleeding, I hope."

She kept the pressure on the dog's fur as she peered around the pen. In his happiness, the dog kept trying to lick her hand and her face. She wished she could be happy, too, but she was too worried to give in to the good feeling. "The Wiegles will just lock you up and turn you mean like those poor wolf-dogs. I've got to get us out of here. But how?"

The wind suddenly raged louder and much more wildly, whisking Annie's long hair across her face. She shivered and plunged her hands deeper into the white dog's fur, her stomach aching from worry.

Annie and the dogs spent the rest of the day out in the yard. Finding no backflip progress, Mrs. Wiegle refused to let Annie inside. She barely even noticed that a third dog had appeared. Annie pounded on the door. She begged. But Walden and his mother just turned up the television so they wouldn't hear her cries. There was no way they were letting her back in the trailer until she taught the dogs to do the impossible. To be fair, the wolf-dogs tried to flip but they were too big and too heavy to do little dogs' circus-style tricks and kept flopping onto their backs and thudding on their sides.

Eventually, as it grew darker Annie gave up and focused instead on surviving the night. She found some dog biscuits in a coffee can in the yard and split the contents between the three dogs. It wasn't enough but it was something. She dragged a blue tarp to a corner that seemed the most sheltered from the wind. The dogs huddled over Annie to keep her warm. The white one seemed to boss the other ones around and kept nuzzling Annie and blowing in her face to keep her skin from freezing. Still, the cold seeped into her bones.

The wind smashed harder, bending trees. Something moved in the woods just beyond the dog fence. All three dogs bolted up, standing in front of Annie, staring ahead at the woods. Shivering, she scrambled to her frozen feet, and clung to the white dog, trying to stay upright.

"We have to get inside," she yelled. The wind swallowed her words. She struggled backward with the dog, trying to use the trailer as a wind block. Inside, Walden and his mother laughed at a television show, nice and cozy, oblivious to what was going on in the wolf kennel.

Annie glanced up at the forest. She hoped the trees wouldn't fall on her or the dogs or the trailer. *Okay, it would probably be an improvement if a tree fell on the trailer. But what is that moving toward me through the woods? Is it a man? A bear?*

She pounded on the trailer door. "Mrs. Wiegle! Mrs. Wiegle, let me in!"

The laughter inside continued. They wouldn't come. Annie was alone. She threw her arms back around the white dog, who stared at the woods expectantly, tension rippling through his muscles.

"What is it?" she whispered into the dog's ear. "What's out there?"

He growled. Whatever it was came closer. Annie swallowed hard. There was nowhere to run.

Horrifying noises from the woods thrust toward them. Frantically, Annie searched for a way to get out of the dog pen.

"Dogs!" she yelled and steered them toward the fence closest to the driveway. "We are going to knock this over."

For a moment, she felt bad about breaking the fence, but she had to survive. Working together, the dogs and Annie heaved and pushed. One gray dog threw himself into the fence, over and over again. It rattled from the force of his weight, but didn't buckle.

A nearby tree crashed to the ground.

"Hurry!" Annie kicked at the fence.

The dogs whimpered and cried, and then, as if realizing there might be a better strategy, they all began to dig in the same spot. Snow and hard clumps of mud flew up in the air behind them. Annie watched the woods, eyes wide with horror. Trees fell over as if shoved by a mighty hand. The path of destruction was coming closer and closer, headed straight for the dog pen and the Wiegles' trailer. She froze.

Something wet wrapped around her hand. The white dog's mouth was pulling gently but urgently on her fingers. The other wolf-dogs had already crawled through the hole and were racing down the driveway, not glancing back.

Annie slammed onto her belly and scurried through the hole. The white dog followed behind her. She tried the front door, which was unlocked, and screamed into the trailer, "Something's coming! Something dangerous!"

The little dogs streamed outside, scattering. Annie grabbed her coat and shoes, smashing them onto her wet feet as quickly as she could. "You have to hide!"

Mrs. Wiegle appeared in the living room. "I told you to be quiet! What are you doing in here? Where are the dogs? What did you do with the little dogs?" She held the TV remote in her hand like a weapon.

Annie tried one more time. "You have to run! There's something in the woods!"

The rumble of destruction came closer.

"Hurry!" Annie yelled and raced out the door with the white dog at her side. She rushed ahead, down the driveway and away. Behind her, metal ripped away from metal. A roof thudded to the ground. Windows shattered, spreading glass into the snow. It sounded as if the Wiegles' trailer was being torn apart, but she didn't dare stop to look, or even turn, because whatever could do that to trees and a trailer, could do much worse to a girl and a dog.

Annie and the white dog veered off the main road. She figured there would be more places to hide there. The snow made it harder to run, but they kept at it for a while before she finally allowed them to slow down.

Annie reached out for the dog and plunged her fingers into its thick fur. He was still hurt. She had to do something. She stopped walking.

"I need to peek at your wound," she said.

The dog gave her big, brown, sad puppy eyes, but sat down and moved so she could see his shoulder. The skin around the cut was ripped and a bit ragged, but not deep.

"Does it hurt?"

The dog shook his head. Annie gasped.

"Do you understand what I'm saying?"

The dog nodded.

The shock of it all knocked Annie backward a few steps. "That's amazing! Oh my gosh. You are THE MOST amazing dog, ever!"

She reached her hand out slowly. The dog licked it, which made her giggle despite everything—despite the fact that they had no home, that they were lost in the middle of the cold, that they had been attacked. A dog's lick can make you forget all that.

"We have to fix up that wound. I don't have any bandages, though, and I think the snow has cleaned it out. It's sort of scabbed over, but I don't want the scab to come off." She searched around for something to cover the wound, but it was all just snow and tree trunks and tree branches. *Oh! My socks!* She was wearing long soccer socks that were super stretchy. She leaned against a tree to keep her balance and took off her shoe and then her sock. First one, then the other. The frigid air stung her skin. The dog whined in protest.

"Nope. I'll be fine," Annie reassured him as she wrapped the socks around his frame, covering the wound and tying the ends together. Once she was done she wiped her hands together proudly and ignored the stinging pain in her feet. "Good. Let's go."

The dog whimpered at her.

"No protesting," Annie said. "You have to be taken care of. Everyone needs that. Everyone except me."

The dog lifted an eyebrow.

"I mean it. I am just fine taking care of myself, but you . . . You're hurt and it's going to be dark soon." Annie's voice grew concerned. "It will be colder even than right now. We have to find somewhere for shelter."

If she couldn't find shelter, she and the dog would die from the cold. One of her foster dads, Mr. Sundberg, had been heavy into television survival shows like *Naked and Alone, Terrified on an Iceberg,* and *How to Survive Everything When You Have Just a Toothpick.* In the survival shows, when they were in winter-frozen places, they would make a shelter out of tree limbs and snow. First, she had to find a flat spot, which wasn't easy since Maine is a hilly state and there are a lot of little mountains in Mount Desert. Finally, she found a spot that seemed okay. She lifted her head to the sky, to determine where downwind was, since she didn't want the snow to fill up the hole. Then she plopped onto her knees and started digging a cave tunnel. The coldness of the snow seeped through her knees and her hands.

"We need it to be about a foot longer than me, maybe, and about three feet wide."

The dog helped, but it was cold, hard work, and she was shivering fiercely, trying to find some sort of body heat.

"It's so cold," she said, and tried to make her voice light and cheery. "But we'll survive. We'll totally be okay."

Annie crawled into the whiteness of the snow cave and hoped she wasn't lying. The dog scooted in beside her and pressed his doggy bulk into Annie's side for warmth, nudging his long muzzle beneath Annie's head so she could use it as a pillow.

Wrapping her arms around his fur, Annie said, "Thank you. You are the best dog ever."

She breathed in the smell of wet dog and snow, and actually, despite everything, happiness dripped into the corners of her unloved heart. She'd escaped the Wiegles and whatever had been in the woods. A dog nestled into her side. She was sort of, kind of, warm, and she felt sort of, kind of, safe, and then even though it was still quite early in the evening, she fell sound asleep.

6

Running Away

Jamie eyed his house warily as he walked away from the library. He had spent all day in the cozy place, reading all the books about trolls that he could, and it was dark already—long past when he was supposed to have been home. The windows of his house, and of the other dwellings on the street, glowed with yellow lamplight. A terrible quiet encased the world.

Shivering, Jamie contemplated what to do next. Mr. Nate had said it was dangerous for him at home, and deep down he absolutely knew that was true. He and Mr. Nate had agreed to meet again at the library tomorrow. But after that, what then? Where could he go? How far would he have to run to escape his family? There were a lot of factors to think about.

a. It was the middle of the winter.

b. He was pretty sure it was some kind of illegal to run away when you were two days away from being thirteen.

c. Running away right this second didn't seem an intelligent thing to do in the dark. Things are always worse in the dark. Those trolls came last night in the dark.

d. Staying in a house of trolls wasn't a good idea either.

He hauled in a deep breath. The cold stung his lungs. There was no way around it. He'd have to spend at least one more night with his family. He was almost thirteen. That meant he'd already spent over 4,105 nights in the house with them anyway, and he'd survived, right? He was all in one piece, right?

Right, he told himself. *Right.*

Still, his hand shook as he turned the doorknob and creaked open the front door. His heart beat a hopelessly scared rhythm against his ribs as he stepped into the front hall. And his lips pressed together in a hard, frightened line as he shut the door behind him, stomped the snow off his shoes, and gazed at the little-man figurine.

"Everything going okay here?" he whispered to it.

It didn't answer.

He was pulling off his shoes when a loud voice boomed just above his ear. One shoe dangled from his hands as he turned to see the large, jowled face of his father.

"You took forever, boy! Out gallivanting, huh? Well, we're hungry. Get out of sight while we eat dinner!" Mr. Alexander smiled as he spoke, but it was not a nice smile. It was a predator's grin. Jamie couldn't believe he'd never noticed that before. His father's leer broadened, showing thick, solid teeth. "Better hurry, before we give up and just eat your skinny butt."

Jamie's face must have fallen, because his dad reached out and punched him heartily in the shoulder. "Just kidding, boy! Just kidding."

But as his father turned away, Jamie doubted it. The Alexanders really didn't have good senses of humor.

It wasn't until bedtime that Jamie got another chance to think. He'd been too busy avoiding the jabs and stings of his father's and grandmother's words. He could only stand being called a "tablecloth of a boy" so many times. He didn't even know what that was supposed to mean. *A tablecloth?*

From his bed, Jamie listened to the sounds in the house. His father belched in the living room. His grandmother stomped around in the kitchen. Jamie slipped out of the bed as noiselessly as possible and began to pack his things into some plastic bags from the grocery store. He had stuffed the bags into his pants and smuggled them up from the kitchen right before bed.

Jamie crammed all his socks, underwear, shirts, and pants into the bags. It wasn't much, really. He tied the plastic bags to his backpack full of school supplies and books, tugging to make sure they were secure. He wished he had money. He would have to find a job or something. Maybe Mr. Nate would help with that.

Creeping to the window, he lifted it open. Paint chipped off the sill. He dropped the backpack and bags over the side. They fell softly into the snow. He crossed his fingers that nobody would see them and scurried back into bed.

Down below him, in the living room, his grandmother yelled, "I'm hungry."

"Me, too . . . me, too . . . ," his father answered.

"Soon, right?"

"Soon," his father agreed. "We feed well soon."

Lifting the covers to his nose, Jamie tried very hard to sleep.

———

Jamie's last night with the Alexanders wasn't easy. He kept waking up with the feeling that someone was standing just outside his door, listening. And then there was the slightest sound of sniffling coming from downstairs—a sound like muffled crying.

Jamie stayed in his bed and kept as still as possible. He slept fitfully, dreaming of tablecloths and crows, hidden back rooms in libraries, and gnomes, snowstorms, and trolls. When it was finally time for school, he was grateful to be up and ready to go, even if he did have to watch everyone else eat breakfast. Honestly, he had to admit that he was ridiculously happy that *he* wasn't breakfast.

Managing to grab his backpack with the grocery bags tied on, Jamie slipped out of the house and headed off to school. He stashed the bags behind one of the library hedges, and then walked the rest of the way with just his backpack. Throughout his morning classes, he held his secrets inside his brain, but they scrambled around and around in there. When the dismissal bell finally rang, Jamie grabbed his pack, scooted down the sidewalk and across the icy street, and ducked behind the hedges of the library to grab his bags.

For a second, doubt overtook him. He still didn't have a place to go. And it was cold. The wind seemed to be gusting especially hard.

He bit his lip and stood, leaving his bags where they were hidden in the hedge. He'd be back for them. First, though, he was going to meet up with Mr. Nate, ask him where he should hide, and find out what sort of danger he was really in. He knew his family members were monsters, but they hadn't eaten him yet, right? So maybe he could take a little extra time, maybe think a bit more about exactly how to run away. It was a monumental, life-changing, scary task, and he didn't want to mess it up.

He clomped the snow off his boots at the front door of the

library and then stepped inside the building. Warm air blanketed him as he strode over to the front desk. The librarian on duty was dark skinned like him, and had hair that sprang out in all directions like a halo of black coils.

She squinted at him, but kindly. "Can I help you?"

Jamie had to stand on tiptoes to see over the circulation desk. "Is Mr. Nate here?"

For a moment the librarian studied him. Her eyes softened a bit and she whispered, leaning forward, "Are you Jamie Alexander?"

Jamie nodded.

She slipped a white envelope across the counter. Jamie's name was written across it. "You can go read it over there."

She moved her head to indicate a place behind the stacks. Jamie thanked her and trotted over. There was a big red chair, overstuffed and ready to burst. He sat down without even taking off his backpack. His heart raced as he ripped open the envelope. A piece of thick yellow paper floated to the floor. Jamie snatched it up, just as a strange bird-looking woman walked by. She paused at the poetry books in front of him. Jamie didn't know why, but she freaked him out. He slipped the piece of paper beneath his leg and waited. After a minute she grabbed a book and moved on, humming under her breath. As soon as she was out of sight, Jamie opened the paper.

Jamie,

If you are reading this, then the danger is greater than I had initially thought. You must go now. Anywhere. Do not return to your house. Or your best friend's. They will find you there. That is too obvious a place.

Do not search for me. I will find you. Please, I cannot impress upon you enough that you must leave now. You must not be at your house on your thirteenth birthday or past it. It is of the upmost importance. Trust no creature unless it knows the password, which is CANIN'S BREATH.

Godspeed,

Mr. Nate

Jamie carefully put the paper back in the envelope and placed it in the front zipper part of his backpack. *Why my thirteenth birthday?* That was tomorrow. He hadn't thought about it much because his family never celebrated it. He'd never had a cake or a balloon or anything like that. But he barely had time to think about it before sirens echoed throughout the building. He jumped up and rushed to the front desk. The nice librarian gave him worried eyes.

"Is that a fire alarm?" he asked.

She shook her head. "Not here. Down on Main Street."

"That's where I live!" Jamie rushed out the door without saying good-bye.

The sirens were even louder on the street. His ears throbbed from the noise of it as he rushed down the hill toward his road. Kids were running toward the fire, too. Great black smoke clouds rose above the snow-covered roofs. It wasn't until he was on his block that he could see that the fire wasn't coming from his house, but from Mr. Nate's little white home. Orange flames burst through holes that were once windows as firefighters frantically worked the hoses, trying to stop the fire's path, but it was obviously too late. Flames poked up beneath the roof.

Mr. Nate!

Jamie's mouth dropped open in shock. His brain barely processed everyone's talking around him.

"Is he in there?"

"If he is, he's a goner."

"Stand back. People! Stand back."

The voices seemed to come from everywhere. Neighbors rushed out of their homes to watch. Volunteer firefighters and police officers tried to control the crowd. Jamie walked backward, mouth still open. He grabbed the elbow of the woman closest to him.

"Was Mr. Nate still in there?" he asked.

"I don't know," she answered.

He ran to a firefighter, Bruce Walton, who was talking into his radio with a determined tone.

"Was Mr. Nate still in there?" Jamie shouted over the sirens.

Bruce Walton raised his shoulders, and shooed him away. "I don't know, Jamie. Back up. We have to take care of this."

Another ladder truck, this one from the town of Bar Harbor, came screaming up to the scene. People staggered out of the way. The house cracked and popped.

"It's a total loss," one firefighter yelled. "Just try to keep it from spreading."

Something horrible and hard welled up in Jamie's throat. He couldn't even begin to swallow. There was no way Mr. Nate could have survived that if he was in there. No way he could have—

A large, strong hand yanked Jamie backward by his arm. He stumbled, but managed not to lose his footing. His grandmother towered over him.

"What are you doing here?" she hissed. Spittle came out of her mouth as she talked; she was that angry. "You're to come straight home after school. You know that."

She yanked him away from the crowd and up the street, yelling at him the entire time. He could only make out a few phrases here and there. *Stupid boy . . . Can't trust you further than I can spit. Thirteen years of you is hardly worth the reckoning . . . Stupid . . . Stupid . . .*

She kept at it as she hauled him up their walk, into their house, and up the stairs. She flung him into his bedroom and locked the door. He landed hard on the floor, listening as she bellowed out, "Can't imagine you leaving the day right before it has all paid off. The nerve of you! You're staying in there till tomorrow. Got it?"

She didn't wait for a response. She never did.

"All I have to say is you better be tasty if you don't turn!" she said, and her feet thundered down the stairs.

Tasty?

Turn?

For a moment, Jamie couldn't move at all. He simply could not will his body to do anything. The sounds of his grandmother breaking dishes and yelling in gibberish that he couldn't understand echoed up the stairs. Jamie zoned her out and scrambled over to the window. He got there just in time to see Mr. Nate's house fall into itself. It seemed like a card house, no longer solid or real.

Jamie's stomach seemed to fall into itself, too, just drop a few inches from where it should be. He leaned his forehead against the cold pane and closed his eyes. He was trapped in here, and tomorrow was his birthday. Mr. Nate had written that he couldn't be here on his birthday. He swallowed hard, wondering why.

After a minute he glanced outside again and saw that there were footprints glistening on his lawn. The moving pattern of letters magically formed words that could only be read from above. Jamie caught his breath as he read the message trampled in the snow:

THEY WILL
EAT YOU.
GET OUT NOW.

7

Snowmobiles That Hover

For hours, Annie and the dog wandered through the thick woods, searching for a road or a house or a way out, circling back on their own tracks again and again. After they had woken up, Annie had felt hopeful. The storm had stopped. The sun shone. They survived the night, but then they just couldn't find the way out. Shadows crawled up trees. Cold resettled in their bones. Clumps of snow clung to their legs. As they wandered through the snow-covered forest, something crashed.

Annie paused.

The dog sniffed the air.

Something through the trees, just a little bit in the distance, thudded.

The dog bared his teeth.

Something shuffled and belched. A foul stink of egg and raw chicken filled the air.

Annie grabbed the dog around the neck and whispered, "We have to hide."

There was another sound. It wasn't a rumble exactly, more like a deep voice full of scratches and dents. It was not the sound of something normal, not an animal, not the wind. Annie thrust the dog toward a gully behind the tree. But their footprints . . . She wished as hard as she could that their tracks would vanish somehow, so they wouldn't be found. She wished so hard her body trembled from it. Her hand swiped across the snow as if she were drawing the tracks away.

"Stay low," she whispered to the dog as she flattened herself out onto the ground. The cold of the snow sank through her clothes, and her trembles became full-fledged shudders.

She stared into the whiteness of the snowbank, arm draped around the dog's back. His muscles tensed like he was getting ready to spring. She cooed at him, moving her fingers across his fur. Heavy feet moved closer, out of the trees, and almost right in front of them. A tree cracked and fell. Annie imagined that it was rammed by a mighty hand.

"Trail stops," something grumbled.

Who is it? What is he talking about?

"They can't vanish," another voice answered. "Food can't vanish!"

"Trail stops!"

"How will we get her if we can't find them?" the first voice said. "We have to find them. We're so close I can taste it. Dog. Human."

"No tasting. You know we have to find the magic place."

"I know. I know. We're not allowed to eat her. We never get to eat the good ones."

Annie swallowed hard. *Eat? Magic place?* Their trail was so obvious in the snow. *How could they not see it?*

"And it takes thirteen years for them to even be worth it. Such a waste. Stinking curse. We can eat dogs, though."

Terror froze her fingers. She would not let them eat her dog. Not ever. The dog growled, a low warning tone.

"Do you hear that?" one of them yelled. "I heard dog. We could eat dogs."

"I still have feathers in my teeth from the chickens."

The creatures tromping through the woods sounded large. Too large to be people. Annie bet if they got close enough they could simply glance down and spot her and the dog. There was no getting around it. They would have to run.

"On the count of three," Annie told the dog, tensing and getting ready. "One . . . two . . . three!"

She sprang up and ran. The dog followed.

"Come!" she willed him. "Come!"

Darting behind trees and zigzagging across the forested landscape, Annie ran as quickly as she could in the deep snow. It was hard to get traction since her legs were so short, but she'd been running all her life and it helped now. The dog caught up to her again and urged her onward with his nose. Finally feeling brave enough, she turned to peek behind her. She wished she hadn't. Two large beasts, easily eight feet tall with bulbous noses and hands that seemed encased in boxing gloves, stood amid a circle of smashed-over trees, obviously searching for her.

"Don't see us," she murmured, wishing with all her might. "Don't see us."

The monsters saw them. One pointed and lunged forward, its giant foot crunching through the snow.

"Food!" it yelled.

Annie drove the dog ahead. They were close, closing in. There was no way she could outdistance them. Their legs were too long. She tried harder, forcing her muscles to move as quickly as possible. She couldn't just give up. No way. No how.

Thud!

She fell over backward, smacking hard against the snow.

The white dog leaped on top of her and turned, standing exactly over her, its doggy legs straddling her. He growled at the approaching monsters.

"No! Run! Run! They'll hurt you." Annie shoved against the dog's legs, trying vainly to move him aside. His lips curled into a warning snarl and he refused to budge. She scrambled out from beneath him, turning to thrust herself up off the snow. Something loud rumbled to the right.

The dog's tail wagged the tiniest of bits. The monsters stopped their approach and stared toward the oncoming noise, distracted. A dead chicken dangled from one of their hands. Annie's heart broke. She scrambled up into a standing position and began to run but stopped, falling again, just as a new rumbling noise broke the cold air.

A dark oversize snowmobile raced out of the trees. It flew close enough to the beasts to unbalance them, and they both tumbled sideways into the snow. Their ugly feet waved in the air.

Annie's mouth dropped open in shock. The shiny snowmobile had glittering pictures of golden dragons painted onto the sides and hovered a good five inches above the snow. The rider pressed a button, and the sled dropped to the ground next to Annie.

"Um . . . ," Annie started. "Help?"

As if she had all the time in the world, the rider whipped off her helmet and beamed at Annie. Her pigtails smacked across her face. She shoved them away, muttering, "Ridiculous things."

"You're a girl," Annie said, realizing the moment she said it that it was a dorky thing to say, especially when they should be trying to escape.

"Duh. And *you're* Annie, right?"

"Uh-huh."

"Annie Nobody? You're sure?"

Annie nodded as the girl surveyed her. The wind blew a passionate gust, and they rocked with it but didn't fall. The girl's face solided up. She was small but rugged and seemed like someone Annie would not want to meet on a dark playground. There was something firm about her, too, as if she would always have your back. Annie wondered what the girl was thinking about her—if she thought Annie's hair was too long, that she was too skinny, or if she seemed terribly un-special.

Annie's fingers tightened in the dog's fur. Fear of losing him forced her words out, "We have to go . . . Those things . . ."

As she said it, the creatures righted themselves and lunged toward the girls.

"Trolls. Uck. Hop on," the girl ordered.

Annie climbed onto the snowmobile. The dog hopped on behind her and rested his head on her shoulder.

The driver finally grinned again. It lit up her entire face as she said, "I'm glad Tala found you."

"Tala? What's Tala?" Dizziness overtook Annie, and she felt even more confused. "Your snowmobile was . . . was . . . hovering?"

"It's cool, isn't it? My dad tinkered with it." The girl started the engine as the trolls got even closer. "The dog's name is Tala. I'm Eva Beryl-Axe. Hang on. We need to get you home."

"Home?" Annie whispered. "I don't have a home."

Eva snapped her head to stare at her, stunned. "Of course you do. Aurora's your home."

"Aurora?" Annie repeated, but her voice was lost underneath the torrent of the snowmobile's engine.

"See you later, alligators!" Eva yelled. She squeezed the handlebars, and the snowmobile roared to life. She pulled it around in a circle and zigged it off across the snow and farther into the woods.

"Food, come back! Food!" the trolls bellowed at the retreating snowmobile.

Eva made a sharp left and then another through the trees. She revved the engine and zipped back into the woods, muttering under her breath, "Trolls. They think they're so much better just because they're tall."

"I'm not tall," Annie said, swaying on the back of the snowmobile. She couldn't believe she just said that. *I'm not tall?*

Eva lifted her hand from the handlebars and gave her a thumbs-up sign, and they continued through the forest, passing a giant boulder that resembled a dragon and another that resembled an egg. Trees blurred as they sped past.

"What jerks!" Eva yelled over her shoulder as the snowmobile moved farther into the woods, spewing up snow.

"Y-y-yeah," Annie panted out. She clasped Eva's sturdy back as pigtails whipped into her face. She steeled herself as the snowmobile darted between tree trunks and branches, ducking every now and then.

"Hold on. I'm going to go into hover mode. Okay?"

"Okay!" Annie wanted to do a happy dance it was so okay. She was all for her and Tala leaving the cold forest and the Wiegles, and never glancing back.

Boom! The snowmobile jolted forward and backward. It sputtered and kicked. It let loose a gigantic roar and stopped altogether. *Boom!* Annie rocked into Eva's back, and Tala flopped off into the snow.

"Tala!" Annie screamed, getting ready to dive off the snowmobile. "We lost Tala."

Eva smacked the handlebars with her fist and bellowed, "Vampire milk!"

Her curse echoed through the empty woods.

"Vampire milk?" Annie squeaked.

Eva hopped off the snowmobile and lifted up the front part and crankily explained, "It's how I swear, okay?"

Annie examined Tala, who gave her a few well-placed doggy kisses. "Okay."

"Vampire milk. Goblin goo. Troll cooties!" Eva slammed her fist into metal thingamabobs inside the snowmobile's hood. "Crud cakes. Werewolf weenies. Unicorn turds!"

Annie stepped away and gave Tala a hopeless frown. He rolled his eyes.

"Um, so could you tell me where you're taking us?" Annie asked.

"You really don't know?" Eva glanced up for a second and

started grumbling, hiding her head behind the mechanical engine parts.

"No. You said something about Aurora."

"You've never heard of Aurora?"

"No."

"Never heard its name whispered to you in your dreams?" Eva's face became visible again. It was streaked with grease. She scrutinized Annie. Annie scrutinized her back, feeling a little bit like a failure.

"No."

Eva stepped toward her, voice serious, hands on her hips. "You do *have* dreams?"

Annie lowered her voice. "All the time."

"Phew, you had me going there. I was worried you were one of those people who don't dream, don't believe, don't anything." Eva shuddered and slammed down the engine hood. "People like trolls."

"I would never be like them!" Annie's hand shot up to cover her mouth. "Sorry. I didn't mean to shout."

"What's wrong with shouting?" Eva asked, shouting. "I shout all the freaking time! So, anyway, Aurora is a town. It's magic. There's this great old lady there, Miss Cornelia. She is made of awesome, like myself, and she sort of keeps it all together somehow. I don't know how. It's all beyond me. I'm good with my hands. Not with my head. You should see my social-studies grades."

"*Magic* town?"

"Yeah. Magic. Those of us who don't fit into the human world can choose to live there together. It's sort of like a safe haven." Eva snorted. From her jacket pocket, she pulled out a dark candy bar and bit off half, holding out the other half to Annie.

Annie's stomach growled. "Thanks." She took a bite. It melted in her mouth. "It tastes like honey."

"Really? It tastes like mashed potatoes and stuffing to me," Eva said, still chewing. "It's a 'What You Want' bar. It tastes like whatever you're in the mood for."

"It's so yummy. How does it do that? Taste like what you want?" Annie said. She took another nibble and let the honey taste warm her mouth and puff up her tongue. Her stomach began making happy noises. Then she remembered what they had been talking about.

"So, you live in Aurora, which is a place for people who don't fit in?" *Like me*, Annie thought. *I never fit in.*

"Yeah. But I don't know how safe it is since Miss Cornelia makes us go to school with humans, and well, lately—agh . . . That's not something I should be telling you yet."

Annie shook her head, trying to figure it all out. "You say that as if you aren't human."

"I'm not."

Annie took a step backward. "You're not—"

"I'm a dwarf."

"A dwarf."

"A dwarf. 'Dwarf' is not a dirty word. According to the *Multiple World Encyclopedia of the Fae*, we are 'a hearty race of industrious workers, inspired tool smiths, fantastic diggers, and jewelry makers.' Plus, we are darn good dancers," Eva boasted and began to two-step in a circle.

Annie laughed while Tala covered his eyes with his paws. "No, really?"

"Really," Eva announced. She bowed. "Don't tell me you've never met a dwarf before?"

Blushing, Annie apologized. "I don't think so."

"Well, I'm betting you have. There are tons of us around. We don't all live in Aurora. Lots of magics live in the world with regular people. Some just don't ever find their way home to Aurora or the other places like it."

"And that's where we're going? Aurora?"

Eva stared for a second, seeming a little disgusted by Annie's slowness. "Yeah, that's what I said. Aurora."

"And it's magic, like *magic* magic?"

"Yeah. It's *magic* magic, but some of the magic has faded a bit, which is why it was so important we bring you back before everything goes kablooey. Personally I'm just glad you're not dead or stuck in some other dimension or something, which would suck," Eva explained. She ripped the band off her left pigtail and unthreaded the braid. Then she started tightening it.

Annie tried to figure out which question to ask first. "And why is it going kablooey?"

"The Raiff. He's this guy—really bad news if you ask me. I mean, he used to be one of us before he turned to the dark side or whatever . . . and he's super scary-looking, too, all thin with platinum blond hair and eyes that lack any light, eyes like the bottom of a mine, you know? And it's all because of him that things ain't been right . . . sorry, things *haven't* been right . . . I'm not supposed to say 'ain't.' It drives SalGoud wild. There was this epic battle twelve years ago, right after you were born. The Raiff took all the elves away. It really was bad. First it was the Daisies who disappeared, then the Pines, and then Bloom's parents and all the rest of them. Everything was a mess." Eva paced back and forth, her fist hitting her hand and her pigtails flip-flopping in the wind as she became more and more worked up. "And then there was an all-out war. I was too freaking young to be in it, which is a darn shame if you ask me. I bet it wouldn't have ended in a stalemate if they'd let me fight. So what if I was only two years old? Big deal. Dwarfs can fight from birth!"

"And dwarfs live there, in Aurora?"

"All sorts of fae live there," Eva announced. She calmed down a bit, and her fingers moved lightning fast, rebraiding her loose pigtail. "But not elves anymore, except for Bloom. The Raiff got all but one of them in the Purge. Now let's get you back on the snowmobile before I get in trouble."

"In trouble?"

Eva's face reddened. "Well . . . Canin and Tala actually found you when they were searching for the gnome. Nobody even knew to try to find you, you know? We all thought you were dead. But Tala recognized you right away with his keen doggy senses and insisted on staying and keeping you safe. Canin went back to tell everyone, and everyone started debating on whether the girl they found could possibly be you. And then the trolls came, and I couldn't just hover there. So, yeah . . . it wasn't my job to save *you*. Mr. Nate said I was supposed to rescue this skinny kid who goes to my school, which should have been an easy pickup, but there was a freaking fire on the road. I couldn't just race right in and save him on this. And then there you were, about to be eaten by trolls."

Annie eyed her. "So *you* saved *me* instead."

"Yeah, suppose so." Eva bit the corner of her lip.

Relief filled Annie. She balled up the candy wrapper and put it carefully in her pocket. "I don't completely get why anyone would want to find me in the first place, but I'm totally glad you did."

"Really?" Eva's face lit up.

"Yeah," Annie said enthusiastically, since she noticed that Eva really perked up when she was complimented. "Thanks for rescuing me. You were really heroic, really tough."

Eva's smile got even bigger, and then she started to blush. "You think? 'Cause sometimes I pass out when I see trolls."

Annie grinned back at her. "I don't think. I know."

They hopped on the snowmobile, except for Tala, who refused despite Annie's pleas.

"He's stubborn like that," Eva explained. "You just have to go with it. He'll be fine. He's super tough. He just hates hovering. All dogs do. They'd rather run. I'm surprised he got on before, actually. He must really love you to do that."

"He's the best dog ever." Annie swallowed hard and leaned forward, circling the conversation back to what was tickling at her brain. "And why am I supposed to go to Aurora?"

Eva revved up the engine, which now seemed to work fine. "Because you are the only one who can save us, save Aurora, and save magic. Duh."

Annie's breath leaped inside her chest, taking her words away. Stunned, she clutched Eva's back more tightly and finally said, "I think you have the wrong person. I'm not the sort of person who saves people. I'm not special like that. I'm just . . . I'm . . . uh . . ."

But Eva didn't hear. The dwarf pressed a button, and the snowmobile lurched and hovered, then zipped off through the trees, screeching through the air like it had never been broken. Annie closed her eyes and held on to the little dwarf, hoping that Eva knew where they were going and that nobody—human or dwarf—would fall off.

8

Out the Window

Jamie staggered backward away from the window and the horrible blaze. In all his almost thirteen years, Jamie knew that his family wasn't normal. The signs were there:

1. He was too embarrassed by his weird family to bring friends home.
2. He had never seen a picture of his mother, ever.
3. His family was terribly, ridiculously mean.

And, in all his almost thirteen years, Jamie knew that he didn't fit in with his father and his grandmother. The signs were there for that, too:

1. They were quite large. He was quite small.
2. They were quite loud. He was quite quiet.
3. They were quite pale skinned with a greenish tint. He was quite dark skinned with a bluish tint.
4. They were quite evil. He wasn't. He knew he wasn't.

And now there was number five:

5. They thought that eating boys (specifically him) was quite acceptable. He was quite sure that it wasn't.

He remembered all the horrors he had seen, all the ways they'd hurt him, and he knew that they most certainly *would* eat him, just totally gobble him up like he was potted meat. "Jamie! Get down here!" his grandmother bellowed from the bottom of the stairs.

Jamie Alexander preferred not to be anybody's dinner.

"One second!" he yelled back, trying as best he could to sound like a normal boy who wasn't about to be eaten or devoured or ingested in any way.

He opened his window and let the cold air and smoke from the fire billow into his room.

"I will not be eaten," he sputtered as smoke filled the air. "Not now. Not ever."

Coughing, he yanked the sheets off his bed and tied the ends together as tightly as he could. Then he added a jump rope to the end and dangled it all out the window. He secured one end to the bedpost, hoping that it would hold.

"James Hephaistion Alexander! We are hungry!" Grandma Alma Alexander yelled.

"I know! Coming!" Jamie lied as he pushed his body out the window. His feet dangled over the edge. Reaching back, he grabbed the sheet and turned so that his feet hit the grayish-white siding of the house. He was suspended there, just hanging for a moment, gasping from the joy of being outside, of escaping.

"I can do this," he whispered. "I can do this."

He began rappelling down the side of the house. *It isn't really that far*, he convinced himself. *And it would be better to fall and die than be eaten, right?*

"Right," he murmured, just as the knot attaching the sheets loosened and he plummeted to the ground below.

Phlump!

Jamie landed on his feet and then flopped onto his back. The air ricocheted out of his lungs as he lay there in the snow, staring up at the smoke-filled sky.

"I am dead," he muttered, but then he realized that dead people didn't mutter. Sitting up, he brushed the snow off his back and admitted, "I am not dead."

"JAMES HEPHAISTION ALEXANDER!" His grandmother's voice bounced around the house and into the outside air. "I am going to count to three, and then I am coming upstairs to get you!"

Crud. He skittered backward on the snow, trying to get enough strength to actually stand up. If she came upstairs and found him gone . . . he couldn't even think about how horrible things would be. He had to go—now.

"One!" she yelled.

Horrified, he managed not to faint. Terror blazed into him, a weight right between his shoulder blades. She would catch him. She would . . .

From his left came the sound of a rumbling motor. He turned. A snowmobile flew up the side yard and skidded to a stop beside him. Two small girls sat upon it. The passenger shivered and seemed frail. The one driving the machine was squatter, more solid, and Jamie thought she seemed familiar. *Maybe from math class?* She eyed him just as a huge white dog appeared and wagged its tail at him before sniffing at the passenger and licking her hand.

"Are you Jamie?" the driver asked. Her voice was like a horn, it was so loud.

Jamie was too stunned to speak. He managed a nod.

"Get on," she ordered. "I'm Eva. Sorry I'm late. Had to rescue Annie."

Get on? Get on the snowmobile?

"TWO!" his grandmother bellowed. "Do not make me count to three, young man! You do not want me to go up there!"

He struggled to his feet. Annie hopped off the snowmobile, put her arm around his waist, and helped him on.

"Do you know the password?" he stuttered.

Annie stared at him. Her lip trembled from the cold. "Password? Eva, is there a password?"

"Canin's breath." Eva's eyes grew desperate. "Hurry up!"

"It'll be okay," Annie whispered as she settled him onto the snowmobile. "I think. I mean, I actually have no idea what's going on, but I am pretty sure that—well, it's got to be better than—"

"THREE!"

Jamie found his voice. "Go! Please . . . please . . . hurry!"

"Anything you say, partner," Eva yelled.

With her thumb, she gestured to the rear of the snowmobile, and Annie hopped onto the back, making it all pretty crowded.

"Now, hold on," Eva ordered over her shoulder. "We're heading to Aurora, and sometimes this here sled doesn't give the smoothest of rides."

Jamie barely heard her. He was too busy staring back at his upstairs bedroom window. His grandmother's bulk leaned out the window. She was screaming at him. In her hand were a fork and a knife. And her mouth? It was drooling.

9

Aurora

Three people are a lot for one snowmobile to carry, even if the people are somewhat small. Annie apologized to Jamie as they bumped and zipped across the lawn of the house. It didn't seem right to be clutching a stranger, especially a boy stranger. The first time she tried to apologize he didn't hear her over the roar of the engine, so she cleared her throat and tried to yell, even though she hated yelling.

She shouted closer to his ear. "I'm so sorry that I have to hold on so tightly."

"It's okay," he said.

"Maybe not quite so tight?" she suggested, and her hold lessened as Jamie turned and gawked behind them. His face was taut with tension and worry. Annie wanted to soothe him somehow, soothe him the way she'd always imagined her own mother would soothe her. "It'll be okay, I think. Eva's taking us somewhere safe. At least, she says that—"

Jamie wasn't paying attention, Annie realized belatedly. He interrupted her, his voice urgent and terrified as he frantically tapped Eva's shoulder. "She's chasing us! You have to hurry! Please!"

"Going as fast as we can!" Eva yelled. "No fears! We'll beat her or my name isn't Eva Beryl-Axe of the long line of mighty Beryl-Axes."

Annie glanced behind her to the side lawn. A tall, strongly built woman rushed after them. She held a huge knife in one hand and a fork in the other. Her face was contorted with determination as she pounded across the snow toward them.

"Who is that?" Annie asked, fear gripping her stomach. The woman reminded her vaguely of the Wiegles, but somehow managed to be worse.

"My grandmother!" Jamie shouted.

Annie's eyes widened in surprise. "Your grandmother?"

Jamie nodded vigorously. He started to peer over his shoulder again, but Annie yelled, "No. Don't look!"

Jamie's grandmother let out a roar, interrupting Annie's thoughts.

"Eva!" Annie begged the dwarf to hurry up. "She's gaining on us."

"Got it!" Eva said, driving even faster as they entered the woods. Tala kept up, thankfully, and Eva veered the machine around a tree. Just then, the giant woman threw the knife. It whizzed over their shoulders and stuck into a tree trunk. Annie shuddered as the distance between them and the woman increased. They had come so close to being knifed in the back . . . so close . . . Only when she was completely out of sight did Annie face front again.

"She's gone now," she announced.

Annie still didn't loosen her hold, not for the rest of the ride. Luckily, Jamie didn't seem to mind.

"Almost there!" Eva bellowed as the snowmobile roared out of the woods and across a blueberry barren, heading straight for the intersection of two small roads. "Hey! Look! They've got signs out and everything."

Annie squinted into the setting sun. They were heading straight for a pack of people clustered together in the middle of the road.

Jamie screamed out a warning. "Watch out!"

"Perfect." Laughing, Eva slammed on the brakes, and the snowmobile skidded into a sideways stop just seconds before it would have slammed into the strange-looking crowd standing there in the road, staring at them. Extremely tall people huddled with people as short as Annie's waist. Bright, purple-haired people clustered around a man who seemed to have painted his skin blue. For some reason, they all seemed to be smiling.

"I can't believe we didn't hit anyone," Annie whispered to Jamie as she tried to take in all that she saw.

"I know!" He wiped at his forehead with shaking fingers.

Eva kept talking, addressing the strange crowd assembled in the road. "HEY! I've got the girl! Annie! Annie Nobody! She's alive and here! Right here! And I got her! Me, Eva Beryl-Axe, the dwarf!"

Giant hands yanked Annie off the seat and clutched her in a gigantic hug. A bright-yellow parka was mashed into Annie's face. She couldn't see anything—nothing at all. Hands petted her back. She tried to wiggle free.

No good.

"Eva!" She tried to yell. "Tala!"

She couldn't tell if the yellow-parka person was trying to burp her, hug her, or give her the Heimlich maneuver. If it *was* a hug, well then, it had to be the strangest hug that she'd ever had in her whole entire life. Although, to be honest about it, she hadn't really had all that many hugs to compare it with.

She tried to pull her head away from the big puffiness and find Eva or Tala or Jamie. She pushed her hands against the coat.

"Eva!" she yelled, wondering why she couldn't hear Eva's rough voice over the din of all the other voices around her. "Eva!"

Annie's heart tightened. Eva had left her. Like all the others. A big breath escaped Annie as she moved her head to the side and could finally see around the yellow parka. The snow-mobile's lights flickered, and its treads were firmly planted on the cracked old road. Eva was not on it. Neither was Tala or Jamie.

"Eva!" Annie called.

The dwarf's little face popped into view. She frowned. She bashed the yellow-parka person in the side. "Will you stop hugging her? Vamp dung! Troll spit."

Yellow-parka man spoke. "Eva, watch your language."

"You're freaking suffocating her."

The two hands stopped patting Annie's back. Instead they hoisted her high into the air. They placed her atop the shoulders of a man—she thought it was a man—wearing a red parka. She felt like a football hero, or maybe a veteran returned from war. She peered down. The world spun. She was no good at heights. She squeaked, "Eva?"

Eva waved from far down below. Tala wagged his tail and then spun around in a delighted doggy circle. Jamie seemed as confused as Annie felt. He was sort of walking backward, away from the crowd.

Eva ordered her, "Don't freak out. Don't faint or anything. It's cool. We're just happy you're here, Annie. Everyone's happy, and I'm a hero 'cause I brought you back. Me! Eva, the dwarf! Dwarfs rule!"

Some low-voiced person in the crowd repeated her boast. "Dwarfs rule!"

Annie shook her head, trying to figure it all out. It made no sense. No one was ever happy to see her. And yet, here she was, surrounded by shouting, cheering people bundled in winter clothes, all beaming up at her.

From her new position, not only could Annie breathe, but she could see a lot more. The man was super tall, professional-basketball-player tall, and from his shoulders Annie spotted several old-style wooden and stone houses. They leaned toward the ocean and away from the forest and the barrens. Porches teetered along the tops of the houses, the way Annie teetered on the giant man's shoulders.

"Sir? Sir?" she asked. "Could you please put me down?"

He didn't answer. He was too busy clapping his hands and cheering.

She grabbed onto his hat as the wind bashed against her. She tightened her lips against the cold. Store signs proclaiming World In Store and Full Belli Deli banged against the peeling paint. A Ferris wheel waited in a far clearing, surrounded by carnival construction.

"A carnival. I've always wanted to go to a carnival," Annie murmured.

"She likes carnivals!" the man yelled.

"Of course she does." Eva laughed. She jumped up and down and then strutted in a little circle, boasting, "I found her, you know! I rescued her. Me. Eva."

People cheered again and clapped their hands. They started chanting, "E-va. E-va. E-va."

Eva took a bow. Annie thought Eva's face might split from smiling so big. It was nice to see her so happy. A gray cat with white paws rubbed up against Eva's leg, while little dogs scampered all around her yipping out their joy.

The dogs from the Wiegles? How had they made it here? And what about Jamie? People should be making just as big a fuss over him, Annie thought. *He shouldn't be left out.* She tried to wave him over, but he shook his head. He was standing by a girl whose beautiful, shiny hair peeked out from beneath her pink wool cap. She was frowning, and her cheeks were perfectly white—not reddened by the cold at all. Two women huddled beside her. Their hair flew wildly about their shoulders. They reminded Annie of the kind of witches you would find in Halloween cartoons.

"I don't see what's so fantastic about her. She appears absolutely normal," the girl sneered. "If she's even really Annie Nobody at all . . ."

Annie's heart sank. Someone already hated her. She was barely there, and someone already knew she was boring and normal and absolutely unfantastic and barely worth the checks the fosters got for keeping her.

Eva pounded over to the grumpy girl, hands in fists. "What? Are you doubting me? You think I got the wrong Annie or something?"

The girl lifted one pretty shoulder and didn't answer.

"I got the right Annie, Megan." Eva shook her fist, glowering.

Megan didn't move. "I'm sure you did, but she doesn't look like a Stopper. She seems norm to me, hideously, boringly norm, and we can't have that here."

The crowd started muttering.

Norm? Stopper? Annie's head hurt, she was so confused. "Excuse me, what's going on?"

The people below her stared up, their breath making clouds in the cold.

"She wants to know what's going on," the giant man boomed.

People cheered as if this was some sort of amazing accomplishment. Annie spotted Jamie again. She shot him a questioning glance. He shook his head like he was just as clueless as she was.

"We're welcoming you to Aurora, Annie," the man said.

"Oh . . . Okay . . ." Nervousness raised Annie's voice, and she wiggled a little bit. The world spun again. She really, really wasn't the best at heights. She tapped the man on his head. "You're a very friendly town, which is really super nice and everything, but, um, I'd like to get down now, please. And also, could you welcome Jamie, too? And Tala, the big white dog? He has a wound. Someone needs to help him." She felt a bit bossy saying it like that and added, "Please."

The man ignored her request, but turned around so that they faced a different direction. He pointed. "See that house, Annie?"

Up on a hill overlooking the town was a large, grand house five stories high and at least seven windows across. It had a circular tower and gray siding, and it loomed over everything as if it were an overprotective mother, watching her mischievous children as they played.

Annie closed her eyes, trying to not be dizzy. She opened them again. "I see it."

"That's Aquarius House. You'll be living there. Thank the Stoppers, you're here!" The man's shoulders bounced up and down as he clapped his hands. Annie leaned backward, then forward, grabbing bits of parka between her freezing fingers.

"Whoa!"

The wind picked up. The bite of it forced Annie's heart to speed up, and she shivered from both the cold and her fear.

"Do you see the signs, girl?" the man bellowed.

People hoisted handmade signs written in black permanent marker on big pieces of cardboard. Pastel swirling letters filled other poster boards. Annie liked those signs better.

WELCOME, ANNIE.

YIPPEE FOR ANNIE!

HERE'S TO HOME, ANNIE!

One, written in a young child's hand, simply said HI.

Annie gulped, and something a little bit happy filled her heart. She couldn't believe it, though. Maybe it was all some kind of joke. "Are those signs for me?"

"No other Annies here." The man laughed.

"But . . ." She turned around, confused. "But . . . I'm just . . . I'm not a big deal."

"That's for sure," Megan huffed.

"And what about Jamie? Eva saved both of us. I think we should probably cheer for him, too," Annie suggested again. Guilt seeped into her stomach. They were making such a fuss over her, and poor Jamie was standing there, totally ignored. She knew exactly what that felt like.

A strong voice came from the back of the crowd. It said in a low rumble, "Speech, Annie. Give us a speech."

"Yes, yes," the crowd responded. "Give us a few words, Annie."

She didn't know what to do. She'd never given anything like a speech in her life, except maybe for book reports in language arts class.

She cleared her throat, but it just tightened up.

A blond boy wearing a dark-green cloak gave her the thumbs-up sign. He smiled at her.

Why would he smile at me? Why would they want a speech? Or make signs? Or actually be happy that I'm here? I'm nothing special. Don't these people know that?

"You can do it, Annie!" The boy cupped his hands together over his mouth to make his voice carry. "It's okay."

Eva nodded. She held up a small turtle that nodded, too, and drooled a little bit. "Just do it, Annie. No fears."

No fears.

"Ahem," she finally started, voice squeaking. "It is— umm—it's—umm, good to be here?"

The people gathered around her gave a great, joyous roar. The red-parka man clapped. His shoulders bounced and she wobbled. She wrapped her arms around his head because she came close to falling the good seven and a half feet to the ground. This made the claps turn into laughter and then claps again after a woman in the back yelled, "She's got an angel's balance, she does."

"Let her speak."

"Yes, quiet, everyone."

The people stared up at her, waiting eagerly. Some seemed to have hair on their faces, even on their noses. Some stood shorter than she did, even though she could tell that they were grown-ups. And what was that flitting around a man's shoulders? A fairy? And there . . . in the store's window was a reflection that resembled a man, a man with thin lips and short blond hair and little horns. His eyes met her eyes. The cold inside her suddenly burned.

"This is not normal," Annie whispered to herself. Maybe she *had* hit her head hard enough to imagine things or

Walden put some sort of hallucinogenic drug in her toothpaste. It was possible. He wasn't above that.

Even more anxious now to get down and figure things
out, Annie tried to slouch backward off the shoulders. Big
hands caught her and steadied her. She gulped.

"Um . . . ," she said. "Um, thank you so much for the very
nice welcome and um . . ."

She didn't have to say more because they were cheering
again. She searched for Tala. He just sat there on the ground
wagging his tail. She breathed out and felt a bit better. He
wagged his tail harder and panted as if he were hot despite
the freezing air. He flashed her a lopsided doggy grin. It was
reassuring. She closed her eyes and tried to think.

"An-nie. An-nie. An-nie," the people started chanting at
her. One of them sneezed.

"More!"

"Yes, more, Annie."

"More speech!"

Annie tried to get her frozen lips to move again. The wind
had dried them out. "Um," she began. "My name is Annie.
My friend over there is Jamie . . . Um . . . Ah . . . Yeah . . . I'm
nothing special, and I really don't know why—"

"No!" a sharp voice called out, and a thin older woman
broke through the crowd. "No more speeches. For goodness
sakes, she's just arrived, chilled to the bone, and you all are
having a rally. Mayor, let her down!"

10

Eva the Protector

Jamie didn't mind that Annie was the center of attention in Aurora because it gave him a chance to scope things out. He pushed back to the edge of the crowd and tried to see where Eva had taken them.

At first glance Aurora seemed like every other small town across America. But in many ways, it wasn't the same at all. The buildings were mostly made of white bricks or clapboard, dyed pastel colors and decorated with all sorts of stars and moons and glitter. Some were stone. One shop had a picture of a unicorn jumping over a rainbow. The sign above it said it was the Moony Horn Café. It smelled of sweets. Jamie's stomach rumbled. He backed a bit closer to the building. Maybe he could buy something somehow, or trade for food. He could work for a piece of cake. That might be it.

Although he knew it was unlikely, he was unnerved by the possibility that his grandmother may have somehow followed him here. He tried to figure out the lay of the town, searching for escape routes. The town seemed centered along one main, narrow street. Shops lined the two sides of it. Most were two stories and had a bit of a lean about them. They were all boxy rectangles. Snow covered their roofs. From that street, curving, smaller roads branched out. Stone walls lined them. Gates of wood or iron led to paths that inched through the snow toward front doors.

Eva stood next to him and elbowed him in the stomach. "Like it?"

Jamie nodded. To not nod would seem insulting, and Eva seemed like the sort of girl who would punch you in the nose if she felt insulted. Plus, he *did* like it. The town felt strange, but in a good way. It was as if the air tingled and the road might turn to gold at any moment.

"It's the only town in the entire universe where there are absolutely no norms," Eva boasted. "Not counting you, of course. And maybe Annie. Highly unlikely she's a norm, though."

"Norms?"

"Un-magic creatures."

Jamie's eyes grew big. His heart seemed to thump a bit

too hard against his ribs, the memory of his grandmother's transformation attacking him. "So you mean everyone here is magic?"

"Yep. Pretty much." Eva stared at him. "Why does that make you look all scared?"

"It's just . . . My grandmother—" How could he explain it?

"You think we're all going to eat you?" Eva slapped herself in the leg and started laughing like it was the funniest thing in the world. "There aren't any trolls here. They were banned. The town was founded by Thomas Fylbrigg back in, like— oh, I don't know, forever ago—because he thought we needed a safe place. There were all those witch trials going on and some huge magic world fight. It's hard to hide your magic all the time, you know? Well, you probably wouldn't . . ."

Eva trailed off, embarrassed to mention Jamie's distinct lack of magic. He shrugged and motioned for her to go on talking, which she did. Eva tended not to need any encouragement when it came to talking.

"So," she continued. "Anyway, there are a ton of witches and dwarfs and shifters still out there running about, obviously. They aren't all here in Aurora. But they do tend to cluster in certain cities. There are a lot in Savannah, Georgia. It smells nice there. All flowery. Too warm for me, though. I like the cold. And then there are more in Hammana, Dublin, Prague, Mindoro Island, some random Scottish town whose name I can't pronounce, a place in Buenos Aires, Kolwezi . . ."

"Uh-huh." Jamie glanced away, still searching for his grandmother. There were side streets off the main road they stood on now. Each street had houses and some more buildings on it.

Eva peered at him. "You're shaking. You're acting like you're going to pass out."

"I'm fine."

"You're nervous." Eva paused, trying to put it all together. "Don't you worry. You may not be magic, but you survived trolls. And I promise you, on my dwarf's honor, that I'll keep you safe even if the town ain't hidden no more."

Jamie peered down at Eva, who was standing on tippy toes and squaring her shoulders back to seem more imposing. He closed his eyes and leaned against the wall of the Moony Horn Café. Something grabbed him by the arm, yanking him sideways and backward. Before he could scream, the door of the shop closed soundly behind him. The only noise Jamie managed to make was "Eep."

Eva, his protector, didn't notice a thing.

11

Miss Cornelia

The old woman strode through the crowd and stood right in front of Annie. The gray cat darted under the hem of her eighteen rainbow skirts. Rainbow-colored tights bagged about her ankles, and judging from the crinkled lines surrounding her very blue eyes, she might have been three hundred years old.

She focused all her attention on Annie. "Greetings, dear Annie Nobody. I am Miss Cornelia. I cannot tell you the great joy I feel that it was Tala who located you. It's just so right."

The strangely dressed woman took charge, sweeping Annie in front of her as they made their way through the crowd and down the road. People kept reaching out and touching Annie's arm or hair or face like they were trying to be sure she was real.

Miss Cornelia shouted over her shoulder, "Thank you for your kind work, everyone! We'll just be going home now. See you tomorrow!"

Once they were a decent distance away, Miss Cornelia stopped walking. She sighed, and it seemed to Annie that there was something very sad about the woman's eyes. "I know you've just arrived, but I think I need to give you this now, just in case. It's dangerous times. Dangerous times indeed."

She pulled out a three-bladed dagger from beneath one of her wool sweaters. Light glinted off the silver blades.

Annie gasped, backing up a step. She'd never seen an actual weapon before except at the Tardiffs', the foster home where the dad liked to shoot at small living things like bunnies and squirrels. All. The. Time. She was not too keen on weapons. "I'm sorry. I don't understand."

"Of course you don't. Why would you?" Miss Cornelia bent a little so her face was closer to Annie's. Annie couldn't bear the strength of her gaze. She peeked off to her right at a store that had a sign saying MAKE IT MAGICAL.

Miss Cornelia's voice brought her back. "Annie. You may have a special gift that you might not be aware of, and this gift is terribly important to us, but it also puts you at great risk. Do you follow?"

Annie nodded but the nod was an absolute lie. She had no clue what was going on.

"Good," the woman continued. Wind swirled her skirts. One of the dogs dipped beneath the cloth. "So that is why I am giving you this weapon now, although you are far from ready for it, I fear. Sometimes we have to face things before our time. Such is the way of the world.

"However it may appear, this is not a weapon of the body but of the spirit." Miss Cornelia shook her head. "You must think this is all preposterous, possibly absurd, most likely unfathomable, but I assure you it isn't. This is the phurba or thunder nail. It's been in my family for generations. It is meant to nail evil to the ground, and it has done that quite a few times. Plus, it represents insight. Do you know what insight is?"

Annie gave a thumbs-up but somehow couldn't answer. Her insides shivered just being so close to the sharp, deadly metal.

"Take it and keep it with you. When the time comes, you will know when to use it," the woman urged.

Annie's hand wrapped around the ornate handle of the blade. Images of all sorts of magical creatures were melded into the silver. She wanted to draw them, to trace her fingers on their features. She longed for her pastels, which were still in the Wiegles' wrecked trailer. A serpent and a dragon were the most prominent of the images shifting before her. The handle of the weapon seemed so kind and lovely, nothing like the steel of the blade. She touched the face of what resembled a cherub. It winked. She gasped, almost dropping the dagger.

The woman's hand touched her shoulder. "Put it away for now. Let's hope you never need it."

Annie's heart flip-flopped. She must be seeing things. "I thought it winked."

"Of course it did."

"Oh." Annie glanced at Tala and the little dogs, hoping for guidance. They sat patiently waiting for her to make a move. *The signs? The dagger? The hovering snowmobile? Jamie's grandmother?* Nothing made sense.

The woman's fingers tapped against Annie's coat. "Just don't let Eva see it. She has a hankering for weapons."

Annie thought for a minute. She needed to understand what was going on, but she also needed to make sure Jamie was okay. She tucked the knife in her pocket, staring back at the crowd, but she didn't see him anywhere. "Where's Jamie?"

Miss Cornelia whistled and a dove landed on her shoulder. She cooed to it and made some clucking, birdlike noises. The dove flew off down the hill. "She will locate him."

"Okay," Annie said, shivering from both confusion and cold. "Thanks . . . Um . . . Are . . . Are . . . Are you going to be my foster mother?"

The woman's lip may have quivered a bit as she said, "You could give me that designation—at least until another one is deemed more appropriate."

Annie's mouth dropped open, and she took a step backward toward the crowd. "I think you have to fill out forms or something."

"Don't worry. I have it under control. Human bureaucracy is something I can still manage, thankfully. It'll just take a couple of days." The old woman caught Annie's elbow in her hand and whispered into Annie's ear, "Thank everyone."

"Thank you!" Annie yelled, turning her head back to investigate the crowd.

They cheered again. Eva gave her a double thumbs-up sign. Annie couldn't understand it. Her heart wanted to soar, but when a heart is beaten down too much, too often, it sometimes has a hard time believing in love.

"They're very happy," Annie said as Miss Cornelia hustled her forward.

"They should be. You are here."

"What?" Annie wasn't sure she heard her correctly.

"I said that you are here, therefore they should be happy," Miss Cornelia repeated as she strode farther down the road and began striding up a long hill.

Nobody had ever been happy that Annie was there. And if they were? Well, they didn't stay happy for long. Annie crumbled a bit inside. What had the Wiegles said? If you wanted people to love you, you had to do what they said? She'd do that here . . . She'd follow all the rules and do whatever they needed so she could stay. Maybe she would never belong anywhere, but maybe, just this once, she could manage to not get kicked out.

The wind stopped blowing for a moment as Miss Cornelia continued, "I never should have let the mayor know when you were coming. He can never resist a rally, and goodness knows the people of this town love to make a big hubbub of things whenever they get the opportunity. They're always ready for a party. I'm sure it's all terribly intimidating for you."

The lady stopped in midpace so quickly that Annie ran into her. The wool coat scratched against her nose, and Annie sneezed. Wool always made her sneeze.

Miss Cornelia turned around and cast kind but stern eyes on Annie, and then reached out to place a gentle hand on her head, making Annie's heart calm just the smallest of bits.

To Annie in that moment, Miss Cornelia seemed so stable and strong, like an old tree that's watched over a river for years and years. No one ever touched Annie or hugged her or kissed her cheek.

Maybe this place will be okay. Annie smiled down at Tala.

The dove landed on Miss Cornelia's shoulder. It chattered at her, and she cocked her head to listen and said, "Thank you, friend."

She can talk to birds? First Tala can understand humans and now this? Seriously? Annie couldn't believe how great Aurora was.

Turning to Annie, her new foster mother simply breathed out and said, "Well, we had better wait for young Jamie."

Sweets

"What's your name, boy?"

Brittle and sharp, the voice accosting Jamie's ears was the opposite of the sugary sweet smells of the shop.

"Jamie," he mumbled, staring at the woman holding his arm. Flour dotted her face, which was contorted into an I'm-going-to-kill-you-if-you-answer-wrong sort of expression. "Actually it's . . . it's . . . um . . . James Hephaistion Alexander. People call me Jamie."

The woman sniffed at him, nostrils flaring. "Well, yes, people will do that, won't they? People."

She sputtered the word "people" like it was a curse. Her hair was flung about her head in spiky brown ringlets, and her too-large brown eyes stared at him curiously. There was a tiny dab of sugar on her sharp chin and patches of dark flour all over her flowered apron. She let him go, wiping her hands on the cotton fabric, which sent puffs of flour dust into the air. "I don't suppose you're one, are you?"

"One what?" Jamie asked.

"A person . . . A normal, non-magic person."

"Oh . . . yes . . . I am, sorry. I'm afraid I am." Jamie sighed. He wanted to add "useless." He was a *useless*, normal, non-magical person.

She took a step back toward the counter and grasped a rolling pin, clutching it like some sort of weapon. "Then what are you doing here?"

Jamie stepped back. He had no desire to be bashed with a rolling pin. "Eva, the short girl who seems sort of violent? She brought me with Annie."

The woman's eyes narrowed. "Why would she do a thing like that?"

"I think it's because . . ." He wasn't sure how to admit this, especially to a rolling pin–wielding baker with angry eyes. "Well, my grandmother? She was about to eat me."

"Eat you!" The woman plopped into a chair. The rolling pin fell harmlessly onto her lap. She left it there and sighed. "Is she a troll?"

"I guess so."

The woman leaned forward in her chair. "Are you a troll?"

"NO!" Jamie staggered backward, moving so quickly that he bashed into a table and propelled himself right into a purple-painted chair. "Oh, no! I couldn't be! Could I?"

"Well, you're quite short. And frail. That's not troll-like, but there's no telling really. Most of you don't turn till you're thirteen."

Jamie gasped.

"What? Are you thirteen?"

"I'm only twelve," Jamie explained. "But my birthday's Saturday."

"Happy almost birthday," she said offhandedly and scooted her chair closer to him, peering in his face. "Some change then. But you don't show any indications . . . Quite short . . . No green tinge . . . Thin nose, petite but not bulbous . . ."

Jamie cleared his throat. She was too close. Her breath smelled of almonds.

She sniffed the air around his face. "No foul smells. Good!"

Jamie breathed out as she leaned back and rubbed at some flour that had crusted to her cheek. Relief surrounded him, making him a tiny bit dizzy.

"Well, that's a whole year you've got to stay human. Tell me. Have you lived with trolls all your life?" She leaned forward again, waiting for his reply.

"My dad and my grandmother? Yes, I think so. I mean . . . I don't actually remember when I was a baby or anything."

She scoffed. "People don't remember that. Only witches do."

Jamie thought about what Eva told him about the town being full of magic people. "Are you a witch?"

"Me? Nope. I wish I were so lucky."

Jamie didn't know how to ask politely, so he just forged ahead. "Are you magic, though?"

"Of course! I am a brounie." She wiped her hands on her apron again and said in a half-sad and half-angry voice, "I don't suppose you even know what that is."

"I'm sorry." He felt like a bumbling goofball. He'd never felt so uninformed about things, not ever.

His feelings must have shown on his face because the baker softened. "Oh, you poor thing. You don't need to be sorry, especially since you've been dealing with trolls your whole life. It's a wonder that, *A*, you have any manners at all, and *B*, you are alive. Anyway, I am a brounie. That means that I do not like crowds and prefer to work at night. Descended from the great King Peallaidh, I have the DNA required to enable me to make domestic magic. Some of us do get stuck and cranky, and usually we are at a particular person's house for eternity, but I, as you see, have a place of my own. I'm not quite normal, is what I'm saying. According to Mr. Nate that's due to a molecular degeneration at the—"

"Mr. Nate!" Jamie interrupted.

"Do you know him?"

"I do! I do! He's the librarian and my neighbor."

"Only part-time, sweetie." She stood up and grabbed a cupcake. "Here, eat this. You look thin. The other part of the time he is here. He lives upstairs with me."

"With you." The cupcake glistened in his hand, a pink sugary piece of chocolate-frosted perfection. He couldn't resist and bit into it. Happiness exploded into his mouth, caressing his tongue and teeth before melting into sugary awesomeness. He swallowed and took another bite, forgetting what they were even talking about.

The woman didn't. "We're married."

"You're married?" He took a moment to process this and finished his cupcake in a quick gobble.

She winked flirtatiously. "Sorry to disappoint you."

"No! I—I didn't mean—I—"

"I'm just playing with you, Jamie Hephaistion Alexander. Now it's my turn to say 'sorry.'" She laughed and took a bite of a cupcake. Her expression crashed back down as soon as she stopped chewing. "Nate hadn't told me about you. He tells me everything."

"Well, we're only just . . ." He searched for the right word. "Acquaintances. I'm sure he knows tons of kids better than he knows me and stuff." Jamie's stomach clenched despite the happy sugariness. He wondered if she knew about the house burning down. He opened his mouth to tell her when Eva stormed in, a blond boy just behind her.

"We've been searching everywhere for you! The dove helped," Eva shouted. "Hey, Helena! Cookies? You got cookies?" She rushed across the room and hauled Jamie out of his chair, hustling him toward the door. "Miss Cornelia wants you at Aquarius House. You don't keep her waiting. She'll turn you into a pair of scissors."

The blond boy rolled his eyes at Eva. "I'm Bloom," he said as Eva shoved Jamie at the door.

"Jamie," he said, instantly liking the boy. He seemed familiar, like one of the eighth-grade baseball players at school, the one who was always winning the dunk contests at field day.

"Come on!" Eva insisted, her hand flat on Jamie's back.

Jamie grabbed the door frame so he wouldn't be pushed all the way out into the street.

"Thank you, Helena!" he yelled, remembering to be polite. "Thank you for the cupcake."

"And the conversation," Helena yelled back. "Thank *you*, young Jamie Hephaistion Alexander! Come back anytime."

———

Eva hustled Jamie out of the shop and up the hill. One firm hand on his back maneuvered him past the library, general store, tavern, town hall, and various shops. Bloom, the blond boy, faded away pretty quickly, melting into the disassembling crowd somehow. Jamie didn't even see him leave. People had dispersed into smaller groups and were still chatting among themselves. Bloom must have been in one of those.

Jamie wished he could have taken another cupcake with him.

Halfway up the hill, the businesses became houses. White and rainbow picket fences dotted the yards. Paint shone brightly in all sorts of colors on the houses' exterior walls. Beyond the houses were woods on one side and a field on the other. Jamie could smell the clam flats of low tide. Eva kept mumbling as they walked.

"I can't believe I just lost you like that . . . Way too easily distracted. My dad, he says, 'Pay more attention, Eva . . . You have the attention span of an egret, Eva.' I am not an egret! I am a hero girl . . . blah . . . blah . . ." She grumbled like this while adjusting her pigtails, only taking the occasional break in her ranting to urge Jamie forward.

"I know you're trying to take everything in and all that baloney, but you are the slowest walker in the universe," she told him as they scurried past the cemetery. "Seriously. Your legs are twice as long as mine."

"I just—" Jamie stopped and stood still.

"What is it? You're acting like a bigfoot that just saw a dragon." Eva motioned for him to hurry along. He did. But as he walked, he felt a peculiar, prickly feeling that came with being watched. He shrugged it off.

Finally, after walking and walking and walking some more, Jamie and Eva reached Aquarius House, which was surrounded by a stone wall. A wooden gate opened the way to the actual house. Eleven wooden slats with gaps between them curved upward and framed the flagstone walkway to the large gray house's circular porch. The gate swung open as they approached, and they walked down the path to a white staircase with eleven steps that led up to the porch where Annie threw her arms around the pair of them.

When Annie was done squeezing the life out of him, Miss Cornelia reached out her hand. "You are quite the surprise, Mr. Jamie Alexander. It is nice to meet you. I can see by the frosting on your cheek that you've been to Helena's. I bet you're still hungry, though. Are you?"

Her voice was kind but commanding. He didn't know quite what to think of it. He shot a glance at Annie, who gave him the signal to say 'yes.' Whatever was happening to them, it seemed they were in it together. Jamie admitted he was hungry.

The old woman clapped her hands merrily. "Good! Good! Eva, thank you so much for retrieving them. You are quite the hero of a dwarf today, I would say. Your parents should be proud."

Eva puffed up at the compliment.

"Yes, thank you for rescuing me, Eva." Annie's smile softened her face.

Jamie chimed in, "Yeah. Thanks, Eva."

"Anytime you need rescuing, you ask for me, Eva Beryl-Axe. Got it? Good." She straightened her pigtails and started to go. She stopped and then yelled over her shoulder. "Not Bloom. Me! I am much better at rescuing. He hasn't saved anyone yet."

The threesome all nodded vigorously and yelled good-bye to Eva's small, broad back as it retreated down the hill.

"It's a good-natured rivalry. I am positive Bloom will do a good deal of rescuing someday, once he has the chance. It is in his blood," Miss Cornelia explained. "Now, welcome to your new home."

"It feels oddly . . . It feels . . . familiar?" Annie's voice rose on the last word. She chewed on the corner of her lip. "That makes no sense, does it?"

"Things don't have to be understood to make sense," Miss Cornelia answered cryptically. "Am I right, children?"

They didn't know how else to answer, so they both said the same word. "Right."

13

Aquarius House

The massive red door swung open, pulled by dozens of fairies or pixies, maybe? Annie didn't know what to call the small, beautiful beings. Inside the foyer, a massive winding staircase seemed to be supported by nothing, and beneath it rested a gold fountain that looked like a South American waterfall and led to a pool filled with splashing fish. A tiger peeked through the branches of a wide-leaved tropical plant.

Jamie blinked the scene away with a shake of his head. *Unreal.* The air in the room hung humid against his skin and made him forget he was in New England.

"Can you swim in it?" Jamie asked, touching the water with his fingers.

"The mermaids do in the winter," Miss Cornelia said. "If you glance beneath the surface you will see a couple of them swimming now."

The merpeople glinted in the water. They were having tea. Jamie nudged Annie with his elbow.

"This is too cool for words," he whispered.

Miss Cornelia led them across the marble checkerboard floor to a sitting room to the left and snapped on the light. If Annie and Jamie didn't know better, they could have sworn they were back in the Maine woods. This room resembled an enchanted forest. An overhead light sent shafted rays down through branches of trees and ivy that covered the ceiling, which must have been twenty feet high. Along the walls, thin tree trunks grew, golden flowers and bright purple blossoms twining around the bark. A golden arrow aimed toward a four-leaf clover that was painted against the side of a prancing unicorn. Real clover seemed to lace around the animal.

Annie's small hand reached out to touch the wall. The flowers and the tree trunks felt real. Jamie gasped as one of the flowers moved beneath Annie's fingers.

"It's a lovely room, isn't it?" Miss Cornelia asked. "Quite a bit different from your last accommodations, if I do say so myself."

Annie thought of the cramped trailer. A bird's wings flapped above her. She craned her neck up to see. *Is that a chickadee flitting through the branches?* She remembered to breathe. The air filled her lungs with warmth and flowers.

"It's lovely," she said.

Miss Cornelia laughed, a low, musical sort of laugh. "Thank you. I enjoy it."

Annie sat down on the couch, which appeared to be made of moss that was somehow stapled into the woodwork. She ran her hands over its softness. Through the door, she could see into the entryway. All sorts of colored lights flitted near the fountain, which really did seem more like a waterfall. She rubbed her eyes and looked at Jamie, who shrugged his shoulders, baffled.

"Are we outside or in?" Jamie asked.

Miss Cornelia laughed again and plopped down on the sofa beside Annie. "Why, in, of course. It's far too cold to be out."

Annie agreed, her eyes wide, and pulled a nearby quilt around her. The house was warm, but just the mention of outside chilled her. She seemed to have suddenly and completely lost her ability to speak.

Jamie hadn't, though. "This house must be magical."

"Of course it is!" Miss Cornelia said assuredly, pointing at Jamie with a long, bony finger. "Sound reasoning, Jamie. Sound reasoning indeed."

Aquarius House was not what Annie had expected at all. None of it was. She had imagined her next life would be in another trailer or maybe an apartment over a Subway in downtown Ellsworth, right on High Street where she could hear the logging trucks and the tourists' RVs roar by all year long; where she could listen to the people next door scream their hatred at each other; where she, Annie, could decide all the places where she would never live when she was a grownup. No, this wasn't the place she'd imagined, not at all. In fact, she figured she might actually be dreaming. She snuck her hand behind her back and gave herself a good pinch.

"Pinching never wakes you up," Miss Cornelia said. "It has no effect on dreams whatsoever. Cold water is much more jarring and yields better results when one is attempting to rouse oneself from a dream. I could get a pitcher if you'd like, although then, of course, you'd have to change your clothes and we have yet to have dinner."

Her eyes twinkled mischievously.

Annie shook her head and doodled distractedly with her finger on the couch cushion. The thought of freezing water against her skin didn't appeal much to her after the walk in the cold.

"I feel like I'm dreaming, too," Jamie admitted.

"I can assure you this is no dream," Miss Cornelia said, hands spread wide.

Annie bit her lip. She wanted to believe the fantastic room was real, but it didn't seem likely. A fuzzy brown rabbit hopped behind a long green drape.

"Is that a . . . It's just . . ." Annie couldn't begin to explain.

"I think what Annie's trying to say is that this is all . . ." Jamie paused as if searching about his brain for the proper words. "It's a bit beyond our normal everyday experience."

"Do you like it?" Miss Cornelia asked, slipping off the couch and rushing toward the drapes. Her rainbow-slipper-clad foot poked at a lump behind the fabric. The rabbit darted out quickly, and she caught it, pulling it to her chest. She brought it back toward Annie, and as she did, Annie glimpsed outside, beyond the curtain.

The early-evening gloom cast a shadow upon everything outside, but there in the window's reflection, Annie saw something else. At first it seemed little more than an extra bit of darkness in the coming black. But as Annie scooted back on the couch, farther away, she could have sworn she spotted a man's face in the glass—and not the sort of man she'd imagine her long-lost father to be, the kind who made breakfast in the morning, took her to gymnastics, held her hand when she crossed the street. No, this man's face had a searing chill of ice and hatred. His eyes felt deathly cold. It was like his image was trapped in the window.

Miss Cornelia whirled around, plopped the bunny on the floor, and whipped the drapes shut, but Annie had already turned away from the window.

"He knows you're here already. Oh, my . . . ," Miss Cornelia said worriedly. She snapped her fingers, and all the drapes in the room flapped shut. "My word. Of course he does, what with all the mayor's ridiculous carrying-on. I told him no big to-dos, but did he listen?"

Annie sat as still as she could. All her fears combined with words and gushed out of her mouth. "This is not real. Maybe Walden walloped me too hard on the head and I've got a concussion. That must be it. Or maybe I really am batty, like Mrs. Betsey said. She said it ran in the family. That was why I am in foster care."

Embarrassed, Jamie stared at the floor.

Annie took a good gulp and covered her mouth with her hand. "Oh, I didn't mean that. Oh. I'm sorry."

Miss Cornelia gave her a kind smile.

"Do you know how to read?" she asked, ignoring Annie's rant, and patted the girl's hair.

Annie could smell the breath of her, like mint and red wine and something bitter and earthy underneath it all. It reminded her of the taste of dandelion roots. Dandelions were her favorite flowers because they could grow in anything.

"Yes, of course." Annie loved to read anything and everything. In most of her foster homes there was always a *TV Guide* at least. She'd read that if there was nothing else. Most of the people who took her in didn't have books. There were books at school, though.

Miss Cornelia continued purposefully. "What do all books have in common, Annie?"

"A plot?" Annie asked, flustered and rubbing her hands against her legs. Her lack of a good answer made her forget about the face in the window and even Jamie who was sitting next to her. "I'm sorry. I'm sorry. Wait a sec. Words? They all have words."

Miss Cornelia's lips came together in a tight grimace as she sat again.

"Oh, no," Annie said, scrunching up her face. Already she was messing up. Already, she wasn't being who this new foster mother—or foster grandmother—was expecting her to be. She never was. Not ever. She thought about all her favorite books. Then the weight in her chest lifted.

"A hero!"

"That's right," Miss Cornelia said, and her thin lips parted to become a smile that resembled an upside-down rainbow. "Heroes are important. What do they do?"

Annie thought for a moment, but her brain didn't seem to want to work at all. She startled when the bunny jumped into her lap and snuggled in. She reached down and touched its fur. The softness soothed her fingers and even her heart a little bit. She longed to pick the rabbit up and rub her face in the downiness of it. But no, she had to think.

"They save the day?"

Miss Cornelia stood up, and the entire room got a bit bigger when she did, as if the whole house had sighed in relief. And, just then, as the feeling of relief was about to take over, Miss Cornelia squatted down in front of Annie and leaned toward her.

"That's true. They save the day. Is that all?"

The girl-wizard and her brainy dinosaur sidekick had defeated the evil dragon. The tiny rabbit had vanquished a pig-faced boy who tried to eat his way through town. A young boy became brave enough to face the evil ghost inside his closet.

"They become brave."

"That's right," Miss Cornelia said with such force that her words seemed to solidify in the air. "They are brave. You said, 'become brave,' but in their hearts, they always were courageous. They just hadn't let it out yet. Now, Annie, with all you've been through it seems to me that you should be quite ready."

Annie sighed and stroked the rabbit's fur. The bunny began to thump its leg, and then it quieted and nestled in. It didn't shake at all like most of the rabbits Annie had met. *I'm doing enough trembling for the both of us. I am so tired of trying to be brave. I'd like to just be happy for a while, happy and loved. Maybe that can really, actually happen here.*

Each and every one of Miss Cornelia's bones cracked as she stood up from where she squatted in front of Annie's face. She rolled her neck and then pulled her shoulders back before she slowly stretched out one hand to Annie and another to Jamie, both of whom still sat on the couch, confusion filling their faces.

"Are you ready, Annie?" she asked. Her fingers wiggled. "Are you ready, Jamie?"

Annie took the hand in her own.

"Ready for what?" she whispered. Miss Cornelia's hand felt warm and lovely, still so much better than she imagined.

"Ready to be brave."

"To be brave," Annie repeated, thinking again of the world outside full of people who pretended to love you just for money, of the monsters in the woods, of Jamie's grandmother running after him with a fork, drooling. *Haven't we been brave already? Do we really have to be brave again?*

Jamie scooted a little closer to Annie as Miss Cornelia dropped their hands. Jamie was already brave. Just living with his father and grandmother had made him that way, hadn't it? Or had it made him even more timid, lacking confidence? He didn't know. Could it have made him both brave and cowardly all at once? Does just surviving make you brave? He had no clue. He'd never actually thought about himself so much. It wasn't fun. He coughed and answered the way he knew the strange old woman wanted him to answer. "We are ready."

Annie whispered it, too. "We are ready to be brave."

Jamie's stomach lurched. He was worried that he had just lied.

Miss Cornelia fixed them in her stare. "What you need to understand is that this is a place of no return really. You can choose to stay here with us, or you can move on. If you leave, then we will find you homes, good homes, full of normal people and without any trolls. I can promise you that."

Jamie grabbed Annie's hand, mostly because it was shaking so much, and partially because he needed something to hold on to. Her ice-cold fingers seemed thin and fragile between his. He cleared his throat.

"Why would we want to leave?" he asked.

Annie peeked at him without turning her head. He thought she may have even nodded the slightest bit. She didn't say anything, though. He wished she would. He didn't like asking the question. It felt rude somehow.

"Why would you want to leave?" Miss Cornelia repeated. She raised an eyebrow and once it was lowered back into place, she leaned much closer and whispered, "I don't see why you would ever want to leave. I know I don't. There is no better home for me than Aurora. There never could be. But, yes, some do choose to leave and it's a very viable option for the two of you."

She straightened up, cocked her head, and her right ear seemed to twitch a bit. Jamie and Annie waited. Annie's fingers tightened around Jamie's, drawing strength.

"Ma'am, why would it be a viable option?" she asked.

Miss Cornelia's light-blue eyes focused on Annie's face, and she said, "Because it is dangerous to be here. It is always dangerous to be in a place of magic, and for the two of you—the danger is profound. If you choose to leave, you *can* live a normal life. I don't believe it's too late for you. We could wipe out your memory of this place and us. We have done that before. It isn't the easiest of magic, but it can be done."

"But if we stay?" Jamie prodded.

Miss Cornelia petted the head of the bunny in Annie's lap. Her face crumpled for a moment as she stared at Annie, but then she regained her composure. She said simply, "Well, if you stay I shall do my very best to keep you safe, but the town is in peril, not just because of trolls such as Jamie's grandmother, but from bigger, even more horrid things. It's possible you might die in any number of horrible ways. That's always the risk of a magic life. A magic death."

Before either of them responded the doorbell rang. The sound of it scared Annie so much that she jerked, which startled the bunny. It hopped off and hid behind a Cupid statue in the room's far corner. Jamie could almost swear that the statue blinked.

Moments after the doorbell sounded, a bunch of small, pastel tutu–wearing pixies flash-flew into the room, announcing in chirpy voices, "Company! You have company! Guests! We have guests!"

"Well, hold that thought a moment please, children." Miss Cornelia pointedly glanced at each of them. "I must get the front door."

The pixies shut the door to the sitting room behind them.

———

The children sat there for a moment, totally still.

"I think you should stay," Annie said, her voice dangling in the air.

"Me? What about you?"

"Well, with you . . ." Jamie thought Annie was struggling with words. Her lips moved without any sound coming out before she finally finished, "It's just that I saw your grandmother, Jamie. She was horrible. I think she wanted to eat you or at least kill you. She threw a knife at us."

He swallowed hard, and the thought that he didn't want to enter his head came into it full steam ahead.

"I don't want to be like her," he blurted.

Annie jumped back. "You are NOTHING like her. You don't look anything like her, and I bet you don't act anything like her either."

That was true, but still, what Helena the baker said needled him. "Helena said I might become one. Sometime this year. That's what happens when trolls turn thirteen."

He might. He might not. It was up in the air until he was fourteen.

She clutched his hand. "You won't."

"How do you know?" His voice was as tiny and scared as he felt.

"Because I won't let you," she insisted, as if that made it so. "Plus, that *does* mean you should stay here. The place is magic. It seems like the best place to be if you want to learn how NOT to become a troll."

They sat in silence for a second. All his life he'd hoped his existence held some purpose, and now—Jamie didn't know what he was supposed to do, but he knew that sitting on the couch wasn't brave, even if that couch *was* made of moss. So, he slid off. His feet sank into the soft carpet. He crouched down and spread apart his fingers to feel it better.

"Just like moss," he whispered. "Weird."

Little flowers resembling miniature buttercups grew out of the moss. He fingered one, wishing he could pluck it off and see if it was real like the flowers on the wall, but he didn't know what kind of trouble that would get him into. Miss Cornelia seemed nice, even if she was older than dirt.

"I know what Miss Cornelia said, but do you feel like you're dreaming?" Jamie asked.

"Exactly that way!" Annie said excitedly. "And if we're not dreaming—I mean, so many bizarre things have happened today—"

"You're worried you might be losing it?" Jamie fidgeted.

"Exactly."

"Me, too." Jamie thought for a moment and then used the word Annie kept using. "Exactly."

She started babbling animatedly. "The thing is, with Mrs. Wiegle, my last foster, I felt like I might be losing it there, too, because it was so awful. I wasn't ever allowed to touch Walden's things. Walden was her son. He was a horrible wretch ball. I turned on the clock radio in the kitchen the first day, and Walden sat on me! His super-large butt squashed my face into the dirty linoleum floor. Then he stuffed one of my shirts with tissues and put a melon on it for a head before he set it on fire out on the lawn. And do you know what he said? He said, 'This is you-oo.' He sang it in that squeaky-doorknob voice he has. 'This is Ann-ie, who can't keep her baby hands off my things.' Walden always said I have baby hands, because they're small. I am so glad to be gone from there! I don't care if this is a dream or if we could die because of magic. This is better. Believe me, being dead would be better than being with them."

"He sounds awful," Jamie said slowly. The drape by the window moved a bit, and Annie's shudder turned into a shiver. "Don't worry. It's just a draft."

"Was it awful where you were?" Annie leaned forward and handed Jamie the bunny as if he might find comfort in it. "Your grandmother . . . She looked—"

Annie suddenly seemed at a loss for words.

"It was bad." Jamie's face closed off.

Annie reached out and awkwardly petted his arm. "Oh, you have a splinter." She plucked it out of his hand before he could even react, and then she abruptly changed the subject. "So, do you think we should?"

Jamie's voice shook a bit. "Should what?"

"Stay here in this . . . in this . . . magic place."

He hesitated. A man's face seemed to form in the mirror on the wall. Long lines scowling. Jamie could almost make it out, but it blurred. Even though it worried him, he glanced away, focused back on Annie. "I do. I think we should. I mean, I thought my grandmother was going to eat me and people are so nice here and you . . ."

"My place was horrible. All I wanted was to get away."

"And now we've gotten away."

It almost seemed too good to be true.

"We should vow, Jamie," Annie said, sticking out her pinkie finger. "We should vow to stay here forever, where we are safe, where nobody can eat us, or force us to do despicable things, or throw us outside in dog pens, where no one can make us smell underwear, or tell us we should be invisible because we're so worthless. And whatever happens, we'll stick together and look out for each other. You and me and Tala."

"Deal," Jamie said, and Annie thought he seemed relieved. His eyes lit up.

"Forever friends," Annie said, squeezing his hand. It made her feel better to have him there with her, to not be in this alone. "We should promise to protect this place and each other."

Jamie gave her a slight nod. Protecting this place would give him a purpose much bigger than just feeding his father and grandmother, and it was much more important and exciting than hopelessly existing.

Annie's voice suddenly lost all its bravery. "Okay?"

Jamie hooked his pinkie around hers. "Okay."

"I promise," Annie whispered.

"Promise," Jamie echoed.

They kept their pinkies locked like that for a second, and Annie pulled apart first, awkwardly brushing her hair out of her face before asking, "Who do you think came to the door?"

"Hopefully not my grandmother," Jamie said in an attempt to joke. It didn't quite work.

"Definitely not! Not Mrs. Wiegle or my social worker either." Tiptoeing to the sitting room's threshold, she cocked her head to listen.

Almost as if the visitor heard her, a male voice that neither child recognized said, "It's a noisy night."

"Yes, it is," Miss Cornelia replied with a bit of concern. "Things are about."

Annie motioned for Jamie to join her. He crept over in time to hear the man answer.

"Things?"

"One thing in particular," Cornelia replied in a quieter tone.

"Not—"

"Yes." Cornelia lowered her voice even more. Annie strained to hear. "And now with the gnome gone, it appears all sorts of things will be able to find us."

"And do what?"

"That is the question, isn't it?" Miss Cornelia's voice had a tired edge. "The black bird. There was a sighting."

The man's voice raised in panic. "It's here?! Good goblins, Corny. That means—that means—we could be stuck."

"Shh. The walls, you know, have ears."

"And so do little girls and boys."

This Cornelia lady is far too smart. Jamie started to move backward farther into the sitting room, but Annie grabbed his arm, keeping him there.

"Where is she anyway?" the man asked. His voice was smooth and deep and not the kind to inspire confidences.

"Safe and fine," Miss Cornelia said in a soft voice that made Annie think of mother things like hot chocolate and warm cake and hugs. "Tala did a good job."

"And where *is* Tala?"

"Tala is healed up and is keeping the outside out and the inside in." Miss Cornelia laughed. "He is delighted. He wagged his tail, poor thing. He hasn't been happy since—"

"Well, none of us have. Tell me, do you think she has what it takes?" the man asked.

"She must."

"Are they talking about me?" Annie whispered.

Jamie shrugged and put a finger to his lips.

"She seems small like her—"

Miss Cornelia cut him off. "Well, everyone seems small to you."

The man chuckled. "That's because they are." Then his voice turned serious. "It has been a long time since we've faced such evil. Do you think we will prevail once again? Despite the prophecy?"

"We must," replied Miss Cornelia gravely. "She is at a crossroads where her past, present, and future fatefully intersect. What happens now is up to her. Our very lives depend on it."

14

Danger Approaches

Just then the doorknob wiggled, and Annie and Jamie leaped back, guilty, bumping into each other in their haste to act like they weren't listening.

"Hello, James Hephaistion Alexander!" Mr. Nate pushed the door open and strode into the sitting room. His face was smudged with black. The smell of burned things wafted toward Jamie, who darted up to greet him.

"Mr. Nate! You're alive!" Jamie wanted to hug the gaunt, bedraggled-looking man. Helena had told him that Mr. Nate hadn't died in the fire, but somehow Jamie hadn't quite believed her until this very moment. He caught himself at the last second from wrapping his arms around the librarian.

"Apparently, but only just barely. I had to get past the mayor who is pontificating at Miss Cornelia. That man loves a speech. I barely avoided it." Mr. Nate gestured at Jamie and then at Annie. "And you must be the Annie everyone keeps talking about. It is a great pleasure to meet you." He gave a formal little bow, and Annie giggled.

"Are you hurt?" Jamie asked.

Mr. Nate sat down, explaining that he was fine. His house had burned down, but he'd escaped with a minor injury on his hand, which was now bandaged up, and some smoke in his lungs.

Relief flooded Jamie's body, but he could still sense Mr. Nate's distress. It was a small weight at the base of the neck, worrying him down. Jamie asked, "Where will you live?"

"With Helena, full-time. She'll just have to get used to being near people twenty-four seven, you know?" Mr. Nate petted his stomach. "I expect to be twice this size by tomorrow. That woman likes to feed anything with a digestive system. It's quite an appealing quality in a living creature."

Jamie thought that there were worse things to like than feeding people. One such thing would be eating people. He pushed the thought of his grandmother out of his mind, instead asking the question he wanted to know. "So, all that time at the library . . . you knew about this place?"

Mr. Nate wiped at some soot on his cheeks. "I did."

"Which means you're some kind of magic, too?"

"I am." He straightened his shirt and coughed. "Witch. Wizard. Magic man. Seer. Whatever you'd like to call it. I'm only a bit magic, though. I've hardly any powers to speak of, and when I use them I tend to shake afterward. Not very manly."

Jamie tried to understand exactly what that meant. "So you can . . . ?"

Mr. Nate explained that some people had a genetic predisposition to be a witch or a wizard, to do magic. Usually, it did not involve cauldrons or hats or spells with certain words said in certain orders. Some people were born into magic families, but some just underwent certain mutations in the DNA and—poof—magic was born. Other magic creatures also had similar genetic makeup to that of regular people but with tweaks. Dwarfs, elves, and shape-shifters were like that. For witches, certain abilities were coded into their DNA: power over different elements, flying, telepathy. It was complicated and brilliant, and both Annie and Jamie were totally enthralled.

"What about trolls?" Annie asked, knowing that was the question Jamie most wanted answered.

"You will learn about that soon enough, young lady," Mr. Nate said.

"Please tell us," Jamie urged. He couldn't stand knowing only parts of things.

Mr. Nate took pity on him. "Trolls have a couple of mutations, a few extra chromosomes. There's a lot we don't understand about them. They shift, obviously, into their true selves at will, but usually at night. They hunt in groups, eating large mammals, chickens, and sometimes even trees. They would prefer to eat people, but they know that if they do that too much, people would catch on and hunt them. This happened in northern Europe centuries ago. Trolls were nearly eradicated by humans who had enough of their children being stolen and eaten in the middle of the night. So sometimes they raise people to eat as special delicacies."

"Like me?" Jamie shivered. His hand was clutching the edge of the couch. He forced himself to ease his grip.

"Yes," Mr. Nate answered.

"Which means they stole me from someone," Jamie verified once again. "That I'm not even theirs?"

"Yes."

For Jamie, it explained a lot. Why there were no pictures of his mother. Why he looked so different from everyone else—even his skin color, his eye color, his body shape, his facial features. They had never loved him, he realized, because you don't love your food. But something still didn't make sense.

"Wouldn't they have fattened me up a bit?" he asked. "They starved me. Wouldn't they want more of me to eat?"

"They would if they liked to eat meat and fat, but that's not what they like to eat, Jamie. They like to eat bones and brains."

His bones.

His brains.

"And they had to wait till my birthday to do that?"

Mr. Nate hopped about on his heels. "It is a rule to keep their behavior in check, a curse basically, and a bit cryptic as to its origins as all good curses are. Some say it was a curse created by Thor himself and involves lightning." Mr. Nate shrugged, standing up. "Who knows the thought process of trolls? But let's forget about that for now, birthday boy. I promise you. No one will eat you here. I've been asked to show you around before dinner, so how about a tour? Shall we?"

Annie and Jamie started to follow him into the hallway, but Jamie stopped short at the door. His hand trembled as he reached for Mr. Nate's elbow. "Wait. Does that mean . . . Does that mean . . ."

"What?" Mr. Nate turned, examining his face. Worry made his features scrunch up a bit.

"Does that mean"—Jamie could hardly get the words out—"that my parents are still alive?"

Mr. Nate said simply, "There is always hope, Jamie. You must remember this." He waved his hands in the air as he spoke. "There will always be hope, always be light, even in the midst of the most worrisome troubles. Annie is meant to be our hope, but I do believe that you, Mr. Jamie Alexander, may give this town hope as well. You can be happy here."

Jamie seemed to stand a bit straighter, grinning, but Annie couldn't help but ask, "Why does the town need hope?"

"Well, at this particular moment . . ." Mr. Nate ushered the children in front of him through a maze of hallways and rooms, barely stopping long enough for them to peek their heads in. "Well, there was a gnome. Not a real gnome per se. It was magical and it protected Aurora from detection."

"Detection?" Annie cocked her head. She knew what the word meant, but she didn't quite understand.

"It kept it safe so that humans and trolls and all sorts of savory and unsavory creatures couldn't find us here, but it's been stolen. That leaves us unprotected."

Jamie stopped midstep. "Wait! So we aren't safe now? The whole town?"

"Yes. Why?" Mr. Nate urged them forward again. Annie could hear his stomach grumble.

"It's just . . ." Jamie's sentence trailed off when a terrible rumble began in the hallway behind them, which wasn't dark a moment ago and now looked as if a giant brown fog was thundering toward them.

"Wh-what is that?" Annie stuttered.

Mr. Nate's eyes grew big. He shoved them both away from the approaching fog through the maze of hallways. "Run! Find a place to hide! Now! Go!"

"But . . . ," Annie objected.

"Is it trolls?" Jamie shouted.

"Much worse, Jamie. Run! Stay with each other. Now!"

Mr. Nate, Annie, and Jamie ran for their lives. Pixies and fairies buzzed everywhere. All the occupants of Aquarius House streamed out of doorways, the dark fog pushing them toward the fountain in the foyer, where they realized there was nowhere left to go.

The darkness swirled around the fountain and seemed to settle in it, turning the water black. Several mermaids had evacuated the fountain and were flopping around on the cold floor tiles, creating puddles as they frantically searched for a place to escape. Some of the pixies screamed and Annie stopped still. There was the face of a man in the water, a reflection on the surface.

Mr. Nate snatched Annie and Jamie against his wool sweater.

"Don't look, children," he implored them. "You don't need to see him. He can't be here. He's far away. It's just an image. Just an image, is all."

Just an image or not, the reflection terrified them. There was something wicked in the man's eyes, something more evil than anything Annie had ever seen before. Although she *had* seen him before, hadn't she? *Yes, it was the man in the window*. She couldn't avert her gaze, no matter how hard she tried.

The face in the water stared directly at Annie. His mouth opened, forming horrible croaking words, "Annie Nobody. I will come for you."

"For me?" she whispered.

Jamie shuddered beside her. Mr. Nate clutched her closer.

"Never!" A woman's voice, loud and strong, broke the silence. A giant ball of light hit the water in the fountain. The man's image shook but stayed.

Miss Cornelia strode forward, face taut with tension, hands outstretched. "You will not take anyone. Never again."

The man smirked slowly, completely unfazed by her words. "We shall see."

"Never." Her voice resonated like a bell and seemed to fill the entire house with her power. Across all the walls of the room the word wrote itself over and over in bold, angry writing: **NEVER. NEVER. NEVER. NEVER.**

A ball of light formed in Miss Cornelia's hand. It rushed through the air and hit the water again. The darkness swept up to the ceiling and disappeared. The old woman closed her eyes and bent over a bit, as if terribly tired.

Annie ran to her, wrapping her arm around the woman's thin waist. "Are you okay? Sit down."

She hustled Miss Cornelia toward a marble bench away from the fountain, anxiously gaping over her shoulder.

"He is gone," Miss Cornelia said. "He was never truly

here. He can only appear in reflections now. But he is so strong, stronger than he's been in years."

"You did well," Mr. Nate said to Miss Cornelia, helping some mermaids back into the fountain.

"I am weak." Miss Cornelia sighed and laid a hand on Annie's cheek, focusing her next words on the girl. "This is part of the danger you face, Annie . . . and you, Jamie . . . living here."

For a moment everyone was silent. The mermaids and mermen propped themselves up out of the water, listening. Several pixies landed on Jamie's shoulders and head.

Annie sucked in her breath, terrified. "But, he is gone?"

"For now." Miss Cornelia hauled in a breath and stood back up, her posture restored to its typical ramrod straightness. "And let us pray that he never returns."

15

Dinner

Despite the terrifying experience, Miss Cornelia ordered them all off to dinner, saying she'd meet them there in a moment. Mr. Nate made small talk as he bustled them to a large mahogany door, but Jamie's brain was full of questions.

"Who was that?" he asked.

"Evil," Mr. Nate answered, "Pure, unadulterated evil."

"Miss Cornelia said he took someone. Who did he take?"

"Many." That was all Mr. Nate would say on the matter. "It's important to remember that only his reflection can appear in Aurora. Even without our protection, he has been banished. But if his minions find us, they will destroy everything they can."

Annie grabbed at Jamie's shirtsleeve. Her hand was still shaking.

"When you say 'minions,' do you mean things like trolls?" Annie asked, seeming to read Jamie's thoughts.

"Yes. And worse." Mr. Nate gave them a smile, but it was fragile and weak, hardly reassuring. "Now, let's not think of those things at the moment. Instead, let's think of dinner."

He pushed open the door to the dining room, and once again Annie and Jamie found themselves in a room that looked just like a forest. Tree trunks covered the dining room walls, and long sweeping willow branches, intermingled with Spanish moss, draped down from the ceiling toward a table carpeted with light-green lichen and moss. The chairs were made of wooden sticks tied together, and the chandelier hanging above the center of the table reflected the starlight.

Annie rushed forward into the room.

"EVA!" Annie hugged the pigtailed dwarf. "Are you okay?"

"Of course I'm okay. Dwarfs are ALWAYS okay." Eva pushed Annie away and crossed her arms over her chest. She held a fork in each hand. "Just hungry. Around here, we start with dessert and work our way backward, thank the Stoppers. We get the good stuff first. Brussels sprouts last."

As if on cue, a dozen pies flew through a doorway opposite and settled into the center of the table as a large-eyed

woman called Gramma Doris pointed at them, shouting commands. Annie, Jamie, and Mr. Nate took seats by Eva.

"Cherry, go right and down."

The cherry pie flopped in front of a giant boy with glasses and a stony face who was sitting next to Jamie. Jamie vaguely recognized him from school. The boy winked and whisked his napkin out as another cherry pie rocketed in front of Mr. Nate.

"Banana cream, ninety degrees left and three down. There."

The banana cream pie landed in front of Miss Cornelia. Another landed in front of Eva.

"Apple, no. No! Apple, round about, three o'clock."

The apple pie, flying in a thoroughly confused manner, came to rest in front of an older man with crooked glasses and a stethoscope hung around the neck of his sweater. He marveled at the pie and said, "Absolutely delicious! I love apple pie!"

A plethora of dwarfs applauded as the pecan pies hurtled toward them. A happy-go-lucky fairy sat on one, for a ride.

Bloom hustled into the room and took the seat next to Annie, apologizing for being late.

"Elves are always late!" Eva yelled.

Gramma Doris held up her hands. "Eva. Bloom. No fighting."

Jamie turned to Mr. Nate, his mind on something other than pie. "Why am I here? I'm not—" Jamie didn't want to say it out loud all of a sudden. It felt as if being un-magic was some sort of curse or oddity, something to be ashamed of somehow.

"We had to save you from those trolls," Mr. Nate answered as he lifted a forkful of cherry filling. "But there may be magic in you yet, Jamie Alexander. You never know. And we do allow those who have knowledge of magic to shelter here. You weren't safe at home, so the Council voted to bring you here."

Annie was just diving into her pie and Bloom was halfway through his when Gramma Doris relaxed and sat down again. She cast an appraising gaze on Jamie and said, "Name any sort of pie you'd like."

"He looks like he'd eat anything," Eva announced, splattering yellow pie filling all over her shirt.

"Eva!" Bloom scolded.

"It's okay. I would." Jamie smiled as three pies whisked through the air and landed in front of him. One was chocolate. One had some sort of fruit. The other one was green. "Thank you."

He barely got out the words before he couldn't resist any longer and started forking up the food.

"As I was saying, the Council," Mr. Nate continued, leaning back in his chair, "runs the town. We have representatives of all the major species—"

"Dwarfs. Giants. Witches. Hags. Fairies. Vampires. Shifters. Magical humans," the boy with the stony face announced, reaching out his hand. "I am SalGoud, by the way, a stone giant. I've seen you at school, Jamie. Nice to meet you, Annie."

Jamie and Annie stopped eating long enough to shake the tall, bespectacled boy's hand. His skin was soft to touch, but underneath he was made of stones, hard granite like the land of Maine itself.

"Just so you know, stone giants have horrible eyesight," said SalGoud, "but warm hearts."

Mr. Nate stopped his town government lesson so that everyone else at the table could be introduced. There was the mayor, whose voice they had heard with Miss Cornelia, and an older man named Ned the Doctor, the town physician and some sort of giant as well. There was Gramma Doris who did much of the cooking, several dwarfs whose names Jamie forgot instantly, much to his embarrassment, a few fairies flitting about, and Tala. The dog stayed pressed against Annie's legs as he wolfed down a meat pie. One man, Canin, ran the town store. He had a grizzled beard and a gruff voice. When he said hello he sounded like he was coughing. He had dog breath, and the password Mr. Nate gave Jamie suddenly made a lot of sense.

"Maybe I should show them around Aurora tomorrow, since it is the weekend," SalGoud suggested.

"Well, what a good idea!" said Doris, wiping her hands on her apron. "Give them both a better idea of things. Did Miss Cornelia tell you anything about Aurora, Annie?"

Annie put down her fork and stared up at the red-haired pixies dancing on the chandelier above the long, lichen-covered table.

"We really didn't have a lot of time," Annie said apologetically. She peeked to Jamie as if for help.

"Not really," he said, remembering Miss Cornelia's warnings and kindness.

The mayor cleared his throat. "I'm sure Annie will be learning even more soon. On Monday morning you start school again, Annie, but in Mount Desert. You catch the bus at seven o'clock. The stop is just outside the town proper. After that you'll have magic and history lessons."

Jamie's heart sank, and his pie didn't seem quite so appetizing. He didn't want to leave again. He didn't want to *ever* leave this magical town. Maybe he wouldn't have to. The mayor only mentioned Annie.

"School?" she asked, swishing some blueberries back and forth on her plate. "I really have to go to school again?"

"Of course." Miss Cornelia acted shocked. "You and Jamie both."

No one said anything for a moment, and all the forks stopped in midair.

It was Gramma Doris who broke the silence. "Darn

tooting they have to. This town needs its own school, it does."

"Language, Doris." The mayor exhaled and fixed Annie with his eyes. "School reminds us of the rest of the world and keeps us grounded in reality. Plus, you must learn math, science, and all the basics. It's much better to learn them from humans. Humans love that sort of thing."

Eva crossed her arms in front of her overalls, and a ferret peeked out of the pocket in the middle of her chest. She gave the ferret some piecrust, pushed its head back into the pocket, and grumbled, "That's fine for you. You don't have to go."

"I did. Once, even I was young. I know about bullies and being different, Eva. I remember it far too well. But, we can't shelter you completely in Aurora. Children must lead full-size lives. That can't happen if you are stuck in one place," the mayor said.

Eva sulked for a second and then turned her full attention to her pie, gobbling it up with a total disregard for knives, crumbs, or food on her face.

"Do I have to go, too?" Jamie whispered to Mr. Nate.

"Yes."

"But what if my grandmother finds me and takes me back?" The thought of it made the pie in Jamie's stomach feel like lava, threatening to erupt.

"We will keep you safe." Mr. Nate patted Jamie's hand with his own, reassuringly. "I promise."

The conversation turned to the upcoming yearly winter carnival. Then it became a boasting competition among many at the table about who had the best times for the sack race, the obstacle course, the dragon egg toss, and so on.

Ned the Doctor kept taking his glasses off to wipe at his eyes, only to lose his glasses repeatedly. It happened quite regularly, and each time he would place his thickened hand on Annie's arm and say cordially, "Annie, dear, could you tell me where my glasses are?"

And Annie, who was seated next to him, would pluck his glasses out of the pie or the squash soup, wipe them off with her napkin, and gently place them back on his nose while the fairies giggled.

Each time, Ned the Doctor would pat her shoulder with his gentle hand and announce to the table, "Annie really is a remarkable child. Just remarkable. So clever and with just such a gentle soul. I'm so delighted she's here. Well done, Eva."

And then Annie would blush and Eva would gloat and the blond boy, Bloom, would seem to sink a little deeper into his chair. Jamie recognized that feeling. He knew what it was like to feel worthless and a little bit jealous, and wanting to be invisible. Jamie made a mental note: elves are a bit like him.

"Let's have a midmeal blessing. What was I thinking, forgetting that? SalGoud, do us the honors?" Miss Cornelia asked as she unfolded her napkin and placed it on her lap.

The tall boy swallowed hard and began, *"When I sound the fairy call, gather here in silent meeting, Chin to knee on the orchard wall, cooled with dew and cherries eating. Merry, merry, Take a cherry, Mine are sounder, Mine are rounder, Mine are sweeter, For the eater When the dews fall. And you'll be fairies all."*

"Good one, SalGoud!" Bloom said before shoveling his fork into his stew. "Wow. This is good. I'm starved."

"Robert Graves, wasn't it?" Ned the Doctor said, also digging in. "Brilliant choice. Lovely poet. Mmm. Mmm. Delicious meal. Brave company. Life can't get any better than this."

"Did you know I got Annie all by myself? Seriously." Eva bragged while slopping stew all over her shirt. "Rescued her from the clutches of wicked humans, and then we saved Jamie from being eaten—"

"You've told us that a hundred times," Bloom complained, putting down his fork.

"It was a good job heroically done," Miss Cornelia said, causing Eva to blush bright red.

"I could've done it," Bloom muttered.

"Of course you could," SalGoud whispered. "You just didn't have the chance."

Jamie turned to see if Eva heard. The dwarf hadn't. She was monstering into her ham hock without a fork. He thought it was pretty disgusting.

Mr. Nate raised his glass in a toast. "For our newest citizens! To Jamie and Annie!"

They all clinked glasses. Annie blushed. Jamie suddenly couldn't stop smiling.

At one stage, the ferret and Little Mister Number Two and Little Mister Number Four, two of the small dogs that had escaped from the Wiegles, tackled each other and wrestled in the middle of the table, struggling over a leftover appetizer. The dwarfs placed bets on the winners (the ferret was the odds-on favorite) until Gramma Doris snapped her fingers and big, round metal dish covers dropped over each of them, enclosing them in separate containers. This elicited cheers from the fairies, but boos from the dwarfs and pixies.

Canin slammed up from the table, shocking all of them. "You all are carrying on as if our very lives weren't in danger. As if . . . as if that little thing of a girl could possibly save us."

Annie's eyes grew big, and she seemed to shrink in her seat. Gramma Doris wrapped an arm around her thin shoulders and hushed the wild-haired man. "You stop that, Canin. No need to scare—"

"No need to scare them?" he interrupted, laughing harshly. "Fear keeps us alive. We've been safe much too long. Does no one remember the Elf Wars? Does nobody remember what the Raiff—"

"Enough!" the mayor roared, standing from the table and knocking over his chair, causing Tala to bark and several pixies to fly up to the rafters. He ignored them all, centering his attention on Canin's bent form. "Come with me, Canin. Now."

He stormed out of the dining room, yanking Canin by his willowy arm.

"Well . . . ," Gramma Doris said after a pause. "There he goes. His kind can get so cranky and worried. Don't let him and his anxiety ruin your appetizer finale."

And for the second time that night as if on cue, everyone began to eat again. But Annie's eyes seemed worried, and Bloom kept trying too hard to make jokes that just weren't funny, and the adults all talked a bit too merrily and a bit too loudly, the way people do when they are pretending that everything is all right.

For Jamie the conversation eradicated any hope of enjoying the rest of his dinner. His heart beat heavy and fast at the thought of the Raiff, and of school, and his grandmother just a yellow bus ride away. Fortunately, the next day was Saturday, his birthday, and school was a good weekend away. But the Raiff? He seemed a lot closer somehow.

After dinner, Jamie and Annie were whisked off into the game room by Eva, SalGoud, and Bloom. Table tennis was set up in the center, a basketball hoop dominated one end, a pool table the other, and there were a few old-fashioned video games along the walls.

"All it needs is a bounce house," Annie murmured as they entered, giving Jamie big eyes.

They played doubles on table tennis, with Tala picking up any stray balls. SalGoud curled up in an oversize chair, reading *Bartlett's Familiar Quotations*, which Jamie thought strange until Eva explained that stone giants are very into words, quotes, and knowledge.

"Boring." Eva yawned. She whacked the Ping-Pong ball so hard that it bounced off the walls before landing back on the table.

"Foul!" Bloom shouted.

She shrugged. "Whatever."

Bloom and Annie were a team. Jamie and Eva were another. Annie was just as bad as Jamie at trying to hit the tiny white ball, and the game ended up with just Bloom and Eva playing.

"Can you tell me about Aurora?" Jamie asked them as Tala fetched another ball. This time it had rolled beneath the pool table.

"What about it?" Eva asked, wiping the sweat off her forehead with the end of a pigtail.

"How does it work *exactly*?" Jamie's confusion raised his voice.

"It's full of magical people," Bloom said. He took the ball from Tala and thanked the dog before continuing. "It's set up like any other town, though. There's a mayor and a town council. There's a library and a post office. All that stuff."

"But no school," Jamie asked, twirling the paddle in his hand.

"Nope. Freaking ridiculous rules," Eva grumped.

"And when was it founded and all that?" Jamie asked.

She gaped at him. "What would you want to know that for?"

Jamie felt like he was on the spot. "I don't know. It's just . . . well, I didn't even know this was here and now I live here."

"I'd like to know, too," Annie said. She caught the Ping-Pong ball in her hand, stopping the play completely.

"Um . . ." Eva crossed her arms over her chest.

"History is not Eva's forte," SalGoud said from his chair.

"Forte?" Jamie asked.

"What she's good at," the stone giant explained, shutting his book and standing up.

He walked to the Ping-Pong table and stood beside the net. Eva and Bloom put their paddles down.

Tala wagged his doggy tail and then slumped down on the floor, falling asleep instantly.

"Eva is anti-history," Bloom said.

"I'd like to kick history in its neck, if it had one." Eva picked up her paddle again and began whacking the air with it.

Just then the door opened and the mean-looking girl with the blond hair came in.

"Hey, Megan. You just got here in time for SalGoud's town history lesson."

Megan scowled. "Hi, Bloom."

There was an awkward silence. Dark-green clouds circled around Megan's head. She shooed them away.

"That means she's cranky," Eva muttered. "Them green clouds. She's always cranky."

"Maybe if you'd help illustrate, Megan." SalGoud cleared his throat and began.

As he did, Megan's clouds formed into people prancing about on the pool table in between the shiny balls.

"Well, at the end of the fifteen hundreds there were a lot of magical people being killed over in Europe, where the founders of Aurora came from. They were tired of being stoned, burned, and accused of being evil. It was a horrible time. I don't even know how to describe it, actually."

"You describe it boringly," Eva muttered as the eight ball ran over one of Megan's green vapor people.

"Eva!" Bloom barked at her so loudly that Tala woke up for a second.

Annie made eye contact with Jamie and then turned to SalGoud. "It's not boring."

The boy cleared his throat again nervously and paced away before he began talking again. "Magical races lived in constant fear of being found out and tortured or killed. They needed somewhere safe, somewhere new, somewhere they could live together."

"Somewhere they could hide," Megan interrupted as all the magical tiny people scurried into the holes at the corners and sides of the pool table and popped in one by one, disappearing.

"That's right," SalGoud continued. "Thomas Fylbrigg arrived here in 1602 with a group of magics who had been traveling through the new world for weeks, searching for the perfect place to settle, a place that could be hidden and remote, but also close to the growing communities of settlers. There are mountains behind us and a cove in front of us, with forests on all sides. It was the perfect place. After six months, the magical community sent John Rafeal to lead the settlement."

Megan shuddered and stepped closer to Bloom. In the center of the table, a man of green vapor formed, standing there in Puritan clothes, scowling.

"Fylbrigg was given the rights to build a congregation and house of worship. Rafeal became mayor. Fylbrigg continued with his shipbuilding. He was a shipbuilder and merchant. Both men were Stoppers. Rafeal built the first mansion upon a hill and the library. Fylbrigg built the town's meeting house and tower. The two combined powers to safeguard the town from interlopers, casting a protection spell on an item—the garden gnome—which must be within the town borders to work."

"And now the gnome is gone," Megan said. She leaned the upper part of her back against the wall. Her head was next to a rotating dartboard. "And now we are all in danger."

"In danger of what?" Annie asked. Her voice was tiny. It sounded how Jamie felt.

Megan didn't respond for some reason.

"What danger?" Jamie said.

"The biggest danger of all," Megan answered him. "Death. Destruction. For all of this to just be—poof!—gone."

Everything on the pool table vanished: the green man, the balls, even the pool sticks.

The room was silent.

"But she's supposed to save us." Megan pointed at Annie and laughed scornfully. "So, basically, yeah, we're doomed."

16

The Woman in White

W hy?" Annie demanded. "Why am I supposed to save you? What does that even mean?"

Megan's grin grew triumphant. "How stupid is she? How can she not even know?"

"Annie's not stupid," Bloom interrupted and moved to stand in front of her.

"Yeah, and 'stupid' is a hate word. I should know. People who hate me say it all the time." Eva moved next to Bloom, and Annie couldn't see past either of them.

"Children!" Miss Cornelia's voice suddenly echoed throughout the game room. "I cannot believe you are all still lollygagging about, although I cannot say I blame you. But these are treacherous times indeed. Now off to bed, all of you.

SalGoud, Eva, and Megan: Ned will accompany you back to your homes. Bloom, Annie, and Jamie: off to bed now."

There was no arguing with that sort of voice. They scurried off to their bedrooms. Annie and Jamie stood in the hallway for a moment together, darkness hushing their voices.

"Do you like it here?" Annie asked quickly. She was worried about lollygagging more and breaking other, unknown rules.

Jamie glanced up at her. "Yeah . . . it's . . . it's . . ."

"Weird?" Annie offered.

"Yeah. But it feels safer than home."

Annie squinted through the darkness. Her heart ached for Jamie. His voice was so sad.

"But at least I sort of had a home," he added. "You've just bounced around everywhere, right?"

Annie nodded and then realized he probably couldn't see her because it was so dark. "Yeah."

"I think it would stink," he said slowly, as if afraid to say the wrong thing, "to never feel wanted, but that's not because you aren't special, Annie. It's just that they couldn't see how special you are."

Annie's heart seemed to turn into a big ache. Tears edged to her eyes. She would not cry. She would . . . not . . . cry . . .

Jamie's hand reached out through the darkness and grabbed hers. For a moment they didn't say anything. The world felt so still around them.

Annie swallowed hard and then said, "I think it must have been really hard always worrying about being eaten."

"Well, I didn't know, you know, until recently."

"But they were mean . . ."

"Yeah. They were mean."

Annie felt like that was a pretty massive understatement. She squeezed his hand and then let go, grabbing for the handle of her door, fumbling around for it in the darkness. She wished someone had turned on a light switch.

When she thought about it, she and Jamie were so alike in so many ways. They both were never loved, not really. But they were also so different. Jamie was trapped in his house, in that one place his whole life, paralyzed by fear, taught to be powerless, and Annie—her brain hurt from thinking so hard about this—had been trapped by circumstances, instability, never having roots in one place, always afraid to even like a place, because she never stayed, never stayed anywhere long, not really.

"I want to stay here," she said to Jamie as she twisted the cold doorknob. "I want us to both stay here and live happily ever after."

"Happily ever after."

She laughed. "I know. Corny."

"No," Jamie said. "I like it. I like it. It's good."

———

After seeing all the fantastic stuff downstairs, Annie wasn't at all surprised when she opened the door to her bedroom. The canopied bed had large flowers growing all around its frame. The ceiling resembled the night sky with all its constellations. On the ceiling's edge, a small painted dragon with two riders on its back seemed to move. Miss Cornelia fluttered in behind her, Tala at her heels.

"Do you like it?" Miss Cornelia asked as Annie bounced on the bed.

"It's the nicest room I have ever seen. Ever!" Annie announced, heart thudding a million times a minute. "Thank you so much for letting me stay here. Do I have to share it?"

"Not even with the pixies." Miss Cornelia laughed.

"And Tala?" Annie rubbed the dog's soft side. He leaned against her, sighing, and then flopped down onto the floor, resting his chin on Annie's foot.

"Tala stays with you. Aurora is your home now if you want it to be," Miss Cornelia said softly. "It's a place of refuge for those who don't quite fit in anywhere else and no longer want to be where they don't fit."

Annie sighed. She knew what that was about. She had never fit in anywhere, not ever. *Annie Nobody. She's so weird. Annie Nobody, what a loser.*

As if she could hear Annie's thoughts, Miss Cornelia said, "There's nothing wrong with not fitting in, Annie. Sometimes not fitting in is exceptionally good. In books, heroes never fit in."

"Life is not a book." Annie picked up a pillow and hugged

it to her. Often she wished it were, because then she would have a chance at a happy ending.

Miss Cornelia's eyes twinkled. "Quite true. Sometimes it's better."

Above them, stars shot across Annie's ceiling.

"I am extremely excited that you're here with us, Annie." Miss Cornelia snapped her fingers, and a glass of warm milk appeared on the table. Annie gasped.

"Oh, it's nothing much, really." Miss Cornelia waved her hand, and then her tone grew serious. "Annie, you have things you're meant to do for us. You have a place here, and we won't let anything horrific ever happen to you again."

A place. Annie had always wanted a place to belong. Heart warm and full of acceptance, Annie patted Tala, who began to snore. His feet twitched as he dreamed.

"He's chasing trolls." Miss Cornelia wiggled her eyebrows at Annie, then stroked the dog's fur while he slept. "He does that every night, poor thing. Yes . . . Well . . . I hope you'll be happy here with us, Annie."

Annie beamed. She couldn't stop herself. Putting the pillow back down, she leaned across the little table and hugged Miss Cornelia, who felt like a mixture of softness and bones beneath all of her sweaters.

"I've never been so happy. Never. Jamie and I, well, we've decided to stay," Annie said and then blushed. She wasn't the type of girl who hugged people randomly anymore. She used to when she was young, but there had been so many people who didn't hug her back that it made her scared to hug at all. Nothing felt worse than wrapping her arms around someone and not being hugged in return. But Miss Cornelia, no matter how old she was or how peculiar her house, was not one of those people. She always hugged back.

"Wonderful news," Miss Cornelia said quietly in a rush of breath that Annie didn't realize she had been holding.

Miss Cornelia gave Annie a long look before showing her a nightstand drawer where she could store the phurba, and how to turn the lights off and on. You had to say "dawn" or "dusk" or "midday" to get the brightness you wanted. Then she spoke a quick good night and briskly left the room, all business, skirts swirling around her feet, pixies darting around her hair.

Annie swallowed hard, too overcome with happiness to actually get any words out. Except for losing her drawing pastels, life was so amazingly excellent.

She sighed and gazed across the room at a lilac bookcase that rose from the floor in a swirling ascent to the ceiling. The bookcase frame was made up of a series of boxes, each filled with books, and the pattern twisted as the frame went up.

"It's like a staircase," Annie said out loud, tiptoeing over to touch *Dwarf Girls Versus the Dragon*.

"Me, first!" something shouted from the top of the book-case by the ceiling.

"Me!" said another voice.

"Me!"

"No, me!"

"I long to be read. Me!"

"Please choose me."

"Me!"

The books were talking! Some were loud. Some were much quieter. Some were grumbly. Some sort of sang.

"I would very much like to be read," one said primly.

Annie liked that the book was polite. She pulled it out from the box, which was at eye level. It was a slim volume, *Magic Mistakes* by Alia Aquarius.

"There," Annie said.

"Thank you," the book whispered and then went still and quiet in Annie's hands.

The rest of the books seemed to sigh in a disappointed way.

Annie reassured them, "I am a really fast reader so I'll get to all of you in no time. Thank you so much for wanting to be read."

She climbed under her fluffy covers and read *Magic Mistakes*. Once she'd made it to the final page, she shut it, but still couldn't sleep. People kept mentioning Stoppers. She was supposed to be one. Miss Cornelia was one. She needed to figure out exactly what Stoppers were, and the best way to find things out was always a book. She searched her brain trying to remember what book Eva had mentioned when they were on the snowmobile. *The Magical Encyclopedia of the Fae?* Was that it?

She cleared her throat and whispered into the room, "Excuse me. Books? Um, do any of you have any factual information about the nature of Stoppers?"

There was a massive rustling of pages and covers and then a silence. Into the silence came a deep voice with a Malian accent. "I am here. I do."

A thick book of yellowing pages floated from the shelves and landed in her hand.

"Page twenty-two," it said, opening there, revealing letters and images that Annie had never seen before. "It is Arabic. I will translate as you read."

As Annie stared at the page, the letters re-formed to words she was familiar with. *The Stopper is a magical human, capable of great power. Sorrow and overuse of magic makes them weak. To understand the Stopper . . .*

"Thank you," Annie whispered, and then read about herself until she drifted off to sleep.

The next morning, Annie woke with a gasp, rubbing her eyes and snuggling against her pillow. *I wonder what Gramma Doris is cook—*

"Hello."

Annie shrieked and clutched her blankets.

A woman in a white wedding dress floated above her bed. Every part of the woman was see-through, except for the engagement ring on her finger, which glowed and shot off rainbows when the light from the sun that now appeared in the ceiling hit it just right. The woman rubbed her ring with a vanishing hand.

"Yes, it's pretty, isn't it? The Captain gave it to me before he went out to sea." The woman's voice floated about her, and the words caught on their own resonance and clung there, making her sound like a piano whose foot pedal has been pressed down and all the notes have fallen into each other, echoing.

She reached her hand out toward Annie.

"Would you like to touch it?"

"No . . . no, thank you." Annie started to pull the covers over her head and thought better of it. She needed to be brave. She wasn't going to disappoint everybody already.

Annie hauled the covers off but then lost her courage completely. She was speaking to a ghost. A ghost!

She squished her eyes shut tight and pushed her back against the bed's headboard. The invisible hand brushed her hair, she thought, or at least something happened to the hairs on the tippy-top of her head because they now stood on end as if electricity had shot through them, a terribly cold sort of electricity.

"No, no. Mustn't be scared. We're all friends here," the ghost said. "I won't hurt you, I promise."

Annie peeked open one eye. She could see right through the misty-white woman and across the room at Tala. His back nestled against the shut door and the wall. He snored. His feet ran around in midair, caught in some doggy dream.

The ghost put her engagement ring in front of Annie's face again, showing it off.

"I—I—I—"

"Don't know what's happening?" The lady laughed. It sounded like sleigh bells. "Of course you don't. You were gone so long, how could you know much of anything? I can't believe the time it took to find you, and you were right under everyone's noses."

"Um . . ." Annie pulled her knees to her chest. The nightstand clock read eight fifteen. She'd slept late. Maybe she was still sleeping. She could be. In Aurora, it seemed, anything was possible. She cleared her throat.

The woman hovered a good three inches off the floor, twirling around like a little girl until her skirts billowed out. She admired her twisting garments. "It's a lovely, lovely dress, isn't it? I couldn't bear to part with it. It's the only one I wear now, you know. Despite what he did."

Annie gulped. "I'm sorry, I don't know who you are."

"Who I am?" The ghost stopped her twirling and came right up to Annie, nose to nose. "Who I am? You don't know!"

The woman's lower lip trembled as if she might cry. Annie

felt the same way. She shirked away. The tip of her nose was ice cold now, just like the ghost's.

"No, I'm sorry. I don't," she said. "No offense or anything. I don't know a lot of things. I'm sorry."

The ghost flitted to the window and moved the curtain so the natural sunlight came into the room. Annie wondered for a moment how she could do that with hands that weren't really there. The lady seemed so forlorn that Annie couldn't help but go to her. She knew how it felt to be horribly sad and lonely. It felt like you were the least loved person in the universe.

She stood by the ghost for a moment but wasn't quite sure how to comfort her. She couldn't pat her on the back or put her arm around the shoulders of something that wasn't really there. Could she? From the very back portion of her brain something bubbled forward, and suddenly she knew.

"You're the Woman in White," Annie said slowly. She tried to make it sound like a title a queen would have: the Woman in White.

The ghost did a happy little jig, lifting up her skirts, prancing her feet about in midair while her upper torso remained straight and rigid. "That's right! That's right! You remember!"

Annie reached out her hand. "Nice to meet you."

"And you, too. How do you do? I'm fine, thank you. Fine now. Quite fine."

The ghost's hand in hers felt like a cool can of soda on a

summer's day—startling but in a good, crisp way. It was solid for a moment and then gone.

"I'm Annie."

"I know that. Of course I know. And it's time you start your life, wouldn't you say, Miss Annie? Time to begin. Mine's over, thank goodness, but yours is just on the cusp."

Annie bit her lip. It had been a confusing twenty-four hours, and she wasn't completely sure what to expect next.

"Begin what?"

The Woman in White rolled her eyes. "I am no good at questions. No good at all. I'm supposed to tell you that Miss Cornelia is holding a Council meeting at town hall and must not be disturbed for a bit. She gave me an apple for you."

Annie twisted her hands together and her shoulders sank. She'd probably done something wrong during dinner, or maybe Miss Cornelia had realized how un-special Annie was. She knew it would happen. It always happened. But so soon?

Annie closed her eyes. Her chest shook as she breathed in. She wanted so badly to stay, to be hugged again, to sleep in a warm bed in a house full of magic. She wanted so badly to be loved.

"Now where is that apple?" the Woman in White said, not noticing Annie's distress. "Oh, yes, here it is."

The apple appeared out of midair.

"And a banana. We didn't know which you would prefer," the ghost said.

Annie grabbed the banana, peeled it open, and stared at it. Her stomach was a big knot of worry, and she didn't feel like eating. What had she done wrong? She'd have to fix it. She couldn't leave here, not so soon.

"Go ahead. Try it!" the ghost urged.

Annie bit and chewed. She wasn't hungry.

"Is it good?" the Woman in White asked. "I've never had a banana, you know. Not ever. They didn't have them in New England when I was alive. The Captain always promised he'd bring—"

She turned around and stared out the window again, face sad, lips turned down into a frown. Annie told herself never to mention the Captain person if she wanted to get any information out of the Woman in White.

Annie lied. "They aren't all that great—"

"Really?"

"Sure. They taste like, um...bland bread mixed with mango, but not as sugary." Annie imagined the ghost must have been really very beautiful when she was alive. "What is it I'm supposed to do today, or, um, do you know how I'm supposed to be heroic and save everyone, because Megan said—"

"Oh, a question! You know I am no good with questions. No good with questions. Oh, questions are bad—so bad. Instructions good, questions bad."

Annie was getting a little annoyed by the Woman in White, but she tried to logic it out and hold her temper. She'd never talked to a ghost before. She wondered if Jamie was dealing with a ghost in his room.

"The sea is there—right there—haunting me. Oh, how he haunts me. The ache. The ache."

The ghost seemed like she was about to start sobbing. Annie knew she had to say something fast. Anything. Just not a question.

"I suppose that Miss Cornelia is the type of person who would give a ghost some good instructions about what a girl should do after breakfast . . ." Annie let out a deep breath.

The ghost jumped and pulled her gaze from outside. "Yes. Yes. Of course she did. Of course. She said to tell you to make yourself at home. To go outside and explore the town. That's right. That's right. Tala will protect you, not that we've seen anything during the daytime to need protecting from, but you never know. So take Tala, quite the guard he is. You'll meet a friend, she said. Go explore."

Annie decided she *would* like to explore. The town seemed little from up here on the hill. The ocean banged against the rock cliffs, and the town appeared ready to topple down into it. To the right, the land of the barrens rolled toward plenty of woods. She'd get dressed and go right away.

"You must be back before night, little Annie," the Woman in White warned. "You must be back in the house before the sun goes down."

"Like Cinderella and midnight."

The ghost shrugged. "I don't know Cinderella. Did trolls

eat her, too? Silly girl. Nevertheless, you must be here in the house. Remember. No dillydallying. No getting lost. Ever since . . . well . . . bad things stomp about in this town at night lately. Terrible things. You must promise!"

"Okay." Annie couldn't believe a ghost was lecturing her about coming home on time. It was the first time anyone had ever cared enough to lecture her about anything, and now, of course, it was one of the undead.

"Promise me, little Annie."

Annie still couldn't make eye contact, but she swore anyway. "I promise."

The ghost's hand turned solid and cupped her by her chin. She lifted Annie's face to her own, forcing Annie to look at her.

"Good," she said in a strong, serious voice. "We need you safe. We need you to save all of us. You must save our town."

"What do you mean?" Annie blurted. "What do you mean 'save our town'? Is it going to fall into the sea or something? Or are trolls coming?"

"QUESTIONS! Ah . . . The sea . . . the sea . . . Oh, he calls me. Do you hear him? Do you hear him? I'm coming! I'm coming!"

And with that, the Woman in White flung herself through the wall. Annie ran to the window. The woman's shadow floated down the lawn and toward the ocean cliffs.

A small, sturdy hand smashed against the window.

Annie jumped back.

Another hand grabbed the windowsill. The fingers whitened as someone strained to climb up.

Annie ran to her nightstand and grabbed the phurba Miss Cornelia had given her. She held it ready in her hand.

"Let me in!" Eva's face appeared at the window, red and strained. "I can't hold on forever."

Annie dropped the phurba on the carpet and rushed back to the window. "I'm so sorry. I didn't know it was you."

"Ouch," the carpet muttered as Eva climbed through the window.

Annie stared down at the snowy lawn. They were at least two stories up. "How'd you do that?"

Eva brushed off her overalls. "Dwarfs are great climbers. We can't jump for beans, though."

"Can't jump for beans?"

"You've never heard that expression?"

Annie shut the window. "No."

"Ack. You're a sheltered one, aren't you?" Eva stretched out her fingers. All her knuckles cracked. She plopped down on Annie's bed. "I've only got a minute. I'm grounded."

"You hit someone, right?" Annie eyed Eva.

"Darn right." Eva smacked her fist into her palm. "I pummeled Megan the hag on the way home. She deserved it, too, saying that about you."

Annie perched on the edge of the bed next to Eva. "What did she say?"

"It's nothing. Just ignorance, which is why I pummeled

her." Eva snorted happily and then shook her head. "Of course, now I'm grounded, which stinks, but whatever. It's just a day. And it was totally worth it."

Worry lowered Annie's voice to a whisper. "Are you going to get in more trouble for being here?"

"Only if they catch me. And I'm just gonna stay a minute. I wanted to see how you're settling in and to tell you that when anything bad happens or, you know, if things get adventurous, you can count on me, Eva Beryl-Axe. I like to be part of the action. And I'm good with my fists." Eva winked and stood up.

Tala snored in the corner of the room.

Annie crossed her arms over her chest. "I'll call you—"

"Good—"

"If . . ."

"If?"

Annie stood up, too. "If you tell me what Megan said that made you beat her up."

Eva squinted at her. "You're getting tougher already."

"Really?"

Eva bopped Annie's arm with her fist. "Yeah. That's good. You're kind of wimpy."

"I am not."

"Yeah, you are."

"Okay, are you going to tell me or not?" Annie resisted rubbing her arm with her hand.

Eva opened the window. Cold air screamed into the room,

ruffling Tala's fur. "She said that you would 'fall with evil.' That's the ridiculous so-called prophecy part. I told her that's a load of baloney. She said that you didn't have what it takes to save us. I told her she was an ugly hag. She told me that I rescued you for nothing. I told her dwarfs don't do nothing for nothing."

Annie's face paled while Eva became more incensed.

"She's just a jealous hag, Annie. They ain't always right, you know. They've only got an overall future prediction accuracy rate of seventy-six point five percent."

The wind blew Annie's hair against her face. She didn't even try to move it away, just shuddered. "That's pretty good."

"Ah, no, it's not. Real prophets are like ninety-eight percent accurate, and even tranced-out elves and stone giants have a rate of over eighty-five percent," Eva said. She grabbed Annie by the arms and gave her a little shake. "I've got you figured out already, Annie, and you can bet Miss Cornelia does, too, and there ain't no way you'd ever 'fall with evil.' You don't got an evil bone in your body. Okay?"

Annie didn't answer. Eva let go of her arms and started through the window.

"No worries, Annie!" she yelled.

But telling Annie not to worry was like telling the sun not to burn. It just wasn't going to happen.

17

The Letter

Jamie was brushing his teeth and stopped midstroke when he heard voices just outside the bathroom door.

"She will never forgive us for not finding her sooner."

"We thought he had taken her. We believed that she was dead or lost in the Badlands."

"You know that, and I know that. But she does not. She will feel abandoned. In my heart of all hearts, that just breaks me. She must never think that we abandoned her, that we just let her go."

They had to be talking about Annie. Jamie slowly turned the cold-water faucet off, trying not to make noise. He wanted to keep listening to the voices. One of them had to be Miss Cornelia, and the other? He wasn't sure . . . Maybe the mayor?

"And the boy?"

"He seems . . ."

"Of good character?"

"Exactly."

"But how do you know that he won't—"

"Turn troll? I do not know. But I have a feeling. Please trust me on this."

"You ask me to trust you about everything, Cornelia. I do, and see what happens? We had lost Annie for years when she could have been right here, developing her power."

The old woman's voice broke. "Yes, but we thought she had died. We thought that the beast had—"

"We thought wrong then, didn't we? How do we know that we aren't thinking wrong again?"

They must have moved because Jamie didn't hear Miss Cornelia's answer to the man's convoluted question. Jamie's heart flip-flopped all around his chest. They'd been talking about Annie, but about him, too. He knew it as soon as he heard the word "troll." Miss Cornelia didn't think he'd turn, but the man she was talking to obviously had his doubts.

"Never," Jamie vowed in a half whisper. "I will never turn troll."

He capped the toothpaste tube and looked into the mirror, where a note was now taped to the glass.

Dear Mr. Alexander,

Please be advised that your presence in Aurora is conditional to certain terms and advisements, which follow:

　1. Since you are likely a non-magical human, you must vow never to tell of Aurora's location or magical inhabitants to any non-magical outsiders. To do so would necessitate your immediate expulsion from the Town.

　2. Since there is a likelihood that you will turn trollish in the next twelve months, be advised that trolls are always immediately driven from the Town via all means necessary. To resist expulsion would necessitate your death, most likely via pitchfork.

　3. All non-magical humans residing within the Town boundaries are required to be active participants in the life of the Town, which means attending Town Meetings, voting at the appropriate age, engaging in Town activities, and actively protecting the Town from any threats (demonic or otherwise) by any means necessary.

　If you agree to the terms and conditions stated above, you will be allowed to keep residence in Aurora. To comply and agree with these terms, you simply need to sign below in the space provided for you.

Cordially,

The Mayor
Walburga Wakanda
Nicodemus Metal Smith
Cornelia Aquarius
Leodora Lenci Leksi
Arrius Herman
Aelfric Darling, Incubus of Bats and Shadows

A golden pen materialized in the air by Jamie's hand. He grabbed it and signed the paper without hesitation. There was no way he would ever leave here. Ever. And he would never turn into a troll. Never.

With a pop of tiny fireworks the paper disappeared into the air, and in its place was a sparkling word: "Done." After a moment the word drifted away and vanished.

Jamie investigated the room to see if anybody noticed, but he was alone. The voices outside the bathroom were gone. He almost wondered if he'd imagined them, and then sighed. No, no, they were real. This was all real, and he had to get on with today and just believe.

Jamie trod downstairs toward the kitchen, his stomach grumbling the entire way. The hall had ridiculously high white ceilings. The walls were papered with yellow designs, and as Jamie walked down the hallway, messages appeared on the paper.

Hello, Jamie. The first message appeared in red cursive letters.

He stopped and touched the words, cautiously tracing the letters with the tips of his fingers.

"Hello?"

There was no answer.

He walked a little farther down the hall, staring out of the corners of his eyes at the walls.

Across the wall, more words suddenly appeared.

Aquarius House wishes you a good morning.

"Um . . . Good morning?" Jamie said. His voice broke in the middle of the sentence. He cleared his throat.

Doris has left you some goodies in the kitchen. The words were writing themselves quickly as Jamie walked along the hallway. Some pixies flitted up by the chandeliers dangling from the ceiling. *If you could head to town and find Bloom, it would be mu*—the word broke off due to a doorway and finished on the other side—*ch appreciated.*

And Happy Birthday!!!!

The house remembered my birthday? Jamie sucked in his breath. The house actually remembered? And he, himself, had totally forgotten.

———

There were French toast sticks and orange juice and vegetarian bacon waiting for him on the kitchen counter. The words on the walls became arrows, and Jamie followed them through the off-kilter hallways, past a random dwarf or cat, until he got to the kitchen. He gobbled his food down, scrawled out THANK YOU on a napkin, and started to put the dishes in the sink, but they refused to let him wash them. Instead they danced beneath the faucet, washing themselves. Jamie watched, mouth open in astonishment, before he decided to head out. His coat was waiting for him in the front foyer. As he slugged it on, a merman with wild red hair surfaced in the fountain.

"You're James Alexander, aren't you?" *The merman is young*, Jamie thought, *more like a merboy.* He had curious green eyes and a dark-skinned face that was wrinkle free.

"I am," Jamie answered. There was a hat in his coat sleeve, and gloves. He tugged them out and put them on.

"I hear you might be a troll."

Jamie's good mood vanished. "I hope not."

The merboy agreed. "Me, too. You seem pretty human to me."

"Is that a good or a bad thing?" Jamie asked.

The merboy thought for a second. "It's better than being a troll."

An awkward silence descended. Jamie waited.

"I'm Farkey," the merboy said, "and please don't ask me how I go to the bathroom. Humans always want to know how I go to the bathroom . . . You know . . . Because of the fin . . ."

He flipped up a giant fin. It landed on the marble side of the fountain, sparkling with pink—pink?—scales.

"And yes, my fin is pink. Weird genes."

"It looks—um—nice," Jamie offered. "Powerful, like you could swim really fast with it."

Farkey eyed him, as if pondering something. "You're all

right, James Alexander. Even if you do turn out to be a troll, I think you'll be okay."

Farkey dived back beneath the water before Jamie could answer. The boy stood there for a second, wondering how weird one magic town could possibly be, and then he decided it wasn't worth it to wonder. Instead, he made his way outside and down the hill to find Bloom.

18

The Monsters

Annie and Tala hurried downstairs. The last thing Annie wanted to do was stay in her room and worry about prophecies and ghosts.

Doris, SalGoud, and Ned the Doctor were all bundled up in coats and scarves by the front door. The stone giants had swords at their sides. They quickly tried to hide them behind their backs.

"Good morning, Miss Annie. Isn't it lovely?" Ned boomed out. His sword dangled from behind his knees.

"Did you sleep well, dear?" Doris asked. "Did you eat anything?"

"I did. Thank you." Annie hoped she sounded as grateful as she felt, but she was intrigued by all the strange movements and whatever was being hidden behind their backs. "Are you all going somewhere?"

"Us?" Doris chuckled nervously. "Just an errand—nothing much. We should be back in a few hours. You might want to stay inside for a bit."

Annie squinted at them. They were hiding something. SalGoud wouldn't look her in her eyes.

"You aren't going to be in any danger, are you?"

"Nothing in the world is more dangerous than sincere ignorance and conscientious stupidity," Ned said. He appealed to SalGoud, who barely moved in response.

Annie shook her head, trying to figure out what that even meant. Doris bustled over with Annie's coat and helped her into it. "Annie. Since it appears that you may go into town, I ask that you stick to the main road. No adventuring around. You don't want to get lost when you just got here. Right?"

Gramma Doris looked to the giants, who both started echoing her words in an awkward kind of agreement.

"Oh, no."

"Easy to get lost."

"Getting lost is bad."

"Don't want to do that."

Annie's arms stuck in her coat sleeves. Doris reached in and yanked one of Annie's hands through.

"You seem worried. Don't you worry. You will not get lost

if you stay on the streets," Doris said. "Nothing to worry about, right, boys?"

Annie wiggled her other arm free as "the boys" continued to fluster around. Tala sat down on his haunches and grunted.

"Nothing to worry about."

"All is safe."

"Winston Churchill said, 'Never worry about action, only inaction.'"

"'As a rule, men worry more about what they can't see than about what they can.' Julius Caesar," SalGoud added.

"You all seem very concerned about me getting lost. Is there a reason for that?" Annie asked, feeling the outline of the phurba tucked into her pocket.

They didn't hear her. They were all busy being full of fake bluster.

"Must be going. See you soon! Stay safe," Doris said, hustling SalGoud and Ned out the door. "And remember: be brave."

The door slammed shut behind them. It took Annie a minute to move. Tala whined at the door.

"You must have to go out," she said, staring at the dog's fluffy, concerned face. "Come on. We'll stick to the roads. But there's no way I'm letting you out there without me."

Annie and Tala meandered down the road away from the town and toward the blueberry barrens. Despite all those quotes that Ned and SalGoud were spouting, worry tunneled inside her. Miss Cornelia said everything would be okay. How could they possibly be okay, though? She'd run away from the Wiegles to a strange town that was obviously in some kind of danger—a danger so big that she couldn't wander off. There was an evil-looking man who appeared in the fountain and terrified even the un-terrifiable Miss Cornelia. And last but not least, people kept saying "Annie has magic," but she didn't understand that at all.

How was she magic?

"I don't feel magic. What if I'm not? What if I disappoint them? Mrs. Betsey is always disappointed in me—always," Annie told Tala as they walked. "And she would never let me stay here if she knew there was magic. She is the least magic person ever."

Tala nodded his agreement.

"I can't lose this place, Tala. I can't," she said. She buried her face in Tala's fur and wrapped her arms around his body. He licked her cheek just as a cheerful, familiar voice called out to her from a distance.

Jamie was sitting on a rock wall on a hill above town, and Annie ran to him, eager to change her solemn mood. Below the wall were rolling barrens of low-bush blueberries. The road led to a thick forest and back to the town. Smoke rose from many of the houses' chimneys. A bell rang, marking the late morning hour.

"You're sad, Annie," Jamie said. "You okay?"

She sniffled. "I just—I'm afraid of messing everything up, you know? I'm afraid I'm not magic and that . . ."

"That what?"

She quietly explained everything that had happened with Eva and the Woman in White, only hesitating about Megan's prophecy. "I need to find out if I am magic or not. And how I'm actually supposed to help the town. I'm just so worried I won't be able to do anything. Like they have the wrong girl or something. Like they should be searching for some different Annie."

Jamie coughed awkwardly. "I'm sure it's you."

Annie could tell from the way his voice lifted up and turned his sentence into a question that he wasn't entirely sure.

"At least you have a destiny," he offered.

"What do you mean?"

"It's just, all my life, I've been aimlessly floating along . . . I mean . . ."

"You mean that at least if I'm a Stopper I have a purpose?"

"Exactly." He coughed. "I think being magical would be nice."

"I don't think you have to be magical to have a point, Jamie. I think you just have to be alive and willing to participate in life . . ." Her voice lost its confidence. "Or something. You know?"

He wheezed in the cold air. "Sure."

It was not a very convincing 'sure.'

Just when the awkward silence grew to the place where Annie and Jamie both felt terribly self-conscious, Bloom, the boy from the dinner the night before, strode down the road and hopped up on the wall next to Annie. He was sucking on some licorice. She glanced over, wiping her eyes with the back of her hand and said, "Hi. Jamie was looking for you."

Bloom stared at her for a second before breaking into a huge grin. "What are you two doing here alone? I'm glad I ran into you, friends."

Annie's eyebrows lifted. "That's what the Woman in White said before she flew off. She said I'd meet a friend. I thought she meant Jamie."

"Did she go through the wall?"

"Uh-huh."

Bloom sighed and wiggled his eyebrows conspiratorially. Jamie thought that he was probably the kind of boy who was always having fun at everything. Bloom pulled a piece of gum from his coat pocket, broke it in three, and gave him and Annie a piece. The cold made the gum break into bits when he started to chew.

Elves are nice, thought Jamie, adding it to his mental list.

"What flavor is this gum?" he asked.

"It's opposite gum. It tastes the opposite of how you feel."

"So, if I feel bad?" Annie asked, chewing.

"It tastes good."

"It tastes delicious," she said, frowning.

"Then you must feel really bad," Bloom said. "You asked the ghost a question, didn't you?"

Annie nodded. "And I mentioned the sea. She didn't like that. She got all—wiggy." Annie sat back down, tired of being confused. She decided to let the confusion go and not dwell on it. She spit her gum out into a tissue. It was starting to taste yucky.

"She's a bit loopy," Bloom said after a moment. He pulled one leg up to his chest. "She's a good ghost, though, as far as ghosts go. Always willing to help. She lived around here about three hundred years ago. She's one of the few people who doesn't call me 'Our Little Bloom.'" He made a face.

"That's a weird thing to call you. You aren't even short."

"Especially not compared to the dwarfs or the pixies." Bloom tried to make a bubble and failed. "I can never do it."

Annie sighed sympathetically. "It's okay. It's just because the gum is too cold."

They sat for a moment. Doubt crushed into her again. "I just told Jamie about that Megan girl's prophecy."

Bloom sucked in his breath. "Hag prophecies aren't always what they seem."

"She said I'd fall with evil. And basically, the truth is, all my life I'm always screwing stuff up. So this place probably won't be any different. I just don't know the rules here. I don't know how I'm supposed to act." Annie stood up and starting pacing. "I'm sorry."

Bloom shook his head. His voice came out gentle and soft. "It's okay, Annie."

She tried to smile at him, but couldn't quite do it.

"What kind of place is this? Ghosts running about. People treating me like I'm some sort of hero. It makes no sense," Annie said. "I don't think I'm magic."

Bloom stood up and asked, "Have you ever done something and not understood how?"

"No . . ." Annie then remembered the tracks in the snow that disappeared and how whenever she drew rabbits they would randomly show up in the room. "I don't think so . . . I don't know. I'm just . . . I'm going to disappoint her." She tilted her head and her lip quivered as she spoke. "I disappoint everyone."

Bloom spread his hands out. "You haven't disappointed me."

"Or me!" Jamie announced, jumping down from the wall to join them.

"I will. My foster families always expect someone better than I am. Someone cuter or a better floor scrubber." She shuddered thinking about the Wiegles' home. "They want me to be perkier or funnier or more invisible or something—always something more than what I actually am. You know?"

"I know how you feel," Bloom said as Jamie's stomach growled. "I don't know how to be an elf. I don't remember any of them, and all I have to go by is what people say, what

I read, and it's all adventures and magic and bravery." He cringed.

"You don't have to know how to be an elf. You just *are* an elf," Annie said. "Maybe I'm not making sense."

"No," Bloom said slowly. "You are. You are very smart, Annie Nobody. I don't know how you could ever disappoint anyone."

Annie's spirits lifted for the briefest of moments until she looked past Bloom. Beyond the bleak barrens and the carnival construction grounds, a storm brewed out at sea. Great dark clouds rolled against one another. They crashed violently toward the shore like they were trying to attack the town. Something dark and nasty was headed their way.

Tala growled and shoved at them with his nose so urgently that Annie lost her balance. Bloom caught her by the arm. His green eyes were wide.

"It comes."

Bloom hurdled up the rock wall and pulled Annie along. She scrambled over. Her knee scraped on some old prickers, so sharp that they tore her jeans and cut her skin. Jamie vaulted over as well and hunkered down. Tala waited until they were all safely hidden and then bounded after them.

Bloom put a finger to his lips, and the fear in his eyes made Annie tremble. "Stay down," Bloom mouthed. From a leather sheath strapped to the side of his leg, Bloom pulled out a dagger. The guard and pommel were both silver-plated, and images of dragons covered the handle. A fierce face resembling Bloom's own stared out from the hilt. The blade itself had three lobes, and Bloom shakily held it before him.

Faster than Annie could imagine, the black clouds blew in from the sea, casting ominous shadows over Aurora. The sound of a thousand beating drums pummeled the ground as something very large and powerful approached. But it wasn't the dark or the din that frightened the trio; it was the sick feeling of dread that accompanied the hoofbeats. It was the sense of foreboding that crept into their souls. Jamie, Bloom, and Annie knew without a doubt that whatever this was, it was bad news.

Huddled behind the stone wall with two new maybe-friends and a dog, Annie learned that fear in real life is nothing like fear in a movie. Her heart raced and thumped against her thin chest. Next to her, she could feel Bloom's and Jamie's hearts beat, too. She held her breath. She waited. The whole world felt uneasy. The world shook with the knowledge that something terrible was coming.

Out of sheer nervousness, she traced the outline of a bunny on her pants, over and over again. She glanced at Bloom. Despite the fact that he was brandishing a dangerous-looking weapon, he seemed to grow smaller as the sound of hooves drew closer. Jamie, however, seemed to firm up with courage and expectation.

Then something moved by her left foot. A bunny. It squeaked its tiny nose at her and hopped up in the air for a moment. Then he cocked his head at her and started to do what could only be called a hula dance, swaying his little furry hips around. Annie grabbed him and pulled him to her chest so he didn't get hurt.

Annie peeked over the wall just as a huge brown horse with a glistening black mane galloped past them. A black cloud of spiky, sharp feathers trailed behind the massive horse. The feathers flapped against the wind, creating a screeching sort of noise as the cloud formed a bird shape and then became a cloud again. Annie blinked hard. The feathers were once more a bird, giant and full of darkness. Evil rolled off both creatures. The horse's eye had no iris. It was just black. It smelled of rotting flesh and ancient eggs left in the attic too long. *Death*, Annie thought, *it smells of death*.

Jamie and Bloom both yanked her back down before she could get a better look at either of the strange beings. A minute passed, and the noise of the hooves was completely gone before Bloom loosened his hold on her arm.

"What was that?" she whispered.

"Was it the Raiff?" Jamie asked.

"No," Bloom said. "That was some sort of bird monster, and the horse . . . that's an Each Uisge, not the Raiff. The Raiff's been banished to a place called the Badlands. After the Purge, Miss Cornelia trapped him there, and he's been

trying to get out ever since. His reflection can appear in Aurora, but that's all. But it doesn't stop trolls and his other minions from trying to find a way to bring him back. *Those* were his monsters."

Bloom jumped back over the wall and started running down the road toward the town. "Come on, we have to let Miss Cornelia and the Council know."

"Monsters?" Jamie's voice squeaked as he followed him.

"Not just a horse and a really freaky bird?" Annie asked, hurrying behind the boys and holding the bunny.

Bloom's voice was a whisper. "Monsters."

Fear pushed Annie's heart into her throat. Monsters were here in this town, this special magical place that she thought would be safe, would finally be a happy-forever home. The realization made her sick. *How can we keep it safe?*

"What are we going to do?" Jamie asked, taking the bunny from Annie so she could run freely like they were. He stuffed it into his shirt.

"Battle," Bloom answered, putting his dagger away. "There is no reasoning with monsters. This means war."

19

Preparing for Battle

As Bloom, Annie, and Jamie ran to warn the townspeople, they decided to stick together. Numbers seemed a safer choice when dealing with monsters.

They dashed down the street, up another side street, and jerked to a stop in front of a gigantic white town hall, which had a big bell tower at the peak of its steep roof. Tala flopped down on the snow, clearly intending to be their lookout.

Peering into the hall's windows from the outside was Eva, who turned her head to Annie and whispered conspiratorially, "Snuck out. Again. Boo-yah. No grounding keeps this dwarf down. I've been trying to find out what all the brouhaha is in there."

"Eva! We just saw monsters!" Annie said, the words tumbling out in a rush.

"Monsters!" Eva jumped up and down, closing her hands into fists. "Did you clobber them? Let me at them. I'll put another notch in my ax."

"You have no notches in your ax," Bloom scolded and advised the others, "She only gets a notch if she kills a monster."

"That means you just let them go!" Eva fumed and stomped her foot. "How could you let them go, Bloom? How?"

Bloom glared at her. "That doesn't matter. What matters is that *there are monsters within our borders*. The town needs to be on alert, to be ready."

That was all Eva needed to hear. She smashed open the heavy wooden doors of the town hall with her fist and bellowed into a huge chamber that seemed almost like a church, full of pews and hardwood floors and long windows that let in slanted light.

"COUNCIL! I AM EVA BERYL-AXE, AND I AM HERE TO TELL YOU THAT WE MUST ARM FOR BATTLE!"

The doors banged noisily behind them, and the entire room at once grew silent as dozens of heads turned to look at the newcomers through the swirling dust particles that swamped the hall. The entire Town Council and many of

Aurora's key citizens were gathered and clearly in the middle of a debate . . . which Eva, Annie, Jamie, and Bloom had interrupted.

Annie swallowed. "Um, we're sorry to disturb you, but—"

"Monsters have invaded Aurora!" Bloom shouted anxiously. "They're coming for us!"

"Trolls?" Canin demanded, eyeing Jamie, who cleared his throat nervously. Canin's eyes burned red, bright red. A Red Sox hat was perched on the top of his head, underneath which Brillo-like white hair squiggled out at impossible angles.

"We haven't seen any trolls . . . yet," Annie replied, stepping protectively in front of Jamie.

"Monsters," said Miss Cornelia calmly, as she pushed up from her seat at the head of a long mahogany table that glittered along the edges as if sprinkled with gold dust. "Thank you for the warning, children."

"We've got to take action, or my name isn't Eva Beryl-Axe!" Eva commanded.

The rest of the Council members all began talking at once. Their velvet rainbow robes swished against the table as they gestured animatedly. All wore dour expressions, except for Miss Cornelia, and each of their chairs was decorated with a different marking: a tree for Arrius Herman, a stone for the Mayor, a cauldron for Walburga Wakanda, who couldn't stop wringing her hands, a lion for the blond Leodora Leksi, an ax for Nicodemus Metal Smith, and a bat for Aelfric

Darling, a thin, sallow-faced man who did not seem as if he wanted to be there.

It was Aelfric whose voice rose above the rest. "Dwarf, we know your name. And your kind ALWAYS think we should ready for battle. Nicodemus was saying the same thing." Disdainfully, he motioned toward the small-statured dwarf. And then he noticed Jamie. "Is this the troll?"

"He ain't a troll!" Eva yelled.

"You are quite right, Eva," Miss Cornelia said calmly, shooting a glance at the sallow-faced man. "Aelfric. Please try to hold your criticisms so we can hear what our young people have to say." She nodded curtly at the children. "Do any of you wish to address the Council?"

Annie looked to Jamie, who nodded encouragingly as Annie moved quietly to the front of the room. "We would, please."

She tried to take some calming breaths as Eva yelled, "Duh. Yes. Of course we would!"

Aelfric harrumphed.

"Respectful language, Eva! Make your people proud!" demanded Nicodemus.

"That's the leader of the Aurora dwarfs. My dad has such a man-crush on him," Eva whispered to Annie and then said loudly, "We would like to address the Council, please and thank you, and we don't got no time to waste with this because this is big news. Big!"

Miss Cornelia exchanged a small smile with Leodora, the lionlike woman sitting to her left. "Please do, then. You have leave to address the Council."

"Where's the mayor?" Eva demanded. "Shouldn't the mayor be here?"

"He went for refreshments. It's been a long meeting," Walburga the witch explained, yawning.

"Understatement," Aelfric snapped. "Do get on with it."

Eva puffed out her chest and bellowed, "There are monsters in the barrens! Bloom, Annie, and Jamie saw them headed this way!" She paused, turning to Bloom, and demanded, "What were the monsters?"

"An Each Uisge and a horrible black crow, larger than a normal crow, with feathers that made up its head and screeched as they moved," Bloom explained.

The Council erupted in chatter and outrage. Both Arrius and Nicodemus leaped onto the table, sword and ax drawn. Leodora Leksi and Aelfric Darling transformed instantly into a lion and vampire. Walburga began pulling on her long, tangled white hair as she cackled something they couldn't understand, while Miss Cornelia's voice rang out calling for order. Nobody listened. It didn't help that Eva was yelling even louder than the Council members about wanting to kill the monsters with her mighty ax of awesomeness.

Jamie's stomach growled. He pressed his hands against it and scooted forward a bit toward Annie, overwhelmed by the chaos. He couldn't believe this disorganized crew was in charge of the town and his safety.

With a clap of her hands, Miss Cornelia made all the noise stop. The Council members' mouths moved, but no squeaks or roars or bellows or sounds of any sort came out.

"It's so humiliating for all of us when I have to resort to that," Miss Cornelia fussed and then primly wiped her hands against each other. She motioned for Jamie to approach the stage. "Jamie, please tell me what happened."

"May I speak?" he asked.

"Yes, you certainly may." Miss Cornelia winked at him. "At least now we all know that you are rather calm and most definitely quiet when given alarming news. Just another thing to like about you. Everyone else sit down, or flutter down—Aelfric, I'm talking to you—and once Jamie is done, I'll give you all your voices back."

Walburga grabbed a fountain pen and sprawled out a sentence on a piece of paper and then held it up for Cornelia to read.

"You hate when I do this. Yes . . . yes . . . I know, Walburga. I hate that I have to," Miss Cornelia chided. "Go ahead, Jamie."

As quickly and as calmly as he could, Jamie told the Council what they had seen in the barrens. He stuffed his hands in his pockets so they wouldn't see them shaking from nerves.

"Well, then." Miss Cornelia thanked him and then admonished everyone to stay calm and not talk all at once. Her face was paler than normal, and the crinkle lines by her eyes seemed deeper. "Members of the Council, I propose we fully prepare for battle. No more half measures or time to waste. All citizens must be armed and battle plans ready. Shall we vote?"

She snapped her fingers and Eva snorted. "I'll lead the battle!"

"Eva!" Annie yanked her backward by her arm. "Shh . . ."

Eva stomped her foot but stayed quiet as words exploded in front of each Council member, writing out their votes in large, glittering letters before dissolving into fireworks or snakes, depending on how they voted.

YES, voted Arrius Herman.

NO, voted Walburga Wakanda, who muttered, "Too much panic when you arm everyone. Does anyone truly want pixies running around with machetes? I think not!"

YES, voted Leodora Leksi.

NO, voted Aelfric Darling. "What the witch said. I don't even want that dwarf girl armed."

"I AM ALWAYS ARMED!" Eva yelled, unsheathing her ax and waving it at him. "Do you want to feel the blade of my ax?"

"This is exactly what I mean," Aelfric said, arching a perfectly manicured eyebrow and tapping his nails against the glossy wooden tabletop.

Miss Cornelia cautioned Eva to be quiet. "Two for and two against. All that remains to vote are Nicodemus and me. Nicodemus?"

"Better to be ready." The word YES! exploded in front of the dwarf.

"If Miss Cornelia votes no, it'll be a tie," Eva groaned to Jamie. "Please don't let her vote no. Please don't let her vote no . . ."

A YES YES YES materialized and then pranced away like unicorn fireworks in front of Miss Cornelia. "I feel the same as Nicodemus, I'm afraid. Would the four of you children please go ring the tower bell? The bell will alert everyone of impending danger. Leodora, Nicodemus, let's round up the dwarfs and go to the armory. We have weapons to distribute. Canin, please begin fortifying the town borders with the stone giants and do pass out that nasty-smelling troll repellant. Walburga and Aelfric, gather up the fliers to man the watchtowers. I shall start conjuring up a new protection spell. I don't know if it will hold, but I must try. We'll also need to enlist Helena and Gramma Doris's help. They can bake up some poison pies. Even evil needs to eat."

Miss Cornelia stood up with a flourish. "There we are, then. I guess someone should tell the mayor. Stone giants are great pacifists, you know. They are loath to fight. But sometimes, it seems, we have no choice."

20

Arms at the Armory

Eva rushed up the cramped, narrow wooden stairs of the bell tower with Jamie, Annie, and Bloom close behind her.

"We have to ring the bell," she huffed, struggling for breath. "We ring the big bell at the top, and then the belles come out. They're the town's emergency alert system."

"Like a siren?" Jamie asked as she stopped for breath.

"Exactly."

"Eva." Annie peered into her face. "No offense, but you look horrible."

"Dwarfs aren't made for running up stairs." She leaned over, panting. "Bloom says it's easier to just throw me."

There were a lot of stairs left in the bell tower. Jamie bit his lip for a second. "You and Bloom head back down. Annie and I'll go up."

Relief washed over Eva's face. "You sure?"

"Absolutely. Just tell us what to do," Annie said, nodding to Jamie, and in another moment they were off, charging up the stairs, three at a time.

The top of the stairs ended in a small square chamber that was dominated by a huge brass bell. The ringer was attached to a long rope. Jamie grabbed it, and Annie announced just as Eva had told them to, "Belles! We have an emergency. Please tell everyone to meet at the armory."

Jamie yanked the rope as hard as he could and waited for a giant ringing noise. He'd prove to everyone that he was useful, not some troll-in-waiting, but an asset to the community. It was the least he could do.

The bell was silent. He pulled again, horrified. Was he not strong enough?

Just then, dozens of tiny women wearing bonnets and far-too-large-for-them pastel dresses with hoop skirts flew out of the big bell. They twirled around Annie and Jamie once and then scattered out the tower arches, singing into the sky in the tiniest of voices, "Emergency . . . Emergency, y'all. We have an event in town. Please go to the armory at once. E-mer-gen-cy."

Stunned and wondering how on earth anyone would hear the call, Annie and Jamie watched the belles flitter away and then rushed back down the stairs to their friends.

But, hear them they did. In no time at all, the mayor and townspeople spilled out into the street from Tasha's Tavern and multiple stores to gather in front of the armory's wide concrete doors. Annie and Jamie marveled at the green and red dragons painted on them.

Arrius Herman spoke a strange combination of words beneath his breath and then shot a beam of pink light out of his index fingers. The doors swung open, and Nicodemus Metal Smith jumped in front, shouting, "One at a time, please. One at a time! And only those who do not have weapons at home, please. We want to make sure there's enough for everyone. Hags first."

The children watched as the hags hobbled forward, grabbing bottles of angry green-colored potions and iron claws, which they quickly placed over their own twisted hands.

"That's Fall-Down-and-Die potion," SalGoud explained sadly. "Very toxic."

"Are you getting a weapon?" Jamie asked.

"Stone giants don't fight except in self-defense, and then we just throw stones," SalGoud said, shifting uncomfortably.

"If monsters attack you, it's freaking self-defense," Eva blurted, hopping up to sit on SalGoud's shoulder. "But don't worry, I'll protect you. I'll protect all of you."

Bloom rolled his eyes, and then a group of vampires came up, capes fluttering behind them. Some wore cowboy hats. Others had tutus.

"They have fangs, so they just get swords," Eva announced. "Fangs should be enough. If I had fangs . . . hoo, boy. The world would have to watch out."

Group after group marched through the doors of the armory. The Big Feet were handed dead trees spiked with nails. Brounies were equipped with magical rolling pins, Make-You-Tiny flour dust, and exploding cookie dough. The pixies and fairies were given tiny bows and knives as well as bee stingers and dizzying powder. The mermen and merwomen were handed tridents and ice cubes that froze their enemies, as well as whistles that called sharks to their aid.

"There are no dwarfs," Annie said as everyone finished gathering their weapons. "And not many shifters."

"We all have weapons already. No good dwarf goes around without a weapon," explained Eva.

Once armed, the group stood in front of the armory doors, waiting for further instructions. Miss Cornelia fluttered to the front of the crowd, flanked by Gramma Doris and Ned the Doctor. She clapped her hands, and Arrius Herman blew sparkling red dust at her feet. Instantly, she hovered twenty feet above the crowd.

"That is so cool," Annie whispered. Jamie agreed but didn't say anything because Miss Cornelia had begun to speak.

"Citizens of Aurora! As you now know, two monsters

have been sighted within our town's boundaries. Without the gnome, we are exposed for the time being to evil elements and therefore vulnerable. I beg you to take care of and watch out for one another. For we are not just a town; we are a family."

She paused, and it seemed to Jamie that she tried to look each citizen in the eye, making a connection with every one of them. "Proceed with the rest of the night as you would, and make haste to your homes. Remember that the good in your hearts can never be vanquished by evil. Even in death, the good remains strong."

She fell from the sky, but was neatly caught in Ned's stony arms. He placed her on her feet as Annie turned to Jamie.

"Death?"

He didn't know what to say. His bones felt wiggly all of a sudden, as if shock and fear had weakened them.

"Annie and Jamie, you are to head back to Aquarius House immediately," Miss Cornelia ordered. "That's the safest place for you right now. And you, too, Bloom. I don't want anyone left alone. Not tonight."

"I will escort them and protect Bloom's elfy self from all things dangerous," Eva said, to which Miss Cornelia gave a curt nod.

Bloom let out a hot breath but said nothing.

Eva slapped her hands together and ran toward her dad, who now had two axes over one shoulder and a pipe dangling over his ear. "DAD! CAN I BORROW THE SNOWMOBILE?"

His mustache twitched. "You are grounded, Eva Beryl-Axe."

"Dad," she whined, "there are monsters and I already told Miss Cornelia and it would be so much faster . . ."

Mr. Beryl-Axe seemed to contemplate this and then clapped his daughter on the shoulder with a strong, beefy hand. "You go out there, keep your friends safe, and make the Beryl-Axes proud. What will the monsters eat if they meet you, daughter?"

"My ax!" she announced and punched her dad in the arm before taking off to get the snowmobile. "I'll be right back!"

"Good! Because you are still grounded!" Mr. Beryl-Axe huffed. "And I am busy because I have to go tell Nicodemus how fantastic his recent welding of the mayor's gate was. Artfully done . . ." He turned back once more. "Make your dwarf species proud, girl! And if you see any monsters?"

"Smite them!" Eva yelled back, pounding her chest with her fist.

"Just no fainting," Bloom mumbled. "She's always fainting."

Five minutes later, they all piled onto the hovering snowmobile. Ten minutes later, Eva took a sharp turn to avoid a tree and Annie toppled off, gashing her cheek on a rock.

Fifteen minutes later, back on the snowmobile again, Bloom told Annie to close her eyes and be ready.

The snowmobile smashed to a stop at the fence surrounding Aquarius House, but Bloom and Jamie both made sure Annie didn't fall off again. Tala came bounding out to greet them.

Annie turned to Eva. "Thanks for giving us a ride and everything."

"Sorry you fell off. You need to hold on better," Eva grumped.

"You can say that again." Annie shuddered. Her hand fluttered to her face. Touching the cut gave her another piercing pain. She pulled away her fingers, revealing blood. It dripped.

"That is SUCH a cool war wound. I never get war wounds." Eva leaped off the snowmobile and crossed her arms over her chest. "You should see Canin's. He went one-on-one with an orc during the Purge. He's got bite marks all down his back. And my dad—he's got a huge scar across his calf from a machete-slicing vampire—the evil kind, of course."

"You're not supposed to want war wounds, Eva. They are the mark of a weak warrior." Bloom cringed and then apologized, "No offense."

"They're amazingly cool, dorkus! They mean you battled and survived," Eva roared. "My dad is not a weak warrior. He won! So did Canin. Winning comes with a price!"

"So does losing," Bloom said quietly.

Annie wiped her bloody hand on her pants, unsure of what to say. Bloom's face turned inward, and his mouth became just a straight line toward nothingness. Annie had never seen him like that in the short time she'd known him, and she didn't like it at all.

His parents had died. They were gone forever. Just like hers. But his had been killed. She didn't know what had happened to her parents. They might even still be alive and just not want her because . . . because . . . she was so . . . un-wantable. But Bloom, his parents were probably lovely and good like him, and someone had killed them. It was so wrong.

"Do you think Miss Cornelia expects me to do something now?" Annie said hesitantly, trying to change the subject. "I mean, since she thinks I'm a Stopper? How am I supposed to help out? How can I protect Aurora?"

Bloom's face took on a determined look. "A Time Stopper is a very, very powerful being. It's the Stopper who keeps the bad away and our entire world running, really. All the rest of us feed off their magic. And more importantly, they keep the portals to the other realms closed. They keep evil from sneaking over and ransacking the earth, fae and human alike."

"Portals?"

Bloom explained, "Doorways to other places, bad places, places of darkness, like where the Raiff is trapped."

"Monsters?" Annie asked. "Like we saw?"

Jamie's hand clutched the railing. "Monsters like trolls?"

"MONSTERS THAT I SHOULD KILL!" Eva leaped up, brandishing a branch like a sword and stabbing imaginary evil things.

Bloom ignored her and continued. "Miss Cornelia is a Stopper. The Raiff was a Stopper, who used his power for evil. Annie, you're a Stopper, too. The Council has said so for years, and they got their info from a good source—not some two-bit seer."

Annie swallowed hard again, and the wound on her face flared with pain. "I'm really one of them?"

Bloom grabbed her hand. "Yes."

Annie shivered. The trees swayed with the wind.

"I'm really sorry to disappoint you, but I don't think I am," Annie said in a small voice. "There's nothing special about me. Really. I wish I were . . ."

Eva had had enough. "Okay. I know you don't seem like one. Maybe I had my doubts when I saw you, but I think you've got warrior stuff underneath somewhere. You just need to find your power."

Annie leaned forward, holding on to Bloom's hand more tightly.

"Maybe." Eva started scratching Tala's ears. "You just need some confidence and something worth fighting for."

"Like Aurora?" Annie asked.

Bloom's face shadowed. "Like Aurora."

21

Evil Arrives

The moment they walked through the door, warmth flooded toward them, heating their chilled bodies. Eva decided to stay for a cup of hot cocoa, figuring she couldn't get into more trouble with her father since she was already grounded. She'd just tell him she needed to fortify her innards for battle. Bloom and Tala shook the snow out of their hair and fur. Jamie unzipped his coat while Annie stared at the puddle she made on the floor.

"I'm getting everything wet," she said, panicked.

"So?"

"Miss Cornelia will get mad. There must be rules," Annie said, thinking of Mrs. Wiegle's list, all of her foster families' lists, while trying to wipe up the puddles her sneakers had made.

"Of course there are rules, Annie, but that's not one of them," Miss Cornelia said coming down the stairs, smiling. "Our main rule is to try to always be kind."

She snapped her fingers and the puddles disappeared. Jamie jumped back, astonished.

"Wow," he whispered. He reached down and touched the floor. It wasn't wet at all.

"I still have a little useful magic left in me," Miss Cornelia said as she helped Annie up and hugged her, Eva, and Bloom hello. She kissed all three of them right on the tops of their heads. She motioned for Jamie. "You, too."

He didn't think anyone had ever kissed the top of his head before. He'd barely even been hugged. Jamie shook his head. "I still can't believe I'm here."

The mermaids splashed about the fountain and waved.

"Well, you are," Miss Cornelia said, hustling them farther into the house. "Now, let's go in the library."

She ushered them into the room and sat Annie down on a couch. Annie wiped at her eyes with her sleeve. Miss Cornelia snapped her fingers, and a bunny produced a tissue.

"Thank you," Annie said, blowing her nose. When she was finished the tissue disappeared.

"Wow," Jamie murmured again, checking out the room.

Books were lined up in mahogany shelves that extended up to the ceiling. Small pixies flitted in the upper reaches of the room by a ceiling that sparkled like diamonds and kept rearranging itself into pictures from famous books. First there was a scene from *Dragons of the Seven Skies* where the Dragon Boucher brings the children through the sky toward another world. Then there was a scene from *Kelsa in Maryland* where Kelsa jumps into a hamster cage and becomes a hamster hero adorned with a crab cape. Then there was a scene from *Magic Martin* where Martin turns the evil police chief into a wormy piece of corn on the cob.

"Wow," Annie repeated Jamie's word, staring.

"It's cool, isn't it?" Bloom said. "I like the scenes from *Elves for the Win* the best. Have you read *Elves for the Win*?"

Annie said she had. Jamie shook his head.

"It's the only book series where the author actually got the elf part sort of right," Bloom said. He settled into a large chair.

The chair began singing, "Welcome back, Bloom. Welcome back! Let's read an adventure today, please, pretty please? Please?"

"The chair is singing!" Jamie jumped off the couch as if he expected the furniture to grow teeth and munch him. "The chair . . . it's . . . it's . . ."

"Well, it likes a good story," Miss Cornelia said calmly, as if chairs talked every day.

"It's just . . . It's hard to get used to the whole talking-furniture thing," Annie tried to explain for both of them.

Miss Cornelia cleared her throat, pointed at the chair, and announced, "No reading today. We are talking. You may listen if you want."

The chair seemed to pout, but settled down. Tala jumped up onto the couch with them and laid his head on Annie's lap. She plunged her hands into his fur.

Miss Cornelia strode across the room, agitated. She clasped her hands together and stared out the window. "Annie, I am so sorry that you have not been here with us your entire life and once you are finally, miraculously here, you are faced with this—an unprotected town getting ready for battle, monsters tromping through the barrens as if it were their home, so much danger."

She whirled around and stared at Annie, tiny and small, sitting on the couch, dwarfed by the big white dog and all the books.

"That is the only thing that is worth being sorry about, Annie, and that was never your decision and it had nothing to do with you or your worth," Miss Cornelia stated. "I am angry at how horrendous your life has been, Annie, and yours as well, Jamie. I am angry at people and trolls who do not know how to love. I am angry at your blithering idiot of a social worker, and I am enraged, absolutely enraged, that the two of you and Bloom have had to live lives so full of pain. I am angry that I have so little time to prepare you. I am angry at all of this, at my own weakness."

She squatted down to Annie's level and added, "But I am very *un*-angry at you."

Annie braved out a smile.

"I promise you that I shall not let you go back with those dreadful humans. What were their names? The Wiegles?" Miss Cornelia continued after Eva nodded for Annie, who seemed incapable of answering. "I promise, and you can ask Bloom, my promises I always keep."

Miss Cornelia stood back up in one quick motion and gestured at Bloom, who jumped backward into the chair, which said, "Ouch."

Annie's smile became huge and mighty and turned her face beautiful, Jamie thought as Miss Cornelia focused her attention on him. "And I promise you, James Hephaistion Alexander, that for as long as I am the Stopper of this town, you will have a home here."

He swallowed. "What if I become a troll?"

"You won't." She said it with absolute conviction, and Jamie wanted to believe her. "You won't. I vow it."

A rainbow appeared on the ceiling.

"How melodramatic," Miss Cornelia said, but she laughed lightly as she gazed up. Then she turned to Bloom, who was apologizing to the chair, and announced, "Bloom, well done keeping the others safe today and warning the town."

"Me?" Bloom slowly smiled, a full, beautiful smile that seemed to make him glow.

"Yes." Miss Cornelia sighed. "And you may need to be heroic a lot more, very soon."

She turned to Annie. "And you, too, Annie. Remember how I told you that you will have to be brave?"

"Yes," Annie said. She tried to say it loudly and seem brave already. She wasn't sure if it worked.

"Well, that time is now. What you three faced with the monster sighting is only the beginning, I'm afraid." Her gaze caught all of them with its forceful seriousness. "You will have to help one another. You will have to depend on one another, of that I am sure. Will you be able to?"

The children exchanged glances. They gulped and agreed.

"Good," Miss Cornelia said. "Now the four of you, off to the kitchen and get some food. I have to call another meeting, find the mayor, and converse with him about these recent events. There is so much to do and you must be hungry." Absently she added, "Are you hungry?"

Bloom petted his stomach. "Starved."

"And thirsty," said Eva. "But mostly hungry. No, mostly thirsty. No . . ."

"Very well, then." Miss Cornelia's voice calmed back down. "You can show Annie and Jamie to the kitchen. Gramma Doris is still off running an errand. We'll have to make do."

They all stood up. Tala leaped off the couch.

"Don't leave me!" squeaked the chair to Bloom.

Jamie made a mental note to add to his list of elf qualities: they are well liked by furniture.

"I'll be back," Bloom said. He turned away and rolled his eyes, whispering, "It's so needy."

Miss Cornelia hustled them into the hallway and then turned, almost as an afterthought, to Annie. "No matter what happens, you must remember that you are special and that there is magic encoded into every cell of your body. Promise me that?"

Annie twitched away, obviously uncomfortable.

"Promise," Miss Cornelia demanded.

A lump rose in Annie's throat. She couldn't make herself say anything, so she nodded. It was a nod of promise and hope. That was good enough for Miss Cornelia, who pivoted and sped back down the hall.

Jamie closed his eyes and forced himself to breathe out. His heart nearly shattered with relief. They would always have a home. They would, that is, if evil didn't destroy it.

Once in the kitchen, they peeked in some cabinets and found peanut butter and Marshmallow Fluff.

"Maybe we could make sandwiches?" Jamie asked.

"And hot chocolate," said Eva. "Dwarfs love chocolate, just in case anyone wanted to get me a present at some point for being so heroic."

"Great." Bloom handed some carrot sticks to the Wiegles' little dogs that were camped out on the blinking tile floor.

Jamie hummed as he made the sandwiches. There was so much food, more food than he'd ever seen.

"After this," Annie babbled, "I want to draw you guys. I used to have this picture journal. I could write Miss Cornelia's last name in the front of the book—that's where I write all my families' last names—and it would be the absolute last name I will ever have to write. Wait. What's Miss Cornelia's last name?"

She slapped together the sides of a sandwich and handed it to Tala.

Tala wolfed his sandwich down and smacked his jowls. Jamie gobbled his just as quickly.

"Aquarius," Bloom answered. He bit into his sandwich and smiled a peanut-butter smile.

"Aquarius. Cornelia Aquarius. If she adopted you, your name would be Annie Aquarius. Your initials would be AA. Those are good initials." Jamie licked his lips and made another sandwich. His hand tingled ominously.

Annie started humming again. Alia Aquarius wrote the *Magic Mistakes* book upstairs. She and Miss Cornelia must be related.

Miss Cornelia's kitchen was much more normal than the rest of the house. An oversize old-fashioned stove sat in the middle of the room, and a massive fireplace dominated one of the walls. The stainless steel refrigerator seemed modern enough, but when Jamie opened it, the contents inside danced and sang out what they were, reminding him of Mr. Nate's fridge at the library.

"I am cheddar cheese, cheddar cheese, cheddar cheese," a yellow slab sang out in a startling baritone. Tala and the other dogs started yipping along.

"Radishes are delicious," a bunch crooned, twirling around and showing off their deep red color.

"Pr-r-runes kee-e-e-e-eep you-u-u reg-u-lar!" a fruit sang in an extremely high soprano voice that reminded Jamie of opera singers. In the hutch, a wine glass shattered.

He slammed the refrigerator door shut. "It's hard to eat food that sings," he said.

"Maybe that's why they do it." Bloom bit into his sandwich.

They munched in silence for a while.

"I feel worried," Jamie said, staring at his hand, wondering why it was still tingling. "Like something horrible is going to happen."

Bloom paled. "Me, too."

Annie piped in. "Me, three."

Eva was about to argue differently when something creaked in the hallway. None of the dogs stirred.

Bloom's ears twitched. "Lately, Miss Cornelia hasn't been herself. Her powers are just not as strong as they were, you know, Eva? I'm worried some things might be slipping through, and she's not sensing them the way she normally would."

"By 'things' do you mean bad things?" Jamie's skin tingled.

"Trolls. Evil vamps. Things of the night. But we've always been safe inside Aurora. Nothing could get in here unless it's invited in."

The refrigerator engine stopped humming. The kitchen was suddenly silent. Annie's foot shook so much it wiggled the table. She grabbed it with her hand.

Bloom stood up, focused. "Something's happened. Can you feel it?"

Jamie and Annie didn't have time to say they did. The entire house had suddenly turned terribly, terribly cold. Bloom stared at them with panicked eyes, and together they raced out of the kitchen and ran down the hall. Eva took the lead with Tala running at their heels.

"Miss Cornelia?" Bloom panted.

Jamie shook his head in the smallest of nods. He wasn't sure how, but he knew without a doubt that it was about Miss Cornelia, and that whatever it was, was bad. Something had gone wrong, and when they got to the foyer he froze, horrified.

"What is it?" Annie whispered beside him.

"I don't know," he whispered back.

Mr. Nate was standing stock still at the front door, surrounded by a moving mass of feathers the color of pitch.

It's like a cloud of feathers, Jamie thought, *a cloud of moving feathers that's descending on Mr. Nate.*

Tala raced in front of Jamie and stood halfway between the children and the feathers. Balls of light were streaming from Mr. Nate's hands, striking the cloud of blackness. The feathers just absorbed them. Then, as they watched, a beak formed. The pile of feathers had become an actual bird, the same bird they'd seen on the road. And it cackled.

"Mr. Nate!" Jamie yelled.

Mr. Nate turned around, stared at the children in disbelief a second before his face contorted in rage.

"GO-O-O-O-O-O-O!" Mr. Nate screamed. He launched a ball of glowing light at the cloud of darkness. The light disappeared, sucked up into the black. "Children! Run! Just—"

As they watched helplessly, the black cloud washed over Mr. Nate, consuming his words.

22

Hiding from the Horrible

Watching the darkness swallow Mr. Nate was more than enough to convince Annie to run. She grabbed Jamie's hand. "Come on!"

"Where?" His hand squeezed tightly around hers.

Where?

Where?

She had no idea. Tala barked for them to hurry, nudging at them with his muzzle, pushing them toward the sitting room. Annie decided to trust the dog. "Come on!"

Eva, Bloom, and Jamie followed her into the room, slamming the door shut behind them. There was no lock.

"That probably won't hold it back for long," Jamie said. "We need a better place to hide."

"But where?" Bloom asked. The room was just a room—albeit a fancy one. Long, lush drapes, mossy carpet, statues, and glass lamps didn't really offer many hiding places.

A bunny hopped out from behind the pink, velvety couch and gave a little wave, and despite all of Annie's pleading for it to hide, it didn't hop off into a safe bunny place. Instead, it stood its ground and stared straight into her eyes, which Annie knew was not normal bunny behavior. Bunnies are, on the whole of it, pretty much wimps.

Annie stared back at the bunny. Then she reached down to stroke its fur.

"There is a monster," she whispered. "We have to be quiet and we have to hide."

The bunny nuzzled into her fingers for a moment, relishing the affection. Then it bounced backward and stared at her rather impatiently. The bunny thumped its rear left leg on the mossy floor.

Annie reached closer to the rabbit while Eva took up a fighting pose.

"Annie!" Bloom said, frantic, "there is a monster outside. Now is not the time to be fussing with bunnies."

Jamie hushed him. "It's trying to tell her something."

The bunny bounced another step backward. It shook its head and thumped its leg and seemed indeed to be trying to say something. It took another hop back.

"You want us to follow you?" Annie asked.

The bunny hopped straight up and down, excited.

"Annie . . . ," Jamie pleaded.

The creature hopped to the corner of the sitting room.

"Over here? This corner? Is this where you live? Do you have a cute little bunny house somewhere?" Annie asked.

The bunny rolled its eyes and hopped in place.

The Cupid statue stood there looking like a smooshed-down version of Walden Wiegle. Chubby and unfortunately naked, it held a little bow and arrow in its marble hands.

Annie didn't know why artists always made Cupid undressed and pudgy. *You'd think he'd be thin chasing after so many soon-to-be lovers all the time and shooting those arrows,* she thought.

The bunny hopped on Annie's foot to get her attention.

"Yes, it's a very nice corner of the room," Annie told it.

The bunny hopped on the statue and grunted, crossing its front paws over its chest.

The bunny hopped on her foot.

The bunny hopped on the statue.

The bunny hopped on her foot, again.

"Oh," Annie said slowly, enunciating all of her words. "Yes, it is a very nice statue."

The bunny nodded and hopped with extra enthusiasm.

"We don't have time for this . . . ," Jamie said. "No offense. Maybe we should hide under the couch."

"It's a lovely statue," Annie lied, ignoring Jamie. It really looked like some pink sausages put together in marble and then topped with one of those big blond wigs that country music singers used to wear.

"It's an absolutely beautiful statue," Annie lied again, reaching out to pat the top of the statue's golden head. "Yes. Totally lovely. A work of art."

She gave its head one pat, then another. She wondered if any mice were living in its hair.

The bunny jumped up and down.

"Good statue," Annie said, and as she spoke the words she gave the head a final pat and the whole thing began to move.

"Oh!"

Annie jumped back and covered her mouth with her hands. The bunny funked out a happy little celebration dance on the deep-green carpet, twirling around on its heinie as Annie, Jamie, and Bloom watched the statue slide to one side, leaving a big hole where the base once was. The hole led to a small chamber.

Rushing, Annie led them across the room, away from the door. "It's a secret room! Hurry!"

Annie leaped into the hole, pulling Jamie after her. Eva, Bloom, Tala, and the bunny followed.

She felt all around the wall. "How do we close it again? Help me find a lever or something."

Frantically, the children slid their hands over the cold

rock surface. The light was dim, and it was hard to see anything at all. The sound of the gigantic crow cloud echoed in the house above them.

"What is that thing?" Annie whispered.

"I don't know. We've got to find a way to shut the hole or it'll find us . . ." Bloom's voice was eight times higher than normal.

"Did you see Mr. Nate?" Jamie's words were so hurried and broken that Annie had a hard time understanding them. She tried to give him a reassuring pat on the arm.

Suddenly, the hole above them slammed shut, blocking out the only light illuminating the area.

Everything was terribly, terribly dark and terribly, terribly quiet.

"Um . . . Hello?" Annie whispered.

"Shhh! It will find us," someone answered.

"What will find us?" Jamie asked.

Annie reached for him blindly. Five fingers wrapped around her own. Tala's body pressed against her legs.

"The beast." It was Eva's voice, only much higher, much more frightened sounding. "It's freaking freezing people up there. It's—it's horrible."

Annie imagined Miss Cornelia, brave Mr. Nate, and the little pixies all frozen. She shuddered. That couldn't happen.

"Someone should fight it," Annie said.

"We can't. There's no way to fight it. Didn't you see

Mr. Nate? He couldn't stop it," Bloom answered. "There's nothing we can do."

"Says who?" asked Annie. When he didn't answer, she pressed, "But what about Miss Cornelia? The others?"

"Gone," Eva answered. "Like we'll be if that freaking thing finds us here."

"Stop talking," Bloom insisted in a terrified whisper, as if he thought even the slightest noise could lead the bird to them. "Everyone breathe more quietly."

Annie held her breath as her heart broke . . . *Miss Cornelia* . . .

Even Tala seemed to understand the need for quiet, and his doggy pants were considerably softer, but Eva wasn't listening and she rambled in a panicky tone. "It's 'cause the gnome's gone. Anyone can find us. Even if that crow-cloud thing don't kill us, the trolls will probably come get us soon. Everyone'll be frozen, nobody will be able to fight, and they'll just pick us off one by one. We'll be goners. They'll suck the marrow out of our bones and—and—"

There was a huge thud on the floor to Annie's right.

"Eva passed out," Bloom said. "She always does when she's overly frightened."

"She told me dwarfs don't get scared," Annie whispered, squatting down and feeling around for Eva. Annie's hand grabbed a pigtail. She lifted the dwarf's head and rested it on her lap.

"She lied," Bloom whispered.

Jamie asked into the darkness, "What should we do?"

They were silent. Annie breathed again and thought about the knife Miss Cornelia gave her. Was now the time to use it? Was she brave enough to try?

Eva made an occasional moaning noise. Time passed. Seconds blended into minutes. They were terrified and quiet and had no clue what was going on above them.

Then Bloom gasped. "Annie. I'm so foolish . . . You're a Stopper."

Annie flinched in the darkness. "What?"

"You're a Time Stopper," Bloom said. "That's why we needed you here."

"You shouldn't call yourself foolish," Annie said, totally not listening to the rest of what Bloom was whispering.

He squatted down, and his voice was suddenly right in her ear. "No. Listen. You can stop time. Only one out of a million magic people can do that. The DNA is all recessive. It doesn't always come out in a bloodline, but you are destined to have the skill. The Council said so. Even Megan saw it."

Annie could feel his breath on her cheek. It smelled like mint. She closed her eyes the way she always did when she tried to focus, and finally whispered, "I really have no idea how."

"It's magic," Bloom whispered frantically. "It's something inside of you that allows you to stop time. *You* keep moving.

Whoever you touch keeps moving, but everyone else is frozen."

"Isn't that what the bird is doing upstairs?" Jamie interrupted.

"No," Bloom said. "I don't think so. That thing has to touch people to freeze them, but the whole world doesn't stop. When Annie stops time, the whole world will stop except for her and whoever she's touching."

"If I can," Annie muttered. "I seriously don't think—"

"The whole world? Everything?" Jamie whispered right over her. "Birds? The wind?"

"Everything," Bloom insisted.

The monster cackled above them. The sound seemed to come through the ceiling and touch them. They hushed. Something cold and awful seeped into the very insides of Annie's bones.

"How do I do it?" she whispered, again wanting to pull out her phurba. She gently put Eva's head on the floor and stood up.

Bloom stood up with her, dagger at the ready in front of him. "I'm not sure. Ned the Doctor once said that the Stopper focuses, their vision blurs, and they say the word, 'Stop.'"

Even though she'd read the same thing in one of the books in her room, Annie doubted it. "That seems a bit simple. Too simple."

"I know," Bloom agreed rather urgently, staring up at the

entrance to the chamber. "Sometimes Stoppers need to do a tangible thing to make the magic work. Hold a rock. Sing a word. Touch a familiar. Your power, Annie? Has it ever shown itself before? Have you ever made something appear that wasn't there before?"

"Sometimes . . . Sometimes . . . my drawings come to life," she admitted. "I think."

Suddenly, the covering to the hole that they'd come through slid open. Light shone down, illuminating the unconscious Eva, the terrified Jamie, the shaking but brave Bloom, and the growling Tala. Ice flooded Annie's body, and a horrible smell assaulted their nostrils. Jamie gagged. A darkness overwhelmed the light. A wicked beak appeared in a cloud of black feathers. It opened and cackled.

"Found you. I'll take the Stopper."

23

Time Stops

In the future, when he would retell this story, Jamie would never be able to describe the massive terror he felt when faced with the black crow. Words were inadequate. The crow smelled of death, and it was cold, a cold sort of nothingness that was hard for him to think about, let alone describe. It smelled of his nightmares, of asparagus, and a bit like his grandmother.

As the bird stared down at all of them, peering with a dark, ominous eye that shifted into a beak and then back into an eye, Jamie could barely move. The fear was too profound and intense. His hands shook, and for a few seconds his poor heart failed to beat.

Beside him, Bloom clutched something small in his hand

and muttered words that seemed to be in a different language. Annie trembled in front of both of them, easily the closest to the bird.

It wants her, Jamie remembered. *That's what it said, wasn't it? If it takes her, will it leave the rest of us alone?* It was awful to even think it, and Jamie did not want to find out. He glanced about the hole. Solid rock walls surrounded them. There were no doors. No windows. Only one way in . . . and out.

Bloom started murmuring louder and the crow cackled. "Foolish elf. Gibberish won't save you."

The beak lunged toward them, the cloud of blackness swirling behind it.

"Watch out!" Jamie yelled, jumping in front of Annie to protect her.

She grabbed his shoulder. Bloom grabbed his other one, yanking him backward into Tala, who didn't even whimper. The dog stepped on Eva's stomach, and for one quick moment the five of them were touching. The beak was a mere foot away from them, rapidly coming closer, snapping wickedly, open and closed, and Annie screamed so loudly that Eva jerked awake, only to see the beak and immediately pass out again.

"STOP!" Annie's voice yelled the word, frantic and as terrified sounding as Jamie felt.

Nothing happened. It didn't work. Annie wailed in

frustration. Her hand wrapped around the handle of Miss Cornelia's knife, but something told her there was a better way. *What had Bloom been saying before to them? About her powers?*

"Draw it, Annie!" Jamie ordered.

Annie's fingers frantically moved across his arm, as if she were tracing a picture there. Nothing happened.

She tried again, even faster this time. A word appeared on Jamie's skin, surrounded by red drawn feathers: STOP!

Silence descended on the world. It was like they existed in a giant, empty vast space of nothingness. Annie, Bloom, Jamie, and Tala gawped at each other and at the rise and fall of Eva's chest. The crow was still.

Jamie's jaw dropped.

What happened? Did I do it? Did I actually stop time? Annie's mind raced. Jamie started to say something to her, but no sound came out of his mouth.

Annie was trembling. She staggered back against the far wall, terrified and tired as she stared back at them all. Her hands flattened against the surface of the stones. Jamie had promised to be her friend, but he'd not known then that she was magic. Really, really magic. It was somewhat terrifying. So, maybe he wouldn't actually want her to be his friend since he was now aware of her true magical nature. Being magic seemed cool, but not if it meant losing Jamie's friendship.

"Annie?" He whispered her name.

At the same time Bloom whooped. "You did it! You did it, Annie!"

The blond boy lifted her up and spun her around before dropping her back down on the floor. He glowed from happiness. His skin seemed so golden that it matched his hair.

Eva stirred from her position, jumped up, yanked on her pigtails, fixing them, and said, "What did I miss? Did I miss the good stuff?"

Jamie pointed at the cloud of feathers frozen in the air. The word STOP! had begun to fade from his arm.

"Dragon toots," Eva cursed. "I missed it. I always do. Dragon doughnut tooting traitors."

She kept muttering. She yanked on her left pigtail so fiercely that Jamie thought she might actually lose some hair.

"Annie stopped time," Bloom interrupted her cursing.

"I did?" Annie whispered as Tala licked her hand.

Bloom's voice was gentle. "You really did."

She had. She'd actually done it. The bird was truly frozen before them. The dark cloud of it didn't quiver or move. There was no cawing. Nothing.

"But how can this be happening?" Annie asked. "I don't have a wand or a spell or anything."

Eva snorted. "She knows nothing."

"Of course she doesn't," Bloom said. "She's been away from Aurora. It's her first full day here, and she's already stopped time without even knowing how. Cut her some slack, dwarf."

Then Bloom turned to Annie and said in a soft, patient voice, "It's a nonverbal magic. It comes from strong emotions. Only a few can do it, but it tends to be a bit . . . unruly. Focus comes from stones or spells, or for you it must be images and drawing. That's why I was chanting. I was trying to help you focus. I'd heard elves can help Stoppers that way."

"Um . . . ," Jamie said. "How does the world start again? And when? You know? Because . . ."

He cleared his throat and gestured at the beak.

"Good question, runt." Eva stood up and grabbed him by the arm and hauled him toward a tiny gap of light, a space that the cloud did not fill. "It depends on the Stopper. It's Annie's first time so . . ."

"It'll probably just start again. Soon," Bloom finished for her. He pushed Annie ahead. "Hurry. Let's go."

They climbed through the hole, barely fitting through the small space around the bird. Jamie wasn't sure what would happen if they touched it, but it seemed important to not do so. He held his breath and willed the time stop to hold as he snuck through the gap.

Once out, the group realized that the bird's black feathers filled almost the entire sitting room. Jamie could make out a thousand different wings, motionless but clustered together.

"It's so horrible," Annie whispered as they slipped past it, across the room and into the main foyer.

Jamie followed her and turned to watch as Eva and Tala scrambled out of the hole.

"Just hurry," Eva grumbled.

"Stop being so bossy, Eva. At least you didn't pass out again," Bloom admonished.

Jamie breathed a sigh of relief, but the truth was that if time started right then . . . they weren't safe at all. Eva was right; they had to hurry.

They zipped into the foyer and then stopped, shocked by the sight in front of them. There by the fountain, Miss Cornelia and three other figures were frozen and draped in a cloud of black crow wings. Pixies were frozen in midflight, hovering in clouds of blackness. Even the mermaids, even Farkey, were surrounded by the evil wings.

Eva rushed to her father, who held an ax in his hand. The ax was frozen midswing. "Papa."

But it was the middle-size person that bothered Jamie the most. Miss Cornelia stood, hands open and raised as if she was trying to appeal to her attacker.

There is no reasoning with that crow, Jamie thought. It was like his grandmother. There was nothing good there at all.

"SalGoud," Bloom said, waving his dagger toward the boy whose thick glasses had gone askew halfway down his nose. "He is my best friend."

Jamie nodded respectfully. He wasn't sure what else to do, or how to offer comfort to Bloom, who sounded so sad.

"And Gramma Doris," Bloom continued, moving to a plumper figure. Bloom sighed. Then he continued, "She makes the best pies."

Through the crow feathers, Jamie could make out her gray hair and high eyebrows and laugh lines around her big brown eyes. He didn't know what to say and offered half-heartedly, "I guess she got back from her errand."

Tala whimpered and licked Miss Cornelia's hand.

Bloom's face turned angry, hard and lined. "This is so wrong."

"I will kill that crow beast!" Eva shouted. She grabbed the ax from her father's hand, held it above her head, and marched forward toward the sitting room and the crow.

"We don't know how to kill it, do we?" Annie asked in a tiny quiet voice.

"No," Eva admitted. "But I will kill it!"

Annie touched the girl's shoulder. "Not now. Not without knowing how. I don't think an ax will do it."

"What we need is a plan. We need to find someplace safe and then make a plan," Jamie said. "We have to get out of here."

The others focused on him, staring. It was unnerving to have all their attention like that, but he stood his ground.

"But where? What's safe?" Annie asked. She quietly took the ax from Eva. The dwarf didn't seem to notice.

"Nowhere," Jamie said. "But we have to get some distance between us and that—that crow thing, in case time starts again."

They all agreed.

"How about the bakery place? The Moony Horn Café?" he suggested, because honestly, he was still hungry.

"Perfect idea," Annie said. She rushed to the front door, displacing a few frozen pixies and apologizing as she moved. "Let's run."

24

Frozen Citizens

Annie had never believed that she could be more frightened than she was at the Wiegles' house, but that was before she faced the crow and witnessed lovely people like Miss Cornelia trapped, frozen, and surrounded by swarming black wings. But, there were good things, too. She was magic. Somehow she was *unbelievably* magic *and* she could stop time, which was just seriously the most stupendous event in the history of her whole entire twelve years of life.

Yet there was no time to really think about it, to figure out what it meant to be magic, where it came from, or how she even did it. Quickly, she tried to list what she knew. She knew she was terrified. She knew the word "stop" seemed to vibrate throughout her entire being. She knew it had happened. It had really, truly happened. For now, that had to be enough.

"Amazing," she said as they ran down the hill toward the center of town. Tala stuck to her right side, nudging her hand with his nose.

"What's amazing?" Jamie asked. He was keeping pace beside her, legs pumping hard.

Bloom was just a bit ahead, and Eva—poor short-legged Eva—was quite a distance behind.

"That I've stopped time. That I'm with three people I've never met before running to safety from some monster bird. That this place exists. That I'm alive." Honestly, the list could go on forever.

"Yeah." Jamie huffed. His breath came out in a white cloud because it was so cold.

They said nothing else, just ran, and when they were almost to the Moony Horn Café, time started again. It returned with a huge whoosh of noise and wind. But there were no human sounds. No activity behind the lighted windows of the little town. Every so often, Annie would spot people or dwarfs frozen in their homes, usually sitting or standing by their dinner tables, surrounded by the swirling black wings the crow left behind.

She stopped peering in windows.

"Here." Bloom held open the door to the shop.

The light was on, but Helena wasn't there. It was warm inside the bakery, though, and the place smelled of goodness, of sugar and flour and sweets. Annie and Jamie darted inside, followed by a staggering, huffy Eva.

"Hate running," she muttered, and flopped down on a steel bar stool. "Lock the door."

"I hardly think a locked door is going to keep that creature out," Bloom protested.

"Lock the door!" Eva's voice was panicked and her eyes were wide with fear.

For a second, Annie wondered if she'd pass out again.

Bloom snapped the door's lock into place, and then bolted it. Once done, he raced into the back room to search for Helena. Not finding her, Bloom went to the upstairs apartment. They waited for him in the kitchen area. It seemed safer there somehow. Maybe it was the massive cream-colored cooker that had five separate little heating compartments or the happy spa-blue tile along the walls or the gigantic clear jars labeled "Chocolate" and "Brown Sugar" and "Sugar Sugar" that lined marble countertops. Annie wasn't sure. Eva started pulling out éclairs from a white box and tossing them to the others.

"Helena would want us to eat." Eva smiled. Pieces of éclair were stuck in her teeth. "She always wants us to eat."

The éclair in Annie's hand was too tempting to resist. She bit in. The chocolate seemed to dance on her tongue. Sugary sparkles drifted through the air, glistening like glitter and floating the way tiny bits of dust will.

"What is that?" Jamie stuttered, staring.

Eva shrugged. "Helena's food often does that. It's her magic."

Bloom thundered back down the stairs and entered through the spa-blue door to the left of the stove. "She's upstairs surrounded by those wings."

His hand trembled as he grabbed an éclair.

"I looked in the windows," Annie said, still staring at the sugar dust floating in the air between them all. *How could anything like the crow exist when there is something as beautiful as this?* She didn't know. "People are frozen everywhere."

"It went to Miss Cornelia's last, I bet. That's what I'd do because she's the strongest of us and would put up the most fight. It makes strategic sense," Jamie said quietly. He'd finished his éclair.

Eva tossed him a chocolate doughnut. He chewed and swallowed. Chocolate sugar bits danced in the air in front of his face, and then slowly dissipated. "We need to find out how to reverse the spell, find out what the crow is, what it wants, what—"

"It wants her." Eva used her elbow to gesture at Annie. "Nothing has attacked us in forever and then—poof!— Annie's here. Everyone's freaking under siege and surrounded by freaking bird feathers, which is freaking beyond weird, way beyond weird. Holy vile vampire vestigials!"

Annie's throat closed. All of this was her fault?

"Enough, Eva!" Bloom ordered. "This didn't happen because of Annie. It's because the gnome is missing."

Eva glowered at him and threw a doughnut right at his face. He caught it without even looking at it.

"What?" the dwarf said, as Tala jumped onto the counter. "It's true. It's not like it's a bad thing. It just freaking is what it freaking is."

"It is not Annie's fault," Bloom said, hopping up to sit on the counter. Tala made room for him, and crossed his doggy paws in front of his muzzle. "And you said the word 'freaking' eighteen thousand times."

"Whatever," Eva grunted. She tossed a doughnut to Annie. "I wasn't trying to blame Annie."

Annie caught the doughnut, but didn't eat it. She handed it to Tala. "It's okay. I know it is."

Jamie moved to where she leaned against the counter. "You know, I'm new here, too. It could be me."

Annie almost smiled at him. He was so kind. But instead she shook her head. "No, it's me. Plus, the loss of the gnome. We all know it. But we have to figure out why. And we have to figure out how to stop it and get everyone back to normal. What we need is information. Information on monsters."

"Well, that's easy." Bloom hopped off the counter and through a swirl of sugar dust that now resembled rainbow sprinkles, and offered Annie his gold-tinged hand. "I know just the place. Let's go."

They slunk down the street, sticking to the darkness, trying to hide in the shadows. But when the snow began to fall, they left footprints behind.

Annie pointed to their tracks, heart sinking. The crow would be able to find them so easily. They were leaving a trail. She alerted the others, and Bloom quickly muttered some words, holding something in his hand. The footprints disappeared behind them.

When Annie gave him a questioning eyebrow lift, he simply said, "Elfish," and put the item he was holding back into the pocket of his cloak.

Eva snorted and muttered, "He says that about everything when he doesn't want to take the time to explain. Thinks it makes him mysterious."

"Another one," Jamie mumbled so quietly that Annie could barely hear him, "for the list; elves like to be mysterious."

Their footsteps vanished behind them as they walked. Annie kept turning around to check. Jamie mouthed the words, "So cool."

She agreed. It was, but her whole body was a jumble of nerves. Any moment, that crow could find them, and what would they do? She wasn't sure she could stop time again. And how would they fight it? Miss Cornelia and the others had obviously tried to fight it and failed. Their big plan when they saw the monsters had simply been to tell the town about it. Now that she thought about it, that didn't seem like much of a plan. Relying on adults had never worked for Annie before. She had to take things into her own hands.

They abruptly stopped walking. Tala did a doggy lap around them.

"Here we are," Bloom whispered. They had left the main street of town, and before them was a sprawling stone house that was quite a distance from the others. A three-foot stone wall separated its front garden from the road. Ivy, dead now in winter, spiraled up the stone front of the house, climbing all the way to the pointy roof. Three windows rested beneath equally pointy eaves.

"The mayor's house?" Eva grunted. She crossed her arms in front of her chest. "You brought us to the mayor's house instead of the regular, real library. We can't go in there. He's the mayor!"

"I'm sure he's frozen like everyone else. It'll be fine, Eva. Plus, you know he's a monster expert. He's got that book." Bloom pushed on a stone gargoyle's face and opened an iron gate. Eva gave him a blank stare and he continued impatiently. "The book that Ms. Kniha won't allow the library to keep because it's too dangerous."

Eva stopped at the gate. "We aren't going to look at that?!?" Her voice softened and sounded scared. "Are we?"

"Yes, Eva," Bloom said, ushering her inside and shutting the gate behind them. "We are."

25

The Monster Book

Eva nimbly slid two thin picks into the keyhole of the mayor's house and grumbled. "Don't know why the mayor even locks his door. Nobody in town does. Silly nonsense."

To Jamie's astonishment, it took the dwarf less than a minute to click open the latch and swing the door wide, revealing a huge, shadowy entrance room.

"Well done," Bloom whispered, leading the way.

Eva's pigtails perked up at the compliment, and she hustled right after him. Jamie glanced at Annie.

"Might as well," she said, sounding every bit as frazzled and scared as he felt. "I mean, breaking and entering is completely illegal and everything but . . ." She floundered.

"We have no choice?" Jamie suggested, heading inside.

"Exactly," Annie timidly agreed. "I just hope we don't get

caught. If we all survive, I hope they don't kick us out of Aurora because of it, you know?"

The entrance hall was wide, with ceilings so high that two Christmas trees stacked on top of each other could have fit inside it. Leafy gold sconces lit red-velvet-wallpapered walls. Also along the walls hung gigantic gold-framed pictures, all of the same man. Annie raised her eyebrows.

Jamie leaned toward her and whispered, "I think the mayor has a bit of an ego."

"Just a bit," Annie giggled.

It was a good noise, that giggle, a good noise in all the creepiness. Bloom rushed ahead, checking out the house.

He came back quickly. "I don't see the mayor anywhere. Come on. Let's find the book."

They followed him across a dark wooden floor to a room in the back of the foyer. It was too shady to see much. Twinkling string lights hung across a chandelier made of deer antlers. Musty brown books lined the deep wooden shelves. A bearskin and a leopard skin rug were spread across the shiny black floor. Bloom snapped his fingers and the chandelier turned on.

"It's noise activated," Eva explained. "Bloom's not that kind of magic."

The light illuminated the library slightly. Creepy shadows filled the corners. Murmuring came from all the books. They sounded like people in another room mumbling in their sleep. The children all entered the library and stood close together by the door. Only Bloom ventured far inside, as Tala turned his back and guarded the door.

"The mayor keeps the book locked away," Bloom said, moving to a desk with a glass cabinet on top. "The book was originally created by a demon back in 500 A.D. in Turkey. He wanted to catalog the monsters of the world. By naming them he thought he could control them."

"They ate him anyway," Eva interrupted. "Freaking demons. Always think they are unkillable. Always so 'la-di-da, I can control a bunch of monsters.' Harrumph."

"Fylbrigg and the Raiff found the book during their travels, jointly encased it, and entrusted it to the mayor of Aurora to keep safe after the town's librarian refused," Bloom finished. He gestured for them to join him. "Come on."

They cautiously made their way over to him, all of them glancing about nervously. Jamie felt trapped. There were no windows to escape through if the crow came back.

Even though it was beneath thick glass, the book seemed sinister. It had a frightening, dark, deep wood-grain cover embossed with eerie bat wings. The title was simply *Monsters*, but the Gothic lettering was creepy enough to give Jamie chills. He took a tiny step backward, hoping the others wouldn't notice.

Annie, however, took a step closer. Her small fingers reached out and tapped the glass. "Do you feel that?" she asked.

"What?" Jamie moved closer again.

"Like it's calling to you?" Annie's words were breathy.

Eva yanked her away by the arm. "You go over there. We don't need your Stopper magic mixing with this nasty thing. No telling what might happen."

"Eva," Bloom admonished. "You need to calm down. The book is encased in magic glass. It's not going to get out."

A horrible whisper filled the library, "Let me out."

Jamie caught Eva as she passed out. He staggered from the weight. Annie helped him lay her on the red settee, moving a pile of books out of the way to do so.

"Bloom?" he asked as they got Eva settled. "Where did that voice come from?"

"The book," the elf answered. Jamie noticed he didn't seem quite so calm anymore. "It tends to do that when it knows people are paying attention. It tries to will people to release it from the case. That's why Annie was feeling funny, I think."

Annie wrapped her arms around herself. "How would we even let it out?"

"Give it enough blood—enough powerful, magic blood," Bloom quickly added. "Your blood, Annie, or mine because I'm an elf, would charge it up enough to burst right out of there despite the enchantments keeping it inside that box. The only problem is . . ."

Bloom's voice died off, and he made a curious, nervous gesture with his thumbs.

"The problem is?" Jamie prompted.

"It will only tell us about the crow monster if we give it some blood." He indicated a tiny hole right in the center of the glass, directly above the cover of the book. "You put a drop right there to feed it. If you don't, the book just stays closed."

They were all silent for a moment. The wind howled outside, shaking the house. The books' murmurings increased a bit. Jamie hitched up his pants, which seemed to be growing looser the more frightened he became. Still, he cleared his throat and said as bravely as possible, "Well, it'll have to be me, then, since I'm not magic."

"Oh, Jamie . . . ," Annie said softly. "You really don't have to. We'll think of another way."

He held up his hand. "It's okay. I'm good with it. Yep. Um . . . so, how do we get this blood?"

Bloom reached under his cloak and pulled his dagger from its sheath. Bloom must have seen Jamie's stunned expression because he quickly whispered, "It's all right. It was my dad's. It's called *Lann d'amhrain crann*. It's quite sharp so I'll just make a tiny prick on your finger. It will not hurt too much. I promise."

Jamie nodded quickly before his bravery left him. He held out his hand, palm up. Then, as Bloom asked him to, he curled up all his fingers except his index finger. Bloom quickly pricked it with the dagger. It barely pierced the skin. A tiny spot of deep-red blood rose to the surface.

"There." Bloom gave a halfhearted smile. "Sorry to do that."

"Does it hurt?" Annie blurted.

"It's fine," Jamie said. And it was. It hardly hurt at all. What he wasn't looking forward to was putting his hand over the book, which seemed to be fluttering about, all happy that it was about to be fed.

The chandelier flickered across the shelves and the armchairs, casting a strange, ominous light on the unconscious Eva. Jamie shrugged his worry away. *One drop of blood. Already there. What hurt could it do?* He reached his trembling hand across the top of the container and flipped it upside down. A drop of blood spattered next to the hole but not in.

"Oops," he murmured. "I have lousy aim. So sorry. I'm such a—"

"No worries." Annie grabbed a business card from the table by Eva's head and scraped the blood into the hole. It plopped down onto the book, directly on one of the bat wings. The lights in the room flickered and then shut off. The only illumination came from the book, which glowed a hazy sort of green.

It spoke. "Yummy . . . The blood of one not decided."

"What does that mean? Not decided?" Jamie sputtered.

"It means we have yet to see what you are," the book answered.

Jamie's remaining blood turned cold. *It knows somehow, doesn't it?*

"Here is your answer." The book flopped open with a great groan, and then the pages flipped past faster and faster until they stopped. The drop of blood seeped through the cover onto the pages and created letters. It matched the cover in creepiness.

"The crow is called Corvus Morrigan," Jamie read aloud. The book quickly morphed again, pages tearing and ripping until a scene made of paper sprang from the page.

A woman lay dying in her bed. From the right came black birds just like the crow, flocks of them. They entered the door of the paper house and zoomed up to the woman's room. Her soul fled her body.

There was a puff of dust, and the book went flat again, words forming on a blank page as the children watched: *The Corvus Morrigan freezes the souls of the living in a swath of wings. The evil minions of the demon can then easily kill the living so he can take their souls much more quickly.*

"But how do we stop it?" Annie blurted.

"More blood," the book squawked, slamming shut. "More blood for more answers."

Jamie reached out his hand. Annie grabbed it and held it tightly in her own. "No! It's had enough of yours already."

"She's right." Bloom pushed his fingers through his hair. "Too much blood and it owns you. It corrupts your soul. You can't chance that, Jamie."

"Who, then?" Jamie asked. "Annie's is too powerful and so is yours." The moment he said it, the trio realized who was left.

Bloom's gaze went to the still-unconscious Eva, who was stretched out on the red settee, snoring.

"We'd have to wake her up," Annie said. "It wouldn't be right."

"No, it wouldn't." Bloom strode over, but he hesitated and didn't wake her up.

"MORE BLOOD!" the book demanded.

"Shh . . . Shh . . . Things will hear you!" Annie pleaded. "Just hold on."

Bloom swallowed hard. Sometimes Jamie wondered if the elf was more afraid of Eva than he was of the Corvus Morrigan. Even the name made Jamie shudder. Tala whimpered and offered his paw. Annie grabbed it and put it back on the floor.

"MORRRRRRRREEEE BLOOOOOOOD!"

Eva woke up. "What the troll tootles was that?"

Her pigtail was stuck in her mouth. She spat it out.

"It wants more blood," Jamie explained. "I can't give it any more and—"

Eva waved away his complaint and waddled over to the book, seemingly without a second thought. She bit her finger and put some blood on top of the glass.

"Ahhhhhh . . . Yuck. Dwarfs . . ." The book scrunched up a little bit. "So bitter."

"There is nothing wrong with dwarf blood!" Eva huffed. She made a fist and shook it. "Bitter? Bitter, huh? I'll show you bitter, Mister Monster Book."

She wound up to hit the glass. Bloom grabbed her arm.

Jamie ignored both of them and took a step back toward the book. *It's safely under the glass and quieter now, isn't it?* He swallowed.

"Book," he asked. "Could you tell us how to reverse the spells, free everyone, and stop the crow thing?"

"All the same. All the same answer." The book licked its lips. "So dull."

"So answer it," Eva demanded.

Jamie cast a glance at her. She was really impatient and bold when she wasn't unconscious from fear.

The book opened again. Pages fluttered. Words formed out of Eva's blood:

KILL IT.

"But how?" Annie pleaded. "How do we kill it?"

The book fluttered again. The pages twisted and re-created themselves. Suddenly a three-dimensional story took shape before them. First there was a town.

"It's Aurora," Bloom said, pointing at a house on a hill. "There's Miss Cornelia's."

On the front lawn stood a large man. His paper head glanced about, and then he bent over and plucked a statue off the lawn.

Jamie squinted, trying to understand. "What's he doing?"

The paper man tucked the figurine into his jacket, while peeping over his paper shoulder. Other paper figures came out of the front door. One had a swirly skirt.

"Miss Cornelia," Annie breathed.

Another had a crooked walk.

Bloom pointed excitedly. "That's Canin!"

Jamie was transfixed at the paper scene moving before him. The paper man jumped over a picket fence and off the road, running through backwoods until he set the lawn figure down outside the town border.

"That person stole the gnome." Eva swore, turning away from the book. "He stole it and then just left us unprotected? That makes no sense. How would he get inside the town in the first place? Unless it's one of . . ."

But Jamie was still watching the scene. Other figures lumbered out of paper woods. They stomped through the forest, flattening bushes, eating stones, and then one snatched up the statue and carried it off, decapitating random paper chickens.

"Trolls," he whispered as the realization hit him. "Trolls took it."

Abruptly, the pages flattened out.

"But what does that mean?" Annie asked, frustrated. "What does that have to do with saving everyone?"

The words rearranged themselves as the children stared:

RETURN IT. THEN NAIL THE CORVUS MORRIGAN TO AURORA'S SACRED GROUND.

"Okay!" Annie perked up. "We find the gnome that the trolls have, we bring it back, and everything will be okay. That's cool, right? That's not too hard. I mean, I don't know about the nailing part, but—"

Eva punched her in the arm. "Annie! Trolls have it. You've never dealt with trolls, but they are whacked out. Super fighters. Super strong."

"And super dumb," Bloom added. "We can handle trolls."

Jamie thought about his grandmother and doubted it.

"We just have to find out which trolls have it, though," Annie said. "Where do trolls live? I mean, other than the ones at Jamie's old house."

Bloom's voice lowered, and totally distraught, he fiddled with his dagger. "Everywhere. Trolls live as humans all around the world, disguising their evil most of the time."

"The gnome could be in Hawaii for all we know." Eva muttered about hating trolls and bashing them and how she would be a great troll-killing warrior.

Hawaii would be nice and warm to visit, Annie thought. She hoped they had to go to Hawaii.

Jamie knew better. He interrupted their chatter.

"I know where the gnome is," he said.

Annie, Bloom, and Eva all turned to stare at him. "Where?"

"My house."

26

Believe in Magic Skis

The kids all listened as Jamie quickly whispered his experiences of the past days. He told them about seeing his grandmother turn into a troll, how he suspected his father was one, too, what Mr. Nate had told him, and finally about the lawn gnome that was in the front foyer of his house.

"Wow," Bloom murmured. "That's a wicked couple of days."

Annie vowed that if they survived this, she'd somehow make sure the rest of Jamie's life was good.

"So, let's go," Bloom said. "We have to retrieve the gnome from Jamie's old house, and we'll need transport out of Aurora. Eva, can you work that out?"

"Of course." She puffed up.

Jamie turned pale with worry, so Annie pulled him away from the others and said, "You don't have to come, Jamie. If it's too much, you can totally hide here until we come back. Nobody will think worse of you. Nobody thinks badly of Eva, and she's passed out most of the time."

He shook his head. "No. I'm coming."

They made eye contact, and Annie could tell that he meant it, even though he seemed terrified. She felt terrified, too. Trolls . . . She'd have to sneak into a house of trolls, but if Jamie lived with them for years, surely she could handle it for a minute. Plus, the trolls might not even see them if they were quiet enough.

The foursome gathered, turned from the book, and started to leave.

"Wait. There is one more thing you must know," the book called out after them.

Tala emitted a low, long growl and padded out of the room. The others hesitated and slowly trudged over to the book.

Annie wanted to yank them away, push them through the door, and hurry outside. It wasn't just that she wanted to get on with it, to save the town and Miss Cornelia before it was too late. It was something else . . . She didn't trust the book completely. It demanded blood, but it wasn't just that which made it seem so sinister. There was an energy about it—a dark feeling. Still, she followed the others back to the glass case.

The book was cutting itself apart with a new, excited

fervor. Annie checked to make sure that Eva wasn't going to pass out again. Satisfied that the dwarf was steady on her feet, Annie turned back to the pages, which were now assembled in the shape of a thin-lipped man with close-cropped hair. Above his cheeks were two words where his eyes should have been: *PAIN* and *DEATH*. Shuddering, she barely noticed that Eva was clutching her arm.

"It's the Raiff," the dwarf whispered.

The name stirred dread in the pit of Annie's stomach. The Raiff's face loomed large beneath the glass. His eyes seemed to bore into hers. Then his eyes changed to read: *YOUR PAIN* and *YOUR DEATH*.

"I have seen him before," Annie whispered.

"That's impossible. He's gone." Eva glared at her.

"I have, too," Jamie agreed, whispering as well. "In a reflection and in the fountain."

The image crumpled. As the children watched, the paper flew and cut and splintered off, building up a battle scene. Giant monsters hacked down paper trees and lifted up bodies. Smaller figures tried to fight them, throwing paper balls of light and shooting paper arrows. Then the Raiff appeared again. He held two stones in his hand and raised his arms. The people fighting the monsters fell to the ground. The monsters loaded them into a cart, flopping paper body on top of paper body. One little child was missed, halfway hidden in a grove of ferns. Annie wondered if the others saw him there. He was sleeping with his mouth wide open, his paper chest heaving up and down.

And then the scene was done and the pages unfolded themselves back. Bloom's breath hitched. His face had lost its gold glow.

Annie touched his sleeve lightly. "Bloom? Are you okay?"

His mouth opened, but no sound came out.

Eva spoke for him. "Those were the elves, Annie, during the Purge. That's when the Raiff took the elves." She cursed beneath her breath. "Murdered them all, he did. All except Bloom. He's the last elf."

Eva shuffled backward a step as Bloom's body seemed to almost hiccup in pain. Annie went to comfort him, but she didn't know how. She settled for awkwardly patting his back.

"I should kill you for showing us this, you horrid book!" Eva roared. She swung her ax high above the glass.

Jamie caught her by the arm. "Don't! You'll let it out."

"We're being much too loud," Annie whispered as the pages created another scene. "And where's Tala?"

The book's pages folded again. The paper Raiff appeared. He turned and stared up out of the book at the children and aimed his finger at them. Across the pages, the words *YOU'RE NEXT* appeared over and over again. They took up every speck of space and filled the pages, a swirling, horrible promise.

The book slammed shut.

"What . . . was . . . that . . . about?" Eva whispered.

The book cackled out, "The Raiff. He is my master, the trolls' master, and soon to be the master of us all."

"Let's go." Jamie tugged at Bloom.

"Come on," Annie agreed as Bloom shook himself back to normal. "Let's run."

Eva groaned. "I hate running!"

Behind them, the book began to bash itself against the side of its glass container, desperate to get free, and that was more than enough to get even the slow-footed Eva to run.

———

Outside the mayor's house, the sound of the book became a distant thud. Jamie, Annie, Eva, and Bloom all caught their breath by the front iron gate where Tala was waiting and pawing at the falling snow, anxiously. He tried to nudge them forward, farther away from the mayor's house.

"We've got to get to Jamie's," Annie blurted between breaths. The air felt small in her chest, like the book had somehow sucked the life out of her. The rest of them seemed to be feeling the same way. They hadn't run long, and it made no sense that they were all huffing and puffing.

"Jamie's house is too far for us to walk," Bloom said. His hand held on to the metal railing.

Eva was bent over trying to haul in a breath. "You mean it's too far for me. Freaking elves can run forever."

Bloom didn't answer, but he caught Annie's eye. Annie knew from his expression that it was true.

"Do you have broomsticks or something?" Jamie suggested. He'd already recovered his breath and was standing upright again.

Eva harrumphed. "Only witches and hags can ride those."

"Sorry," Jamie muttered. "I was just trying to think of something magical and fast . . ."

Annie felt sorry for him. He seemed always ready to be yelled at, like everything he said might earn him a whack on the side of the head.

"It is a good idea," she said. She stared meaningfully at Eva. "How about your dad's snowmobile?"

"We can't," Eva grumped. After a lot of pressing, she finally admitted, "I pretty much trashed it last flight. It needs repairs."

"Well . . ." Jamie tried to think about what he knew about dwarfs. They liked to tinker with things, to build things. They liked to be boastful, to have their pride boosted. "Your dad did an amazing job with that snowmobile. I mean, he made it fly and everything. Has he ever . . . um . . . you know? Fooled around with anything else?"

"My father does NOT fool— Oh! Yes, skis! Bloom, you remember the skis?" Eva punched him in the thigh. He sort of toppled a bit from the force of the hit but maintained his balance.

"I do. But those . . . They had some kinks if I remember."

Judging from the doubtful expression on his face, there were some serious kinks in the skis.

"A dwarf does not have kinks in his magic!" Eva roared.

Jamie jumped backward and waved his hands wildly around. "Shh . . . the . . ."

But it was too late. Up on the hill by Miss Cornelia's house, the swarm of black feathers had taken to the sky. And it was flying their way.

"One day you will learn to be quiet, Eva," Bloom said.

"Dwarfs don't do quiet," she grumbled, but fear had found a place on her face.

"It doesn't matter. We have to go," Annie said, opening the gate and heading onto the sidewalk. "Eva, where are the skis?"

"At my house." Eva led the way, breaking into a trot down the sidewalk. "Come on."

But Annie knew that unless Eva's house was incredibly close, they weren't going to make it. The Corvus Morrigan was coming for them—and it was coming fast.

27

Trees and Skis Don't Mix

Where's your house?" Jamie's voice was frantic as the crow flew closer, blending into the night sky. "Where is it?"

"Here." Eva pointed to a smooth stone bump that seemed to grow out of the sidewalk. At the front of it was a heavy-looking wooden door with wrought iron bars across it. A statue of a sleeping man, who looked nothing like Eva's father, leaned up against it. Jamie thought it was some sort of street art or a sculpture.

"Eva, let us in!" Annie urged.

The dwarf yanked open the door and they all rushed inside. Bloom slammed the door behind them.

"Hurry!" he ordered. "It'll find a way in soon enough."

Feathers beat against the wooden door.

Eva hustled across a stone floor. The Beryl-Axes' living room was dark walled and lit by large lanterns. Two huge wooden benches waited around a fire pit.

Eva came running back with four pairs of skis. "Put 'em on," she ordered.

"Eva!" Bloom pointed to the fire pit and the open chimney hole above it.

Jamie gasped. A black feather poked down from the hole.

The Corvus Morrigan had found a way in.

The children smashed on their skis, hooking their feet under the straps.

"Now what?" Annie asked.

"Press 'FLY,'" Eva ordered, bending over and hitting a red button on her ski.

She promptly flew into the door and bounced off, falling on her butt.

"Someone open the door!" she yelled as she popped back up to a standing position.

Jamie flung it open and Eva zoomed past him. The crow was dropping down into the room.

"Annie!" he warned.

She peered over her shoulder, hit the button, and zipped out. "Come on, Jamie!"

Bloom followed behind her. Jamie hit his button. Nothing happened. The feathers fluttered closer. It was forming a beak. He hit it again.

"PUSH HARDER!" Eva yelled from the distance.

Jamie could smell the crow just behind him, coming closer. He smacked the button with his thumb. The skis wobbled and then lifted. He leaned forward and directed them toward the door. Before he even realized it, he was out the door and catching up to the others.

Jamie glanced behind him. The crow was following them. It had trailed out the front door of Eva's house and was barreling through the lightly falling snow. Tala darted back and forth to its left side, barking and trying to distract it from the kids.

"Tala, come!" Annie yelled.

The dog kept at it, leaping toward the Corvus Morrigan and then away.

Jamie zoomed ahead, willing the skis to be faster. He tried to imitate the positions of downhill skiers in the Olympics. *They bend forward, don't they? Or maybe that's the speed skaters?* He wasn't sure. He zipped over the road and through the trees behind the others. *Does Eva even remember where my house is?* He hoped she knew where she was going, but how could she when it was dark?

And then he entered the forest, flying as fast as a car. The trees became deadly obstacles, but he couldn't slow down. The beast was coming after him. He could hear the flapping of its feathers and its wicked cackle as it raced toward him.

"Eva!" Bloom yelled in front of him. "What's the glitch?"

"What?" the dwarf yelled back, her stout form seeming pretty solid on the zigzagging skis. Jamie caught up to her. She was smiling.

He quickly focused his attention forward again, which saved him from hitting a massive oak tree.

"What's the glitch with the skis?" Bloom asked again.

"Oh . . ." The dwarf's voice was matter-of-fact. "Only one pair stops."

It took a second for that to sink into Jamie's brain. He was pretty focused on not hitting trees and not letting the Corvus Morrigan catch up. Bloom, however, instantly understood and let out a panicked, nonstop wail. Jamie added that to his mental list of elfish qualities: excellent screamers.

"Only one pair stops? Eva, do you have any idea how fast we are going? We could die if we don't stop. We could hit a tree—" Bloom ranted.

"Technically, hitting a tree counts as stopping," Eva interrupted the elf. "So, if we all hit trees, then all the skis stop. Technically."

Bloom kept yelling right over her. "Annie and Jamie have human bodies. HUMAN! Do you know what that means? That means they are vulnerable. How are they going to stop, Eva? How? Without getting hurt? Explain that to me."

Eva glared at him. "You don't think I have this under control?"

Annie had dropped behind a little bit. She was still ahead of the crow, but just barely. Before them was a small one-lane bridge made of bright-green metal. The brook beneath it was wide, edged with big granite stones that gave way to smaller pebbles. A slight film of ice had formed on the top of the brook, but water babbled beneath.

"No! I am having some major doubts about not just your ability but your sanity!" Bloom yelled.

"Ha!" Eva slammed to a stop beneath the bridge. She shoved out a stout arm and caught Bloom by the edge of his cloak. He whirled around, jerking from the impact, but also stopped.

Jamie's eyes opened in fear. He was barreling straight for them. Eva snatched him by the wrist. His arm practically jolted out of the socket, but he stopped as well.

"There!" Eva said triumphantly.

"Eva?! What are you doing? The monster is right behind us, and Annie . . ."

As Bloom said it, Annie rushed toward them. She smashed into Bloom. Jamie watched horrified as Annie and Bloom somersaulted through the air, a tangle of skis and limbs, before they landed with a painful-sounding thud on the other side of the bridge.

"See! Everyone stopped!" Eva yelled.

"Eva . . . the crow . . ." Fear quieted Jamie's voice, but Eva still heard it.

She muttered a dwarf curse and pulled out her ax.

"You have to stop time, Annie!" Jamie yelled.

Annie didn't answer.

"Annie! Do your thing! Stop time!"

"She's unconscious!" Bloom yelled.

Jamie cast a glance back. The elf was cradling Annie's head in his hands. She was bleeding a bit.

There was no time to act . . . no time to do anything . . . The crow was there. Right there! It was up to him to save everyone.

"Stop!" Jamie yelled.

Eva snorted. Nothing happened. The world kept going. The crow hovered on the side of the brook bed. It formed an eye. The blackness of it was so deep, so terrifying.

"Stop!" Jamie tried again. *If Annie can stop time, maybe I can. Maybe . . .*

"Come closer, you lousy monster," Eva yelled and started to edge her skis nearer to the crow. "Let me have a piece of you!"

"Eva!" Jamie grabbed her arm.

"I'm going to go get that darn thing," she sputtered, but she didn't try too hard to pull away, and Jamie was pretty sure she could break free from his grip if she really wanted to. Her voice broke. "It's been screwing up the whole town. It froze my freaking dad, Jamie."

"But it's stuck," Jamie said. "See? It's not moving across the water."

It was true. The crow was fluttering and flustering along the side of the brook, but it didn't actually cross the water.

Eva preened. "Some monsters are like that. They can't cross running water. Holy cat shifters. That's awesome."

She tugged loose from Jamie and skied right up to the edge of the brook. She stuck out her tongue. "Ha! Aren't such a toughie crow monster now, are you? Can't even cross a baby brook."

The crow morphed its shape. Its feathers formed a giant mouth. "You will die, dwarf."

"Oh, please . . . ," Eva taunted. "You can't kill anyone. You just freeze them in feathers, surround them with your magic, and trolls do the actual killing. What kind of monster are you, really, huh? A wussy monster, that's what. I would totally kick you in the neck if you had one."

The monster roared. The sound filled the forest. Then it smiled.

"Oh . . . scary," Eva said.

"Eva . . . ," Jamie said her name like a warning. He knew taunting a bully never ended well.

"It wasn't meant to be scary," the crow cawed. "It was meant to call the others."

"The others?" Jamie sputtered.

"From your side of the brook. The ones who will finish the killing." It laughed as Jamie stumbled backward. He lost his skis in the cold water and stepped back onto the bank.

"Eva . . . Eva . . . we should go," he urged.

The dwarf caught him up and shoved him behind her, ignoring the crow.

"Is Annie still out cold?" Eva asked.

"Yes." Bloom's lips formed a tight, concerned line.

"We have to go," Jamie said. "I don't want to stick around and find out who the others are."

"Me, neither," Bloom answered, standing up. "I'll carry her. Let's go." He lifted Annie in his arms as if she weighed nothing.

Jamie added that to his elf list: elves are strong.

Bloom started off. Jamie hoped he was going in the right direction. *Maybe elves have good directional sense, too? They seem good at everything.* Jamie would like to be good at everything. He stood on the backs of Eva's skis and held on to her waist. The skis seemed even faster when he wasn't the one in charge.

"Bloom didn't even wait," Eva gruffed as they flew after him. "Freaking elves."

"Hey, Eva," Jamie said. "You didn't pass out when you saw the crow."

He could hear the smile in her voice. "I didn't, did I? Ha."

Jamie smiled, too, but it only lasted a second, because he remembered where they were going: home. *His* home and to *his* grandmother.

Bloom skied up to them. Annie was slung upside down

and over his shoulder like a sack of potatoes. Each duo went around a different side of a tree. "Have you seen Tala?"

Jamie shook his head, remembering the dog trying to bait the monster away from them. "No."

Bloom's eyes narrowed like he was angry and tired and determined all at once.

"We've got to watch out for the crow's friends," he ordered.

"What do you think it meant by that exactly?" Jamie asked through the darkness and the driving snow.

The elf readjusted Annie on his shoulder. "I don't know, but it can't be good."

28

Home Again

Annie opened her eyes, and the first thing she saw was an elf butt just inches away from her nose.

"Wh-what?" she mumbled.

Cold had seeped through her wet clothes. Her stomach bounced against a hard shoulder, and someone or something was clutching her by the legs as the ground flew beneath her upside-down head.

It was a little disorienting, and the others could hardly blame her when Annie screamed, struggled, and fell—plop!—into the snow face-first on the edge of town.

Eva skidded to a stop and swore, yanking Bloom to a halt. Jamie cringed.

Annie pushed herself out of the snow and stared up at the others.

"Oops," Annie said. "What happened?"

They quickly took off their skis and filled Annie in.

"I held the crow back with my ax," Eva boasted. "And it turned back in fear, overwhelmed by the might and ferocity of me, Eva Beryl-Axe."

Annie turned to Jamie for confirmation. He rolled his eyes.

"We've got to go on foot from here," Eva said. "If humans saw us on flying skis, it would raise a lot of questions. And totally break the rules."

"What rules?" Annie asked as Eva hauled her up into a standing position.

"The Stopper Rules," Eva answered. "You seriously know nothing, you know that?"

"Yeah," Annie admitted. "But at least I *know* that I know nothing?"

Eva gave her a blank stare.

"It was a joke. Obviously not a good one." Annie's head spun. Eva would probably think dizziness was a weakness. Annie changed the topic. "Where's Tala?"

Jamie, Bloom, and Eva gazed blankly at each other.

"So, he's frozen, too." Annie swallowed hard, heart sinking with the realization. "The crow got him."

They were all silent for a moment. Annie knew she couldn't dwell on Tala's loss. Dwelling on it would make it more real when she wanted it to be less real. "So where is your house, Jamie? I can't remember."

Jamie cringed. He tilted his head toward the main street of Mount Desert. White houses and small shops lined the snowy sidewalks. The gas station had a Closed for Winter sign on it. The only light came from the scattered street lamps and the reflection of the snow. It was a ghost town. A non-magic town, but a ghost town nonetheless, or at least it seemed that way to Annie.

"I just realized this will be the first time I've ever had friends over," he twittered nervously. "Not that this counts as having friends over. Yeah . . . huh . . ."

They quick-walked down the snowy street. Bloom muttered elfish words, and their footprints disappeared behind them.

"Jamie," Annie whispered as they walked past the First National Bank and the glowing light of its ATM. "Can you tell us about your family? How do we sneak the gnome past them?"

The others listened to Jamie's silent pause. He cleared his throat. A dog barked in the distance. It reminded Annie of Tala, and resolve strengthened inside of her.

We will get the gnome thing back. We will save the town. We will survive this.

"Jamie," Annie prodded as gently as she could. "Tell us about your grandmother."

Jamie kept his head down. "She's evil. That's all. She's evil."

"Not helpful," Eva muttered. "Artichokes are evil. Hamsters . . . zombies . . . trolls . . ."

"She's a troll." Jamie lifted his head and stopped walking. "There's our house."

The two-story house appeared to be just as Jamie had left it. None of the shades were drawn, and a dim fluorescent glow shone through the front porch window out into the late-evening darkness. The structure looked ordinary, normal for Maine. Not the kind of place one would expect to find trolls.

Annie realized she hadn't really noticed the house when they'd rescued Jamie. She'd been too distracted by the fire and the hovering snowmobile and his grandmother—his hulking, massive, hungry grandmother.

"Is your father just like her?" Annie whispered as they all stood there staring.

"Yeah." Jamie's hands balled into fists.

The wind stopped blowing. Silence suddenly took over the town. Annie missed Tala so much it hurt.

"How should we do this?" Bloom whispered. "Perhaps I should scout out the perimeter? Annie and Eva can take the right flank. Jamie can take the left. I'll go in through the door."

"Splitting up is not a good idea," Annie argued. "It would make noise across multiple positions. More for them to notice. One of us should sneak in."

"But that person would be too vulnerable." Bloom shook his head.

The house creaked. A shadow moved across the front window.

"That's her bedroom," Jamie said, voice raised. "She probably saw us out here. She's probably coming down right now. She probably . . . She probably . . ."

"New plan. Eva plan," Eva said, not even bothering to whisper.

"What?" Annie asked. "What plan?"

Eva didn't take the time to answer. Instead, she just rushed the door.

"Eva!" Annie whisper-yelled after her. She motioned to Bloom. He shook his head and started after her.

Eva's little dwarf shoulder smashed open the front door of Jamie's house. She disappeared into the darkness.

"Oh, no . . ." Annie held her breath.

Bloom stopped midway across the lawn. His footprints and Eva's lay visible in the snow. They were past elfish spells now, thanks to Eva.

Several loud thumps sounded from inside the house.

"Eva?" Annie whispered.

More thumps.

A grunt.

"Eva?"

Footsteps, loud and un-shy, came to the doorway. Mr. Alexander appeared. At least, Annie thought it was Mr. Alexander. He was wearing a ratty yellow bathrobe and striped pajamas. But his skin wasn't human . . . and his bulging arms full of muscle weren't human and his teeth . . . His teeth . . .

"Looking for something?" he asked. He lifted up an arm. Eva dangled from it, kicking and trying to punch the massive troll. But her arms and legs were far too short, and her kicks and punches came nowhere near their intended mark.

Mr. Alexander laughed. "So feisty. What do you think? Would she be a better appetizer or dessert?"

29

Dwarfs Are Tough Appetizers

Put her down!" Jamie stalked past Annie and then Bloom, heading right up the stairs before he even thought about what he was doing. His voice was louder, deeper than ever before. "Put her down right now."

He stood below his father, breathing in the horrible rotting stench of him. *How could I have lived here so long and not realized my dad is a monster? How could I have let him treat me so badly?*

I didn't know any better then, he thought.

Jamie knew better now. He knew that you have to fight trolls. He knew if you didn't—no matter how large or scary or mean or hungry they were—they would take you over.

He took a step closer. "I said, put her down now!"

For a moment nothing happened. The air seemed to ripple a bit the way it will right before an explosion happens. Jamie could almost see the tension in it and feel it tremble against his skin. Then his father threw back his head and laughed. It reminded Jamie of the crow's cackle—wild and wicked and horrifying all at once.

"Stop laughing," Jamie demanded. He lifted an uncharacteristically threatening fist. "Don't you dare laugh."

Mr. Alexander's mouth closed. His large beady eyes fixed upon Jamie. He countered the lifted fist with a thick eyebrow raise. "Are you telling your own father what to do, boy?"

"You are not my father," Jamie sputtered. He swayed where he stood.

"Whatever." Mr. Alexander's goggling eyes seemed to lurch in his head. "Did you come back so I could wish you a happy birthday?"

A hand gently touched his arm. It was Annie. "Jamie . . ."

Jamie ignored her calming, warning tone and snorted, "And don't call me 'boy'!"

"Of course I will call you 'boy.' I will do whatever I want. I am your father. I raised you. I fed you. I nurtured you for how many years?"

Mr. Alexander tossed Eva backward inside the house. There was a thud and then silence. The troll stepped forward, closer to Jamie, Bloom, and Annie. "But that doesn't matter. And who do we have here? A girlfriend?"

He stopped and sniffed the air, and his hair stood on end. "Someone smells delicious. An elf? Could it possibly be an elf? How tasty! I haven't smelled an elf in years! Let alone eaten one."

With a roar he leaped off the porch, thudding to a landing behind Jamie and Annie, and much, much closer to Bloom, who pulled out his dagger.

Annie pushed Jamie up the stairs. "Get Eva and the gnome. Bloom and I will hold him off."

Her voice was so authoritative that Jamie didn't argue. He turned from them and raced up the porch steps, scattering "Welcome" mats and old rolled-up newspapers that were still in their plastic wrappings.

His father had left the door ajar. A nasty smell of rotting pizza filled Jamie's nose, making him lift his coat over his nostrils. He had no choice. He rushed inside and searched around for Eva. Darkness pretty much obscured everything, but he spotted her crumpled form halfway up the staircase. She groaned. A cat that didn't belong to the Alexanders skulked about behind her.

"Eva!" Jamie was by her side in a second, checking her for broken bones. "Are you okay? I'm so sorry. My father . . . He's just . . . Are you?"

She hauled herself into a sitting position, and swatted him away. "I'm fine. Dwarfs don't break. You get the gnome?"

He shook his head vigorously as she growled. She reached out and grabbed her ax from the stairs behind her. "Why not?"

"I was checking on you," he explained.

"I am fine. Dwarfs do *not* get hurt." Eva hopped to her feet like a gymnast, landing hard and flat on the floor, then raised her ax above her head like a super warrior from a comic book. "I'm going to go kick your father's butt. You grab the gnome."

Jamie scrambled over to investigate behind the front door. The same pile of shoes and newspapers were there, but no gnome. His stomach seemed to evaporate into thin air. He gulped.

"It's not here," he whispered, frantically knocking over newspaper piles, searching. The papers flopped to the ground, pages fluttering. "It was here . . . But now it's gone."

Outside his father roared something about how much he missed eating elves and how he hadn't eaten any for a decade.

Eva raised her eyebrows.

"I'm going out there. Nobody gets to eat Bloom." She hurried toward the door, stopping at the threshold only to turn and admonish Jamie with a emphatically pointy finger. "You find that gnome. We're only here because you said it's here. You better not have sent us on some wild goose chase and put us all in danger for nothing!"

She was out the door and onto the frigid lawn before he could reply that he knew that. He knew that very well.

Biting on the inside of his mouth, Jamie turned around in the darkness. He lived within these walls for years, but he'd never had to actually find anything in the house before. The task seemed overwhelming, especially when he imagined running into his grandmother.

"I can do this," he muttered. "I can do this . . ."

The cat on the staircase mewed at him.

"Well, you're new," Jamie said, surveying the sleek gray form. It had white paws that looked like mittens or socks. They glowed in the half-light.

Annie screamed. He turned toward the door. He wanted to help. Anything could be happening out there, but he had to get the gnome first. Without it, so many people would die. Mr. Nate, Helena, Miss Cornelia . . . the entire town.

The cat mewed and then turned, silently walking up the stairs. Jamie lost sight of it in the dim light. He swallowed hard and followed, grabbing a flashlight from the box on the stairs. He clicked it on. Nothing. He hesitated and went back to grab another. The batteries must have died. He pulled another out of the wobbling pile inside the box. This one was huge and black and heavy, like the flashlights the cops his father worked with used.

The flashlight cast a circle of light in the darkness. Jamie swished it back and forth in an arcing motion. It illuminated his former home—and that's when he realized that no matter what, even if he didn't die tonight, there was no way he could ever come back here. His father and grandmother were trolls, yes, but even if they didn't want to eat the marrow out of his bones, they were hideous and evil and so terribly mean to him. Nobody deserves that. Nobody needs to feel worthless all the time or to be called "boy" like it's an insult. Nobody deserves any of it at all. Now he had a purpose; he had new people to love and protect, and he had a home with food that wasn't Vienna sausages. He was not going to lose it.

The cat stood outside the door to his grandmother's room.

"I deserve more than this," he whispered to the cat.

The cat stared at him as if he were the least intelligent human—or soon-to-be troll—in the world. Then, the cat shifted its weight to its back legs, reached up, and scratched at the door.

"But that's . . ." He couldn't even finish his whisper.

Jamie had never stepped inside his grandmother's bedroom. It was a forbidden place. Sometimes the nasty smell of asparagus would waft beneath the door and enter the hallway. Sometimes he thought he'd heard high-pitched whimpering noises coming from beyond the door.

I will kill you if you ever go in there, his grandmother had told him. *I will kill you with my bare hands*.

"I can't go in her bedroom," he whispered to the cat. "No," Jamie said, backing away. He bumped into the wall of the hallway, knocking into the family portraits. They rattled. He jumped. "I can't—I just—"

The cat pushed open the door. Horrible smells of rotting vegetables wafted into the hallway. The cat dropped back down on all four legs and trotted inside. Jamie's heart clenched. His grandmother could be in there. She'd eat that cat if she found it in her room. She'd probably eat him, too, if she found him in her house.

"Great." He tiptoed after the cat as quickly as he could. After a moment of internal debate, he decided to keep the flashlight turned on. He couldn't imagine moving around in the stinky, unknown darkness.

The flashlight was so bright. He pulled the bottom of his shirt over it and swept the light along the floor and walls. There were bones everywhere. The centers were sucked out. *Chicken skeletons*, he thought. Along the walls were huge pictures of trolls. There was one of a woman wearing a suit of armor. The caption said "Mother." Beneath a painting of a man in a toga was the word "Grandfather." And then Jamie's light swept over a blown-up photo of himself, back when he was about six years old. It was his first-grade class picture from school. His hair was sticking out around his head. He was smiling, showing the gap where three of his front teeth were missing. He was wearing a huge T-shirt that was far too orange and far too polka-dotted to be cool. But that wasn't what horrified him. What horrified him was the caption on the plaque beneath his photo. It was just one word, but it made him almost drop the flashlight:

"Food."

Food. That was really all he ever was to them. Jamie

tightened his hold on the flashlight and turned away. He moved the beam along the walls, trying to search the room systematically. His nerves were so raw that every shadow seemed like a monster. Every object felt like a crow ready to swoop in and surround him with never-ending darkness. Every breath sounded like his grandmother ready to devour him.

Every breath? He held his breath. And he heard something else breathing, loud and both shallow and deep.

The sound was not coming from the cat.

Jamie slowly arced the flashlight up to the foot of the bed. There was a lump beneath the covers. A green, bulbous foot stuck out over the edge. Hand shaking, he tried to keep the flashlight steady as the beam skimmed over the body and up . . . up past the belly . . . and to . . .

His grandmother snored and snorted in her sleep. Gripped tightly in her hands was the lawn gnome. She clutched it to her chest, a prize teddy bear that she wouldn't part with, not ever.

30

Toppling Trolls

Mr. Alexander towered between Annie and Bloom. The hair on the backs of his arms and his neck rippled and moved. He grew one foot taller and then another. His yellow robe fell to pieces as the seams on his pajama shirt ripped from his rapidly expanding chest and arms. His pajama bottoms were suddenly much too short.

Annie staggered backward onto another porch step. She grabbed the railing, watching the hideous transformation, and wrapped her hand around the handle of the phurba in her pocket. She had to help Bloom. He couldn't possibly face a troll alone.

There were newspapers and skis everywhere. Newspapers and their skis . . . batteries . . . skis . . . *What good would that do? Think, Annie!*

"Annie! Run!" Bloom yelled. "He wants me, not you."

She didn't answer. Instead, she released her hold on the knife, scooped up a pair of skis, and brandished them like a baseball bat.

The troll lunged after Bloom. The boy leaped away and threw a ball of light at him. The troll sidestepped it easily.

"Baby magic," he taunted. "Elfish goody-goody magic."

Bloom's face tightened. He threw another ball of light. Mr. Alexander dodged it and lunged forward. Bloom soared halfway up a tree, bounding out of the troll's reach, but just barely. Mr. Alexander grabbed the tree by its large trunk and started to yank it out of the ground. The roots pulled up the snow, spewing it into the air like a geyser. It sprayed Bloom's feet and pants.

Bloom climbed higher up the tree.

Annie had to do something. She rushed at the troll, holding the skis above her head.

"Leave him alone!" she ordered. The troll ignored her.

"I said, leave him alone!" Annie yelled again, swatting at him with the skis.

Eva shot out of the house, roaring and waving her ax. Annie jumped out of her way.

"Nobody touches my elf!" Eva roared, quickly closing the distance between her and Mr. Alexander.

"I'm not your elf," Bloom shouted from where he dangled.

"Whatever." She swung her ax at the troll and missed. It slammed into the snow. She tried to hoist it back out.

"Eva! Watch out!" Annie yelled.

Too late.

Mr. Alexander chucked the tree right at Eva. Annie watched, horrified, as it landed on the dwarf, a massive thud of trunk and branches. Bloom was caught up in the limbs somewhere and vanished when the tree thundered down onto Eva and the ground. Annie couldn't see either of them in the twist of branches and snow. They could both be dead. *No, they can't be.*

"Ha!" said the troll, wiping his hands together. "That will make them easier to break apart and eat."

He moved toward the tree.

"Don't you dare!" Annie raced to a position in front of him, waving the skis about.

"What?" The troll stopped and laughed, a huge, chortling cackle. "What are you going to do about it, huh? You're just a girl. A teeny, inconsequential girl."

"I've got skis." Annie waved them in his face. "And I'm not afraid to use them."

"Honestly? That's it?" He mocked her voice: "'I've got skis, and I'm not afraid to use them'?"

"Yes . . ." Annie tried to think of something else to say. There was movement in the tree. Either Bloom or Eva was still alive. She had to give them time to get out, had to lure away the troll somehow. "These skis aren't normal."

"They aren't?" Mr. Alexander took a step closer, casually, without a care in the world.

"No." Annie lowered her voice. "They're magic."

"Magic? How?"

This is a bit like talking to a toddler, Annie thought. She'd learned how to do that from a couple of foster parents back when their three-year-old was having a tantrum. Anything shiny or yummy would almost always get her to stop. Trolls were like that, too, it seemed.

"I don't know if I should tell you," Annie said. She stepped backward just slightly.

It was enough to hook Mr. Alexander. "Tell me!"

He stepped forward quickly, which meant he was three booming steps away from the fallen tree and her friends.

"They fly," Annie said in a way that made it sound as if she were trusting him with the biggest secret in the universe.

"No!" His mouth dropped open in shock, and his hand fluttered to his chest.

"Scout's honor," Annie said. She tried to make the Boy Scout sign with her fingers, but she had never been a Boy Scout. She failed. It ended up looking more like an awkward peace sign. Mr. Alexander didn't seem to notice. He probably hadn't been a Boy Scout either.

The clouds broke enough for the moonlight to flicker through the remaining trees, creating bars of light on the snow. A noise in the house made Annie jump. Mr. Alexander cackled.

He sounds just like the crow, Annie thought. For a second she wondered if all evil things sounded like that, but even as she thought it, Mr. Alexander reached forward, yanking the skis from her hand.

"I'll take those," he muttered. He plopped the long skis on the ground and set his feet upon them. They cracked beneath his weight. "It's not doing nothing."

He growled, staring at her.

"You—you have to turn them on," Annie stammered. She pointed. "There's a button, right there on the top of the ski."

Mr. Alexander looked down, moving this way and that to try to get an angle. His considerable size prevented him from getting a good fix on the button.

"Maybe you could just bend over and press it," Annie suggested.

"TROLLS DO NOT BEND!" he roared. Then he lowered his voice. "Not that I'm a troll—"

"Of course not."

"Trolls do not exist."

"Of course they don't," Annie soothed as a random shaft of lightning lit the sky.

"We are not allowed to let the world know about us," Mr. Alexander finished his thought nervously and then reached out, yanking Annie up into the air, lifting her so high that they were nose to nose. Her legs dangled hopelessly. He squinted his eyes. His breath was so foul that Annie had to cover her mouth with her hands. Mr. Alexander sniffed at her, licked his lips, and then dropped her on the ground. She landed on his foot. He did not flinch. "You do it."

"Okay . . ." Annie moved off his foot and out of the way and reached out a trembling hand. She pushed the button.

The skis groaned and bucked a tiny bit.

"It's not working," Mr. Alexander whined.

"Try to think light thoughts," Annie suggested, willing the skis to manage his weight. "Just give it a second."

The skis lurched, lifting up into the air. Mr. Alexander bent forward, and then recovered his balance, managing to stay upright as the skis rapidly skidded ahead. Annie jumped out of the way, giving him plenty of room.

"One thing!" she yelled after him as the skis accelerated.

"Shut up, girl!" he hollered, heading toward the woods.

"But it's important," Annie called.

He ignored her.

"Okay, then, never mind," Annie whispered as Mr. Alexander's skis wrapped around either side of a massive tree in an impressive troll split. He hit the trunk with the full force of his body. The tree cracked and fell while Mr. Alexander bounced back the opposite way. He landed flat on his back in the snow.

Annie watched.

Annie waited.

He didn't move. He was out cold.

"There's no Stop button," she whispered and turned away, heading back to her friends who were desperately trying to free themselves from the fallen branches.

Something thudded inside the Alexanders' house. She stopped midstride. A horrifying scream from inside the house ripped across the cold night air.

31

Cats to the Rescue

The gnome was right there, smack in the middle of Jamie's grandmother's arms.

Now what?

He had to get it. He had to somehow pluck it away from her without waking her up. Jamie looked at the cat for aid. The cat shrugged.

"Not helpful," he whispered. To be fair, though, the cat did find the gnome for him. She brought him right here. "How did you know?"

The cat wound herself around his legs. She rubbed the side of her head against his jeans and started purring. Jamie couldn't believe it. *How could a cat purr at a time like this? How could he even hesitate at a time like this?* The whole town was depending on him. His friends were outside battling his dad, and here he was—being a coward.

Jamie stepped forward. His hands shook.

His grandmother did not move.

Jamie stepped forward again. Sweat broke out on his forehead.

Still, no movement. He put the flashlight in his pocket. The light beamed up at the ceiling, making a circle of brightness in the dark. *I can do this . . . I can . . .*

He stepped forward. His heart seemed to pause.

Reaching out his hand, Jamie held his breath. His fingers grabbed the tip of the gnome's red cap. It was cool and hard to the touch. If he could just slide it out slowly, maybe his grandmother wouldn't notice. He tightened his hold and pulled. The gnome slid through her arms. One inch . . . Another . . . Free!

Jamie grasped it with both hands. He had it. He really, truly had it.

Pow!

A giant hand snatched his forearm. He screamed.

His grandmother sat up, yanking him toward her. Her breath rushed into his face. "What are you doing, brat?"

"I—I—" Jamie tried to escape but she was too strong. Her fingers pushed into his skin, bruising it.

"Trying to take my gnomie?" she scoffed. "Think you could take my baby treasure. You fool. Can't believe you came back here, but I'm glad you did. Oh, yes, I am . . . Know why?"

"So you can eat me on my birthday?" Jamie squeaked.

"Exactly." She laughed, but her laughter choked off into a grunt.

The cat, the gray cat that had led him into her room, had leaped upon her arm and was biting her wrist. Jamie's grandmother dropped him. He plopped to the ground and hopped up on his feet again as she shrieked at the cat, batting it away. "Get off me."

The cat flew across the room but lunged toward Mrs. Alexander again, hissing. As Jamie staggered backward out of the way, an astounding number of cats bounded through the doorway. His flashlight fell to the ground and rolled beneath their paws. They gracefully hurdled over it as they vaulted toward Mrs. Alexander, claws out and yowling.

The first cat peered back at Jamie and tilted her head at the door. He understood instantly. He ran out, clutching the gnome to his chest and scooping his flashlight into his hands as he raced into the hallway.

He met Annie halfway up the stairs. Her hair was askew and her eyes wide with fear. "Jamie, I heard a scream."

"My grandmother . . . Come on . . ." He led her back down the stairs and outside even as more cats sprung into the house via the front door.

"What is going on with the cats?" Annie asked, stopping on the porch. "I've never seen so many cats."

"No idea, but they are keeping my grandmother busy. We've got to go. I've got the gnome. Where are Bloom and Eva? Wait. Is that my dad?" He gazed at the giant form passed out by one of two knocked-over trees.

"Yeah ..." Annie pulled Jamie toward the other tree, explaining that Eva and Bloom were trapped under it.

"We're fine," Eva yelled from beneath a blanket of leaves. "Can't kill a dwarf and an elf. Not with a tree. No sirree! Bloom just needs to remember the stinking spell to get the tree off us."

"I am *trying*," Bloom's voice came from the tangled branches. "But you keep interrupting me."

"Well, that's 'cause you're so freaking slow," Eva shot back.

"I have to concentrate, Eva. I don't want to screw it up."

Annie gave Jamie a help-me face and lifted up her shoulders as if to say she had no idea why they were like this. Just as she opened her mouth to speak, Mrs. Alexander stormed out of the house. She had turned troll and was exceedingly large, too large to properly fit through the doorway. As she burst through it, she broke part of the wall. Cats hung from her clothing, and one even dangled from her hair. She shook them off, and they soared, flailing through the air before landing in the soft snow.

"I want my gnomie back!" she roared.

Jamie clutched it harder to his chest and whispered to Annie. "I don't think she knows what it is. She was sleeping with it like a teddy bear."

"Weird," Annie whispered back as she struggled to move branches out of the way. Eva popped out first.

Bloom followed. He saw Mrs. Alexander and groaned, pulling twigs out of his hair. "Not another troll."

"Where's my ax?" Eva bellowed.

Annie pointed to a place in the snow, a good distance away from the house. Eva thundered toward it.

Mrs. Alexander's eyes narrowed as she watched all of them. "Who am I going to eat first, huh?"

"You're not supposed to eat us. You're not even supposed to let us know you exist. You're breaking all the rules," Annie blurted. Once again winter lightning lit the sky.

"Yeah, well, maybe I'm sick of the rules, and ain't nobody here to enforce them, are they? So . . . pshaw to rules." Jamie's grandmother seemed triumphant in her logic.

The cats began slinking toward her.

She glared at them. "Don't try it."

The cats stopped slinking.

Mrs. Alexander focused her attention on Jamie. "Give that to me."

Jamie's voice was quiet. "No."

"What did you say?" she roared. She'd picked up one of

the abandoned skis and brandished it like a weapon, threatening Jamie.

"No," he repeated.

He scuttled a step sideways. But Annie had had enough of Jamie's bullying excuse for a grandmother. She took a flying leap at the troll and managed to get enough height to grab at her arm. She hung there foolishly and screamed at Mrs. Alexander to leave them alone, that there would be no bullying anymore.

"And no eating! You will not eat anyone. Not on my watch. You got it?" Annie hollered.

Mrs. Alexander raised an eyebrow. She used her free hand to twist Annie's arm.

Annie screeched in pain.

"Watch out!" Bloom yelled.

Annie let go of Mrs. Alexander just as a ball of light smashed into the troll. Bloom smiled triumphantly. Mrs. Alexander howled and lost her balance, thudding down the porch stairs, banging her head on every step. Annie and the cats scrambled to get out of the way of her falling bulk so as not to get caught beneath it.

Jamie helped Annie, grabbing her by the arm. The gnome was secure in his shirt again. He swallowed hard.

His grandmother wasn't moving. *She can't be dead, can she?* He didn't know what to think, what to do. Only one thing—one person—came to mind: Annie. He'd take care of Annie.

"You okay?" he whispered, patting her arm awkwardly.

She sputtered. "I-I—I think so? I— Are you okay, Jamie? I'm worried about you."

Before he could reassure her, Eva came roaring forward with the ax and stopped a foot away.

"A bit late, dwarf," Bloom teased.

"The ax was stuck in a tree buried beneath the snow," Eva grumped. "And I didn't pass out ... That's your cue for applause."

They ignored her. Annie gestured toward Jamie's grandmother. "She's not moving."

"Trolls are prone to head injuries," Bloom explained as Eva prodded the bottom of Mrs. Alexander's foot with the ax.

"So she's not dead?" Jamie asked.

"Unfortunately," Eva grumped. "All this and I don't even get to add a notch to my ax."

They all stood there for an awkward second until Jamie told Bloom, "That whole ball-of-light thing was great."

"Thanks. Elf magic." Bloom stood a bit taller.

Eva rolled her eyes and herded them forward. "Come on. Let's get the gnome back home before they wake up."

Annie, Jamie, Eva, and Bloom left. They left the broken skis and the troll house. They left Jamie's snoring "relatives" flat on the snow. The pack of cats, led by the gray one with the white mitten paws, followed them as they walked down the street and up toward the mountains, and Jamie swore that this time he was leaving for good. He would never, ever be coming back.

32

A Surprise Reunion

Side by side, they hustled down the darkness of Mount Desert, turning off the main street and up the hill by the stone church. The air still smelled faintly of burned wood from the fire at Mr. Nate's house.

The wind gently blew snow against their disheveled clothes and dirty faces. The cold air seemed to wiggle into Annie's aching bones and muscles, making every movement feel a bit slower and more difficult than it should have been. The sky above them was dark. Jamie gave Bloom the flashlight, and he lit the way back.

"I wish we still had the skis," Eva grumbled as they trudged along.

"The skis almost killed us," Bloom argued back.

Eva harrumphed.

Annie walked with Jamie. Her words echoed Eva's. "I wish we still had Tala."

"Me, too." Jamie seemed a bit shell shocked. She couldn't imagine what must be going through his head after what just happened.

"Are you okay?" She whispered low enough so the others wouldn't hear.

He nodded. Then he shook his head no. "I'm—not sure?"

His voice squeaked, and he seemed so embarrassed about it that Annie had to try hard not to giggle.

"You two, be quiet," Eva ordered. "There could still be monsters lurking around anywhere. We've got to hurry and get this back before—"

A voice, rough and low and bossy, came out of the darkness. "You ain't going nowhere."

Annie knew that voice. She stopped midstep, staring into the darkness and trees.

Walden Wiegle stepped out into the road, right in front of Eva. His parka stretched across his chest. His boots sank deep into the snow. A wool hat barely covered up his ears. He pointed at Annie. "I see you, twerp."

Annie swallowed hard. She would not be afraid of him. She would not be afraid of him. She would not be . . .

She trembled.

Jamie grabbed her by the arm. "Is he a troll?"

Annie shook her head. "I don't think so."

"He looks like one," Eva grumbled. "He's tall and ugly."

"Eva!" Annie scolded. Even if it was true, it wasn't nice.

"Shut up, munchkin," Walden said. "I don't even know what you are grumbling about."

"Munchkin!" Eva raised her ax over her head.

Annie caught her by the arm. "Eva!"

"He called me a munchkin!" the dwarf said as if it explained everything.

"That doesn't mean you should kill him," Annie said, pulling her back a little bit. She hated Walden and everything he'd put her through, but that didn't mean it was okay for him to die. She tried to calm her heart and braved herself to stare at him and say, "Walden. We need to get past you. We have something really important to do—"

"You!" he interrupted, scoffing. "*You're* doing something important? Hold on. I have to laugh."

Walden bent over and forced a mock guffaw.

"If he isn't a troll, he really should be," Jamie muttered as Walden continued to cackle.

"No truer thing has ever been said," Bloom muttered, and then his voice took on a commanding tone, "Let us pass."

Walden stood up. "Excuse me, blond boy? You're the little sports star from school, aren't you? Mr. Baseball?"

Bloom shrugged. "You need to leave."

"You can't order me around! Do you have any idea what that nothing, Nobody girl did?" He pointed at Annie.

"No," Bloom answered. "But I know that you hurt—"

"She destroyed my home!" Walden yelled, thundering closer. Spittle exploded out of his mouth.

Annie was suddenly happy Eva had an ax.

"She let my dogs loose and they're missing! She refused to be invisible."

"And well she should," Bloom interrupted.

Annie's heart warmed in her chest. Elves were so nice, even if they did talk a bit funny.

"She refused to do anything right!" Walden finished. "She was a jerk! A lazy, annoying, noisy jerk, and now we have no pets, no home, and no money! My mother had to get a job. An actual, real out-of-the-house-and-do-work job."

Annie felt strange, like something inside her had been pulled too tightly and was about to snap. *Why is Walden so evil? How can he possibly say that I'm the jerk?*

Beside her Jamie twitched like a nervous bunny. "We need to get going."

"I know," she said. "I know . . . Move out of the way, Walden."

Walden raised an eyebrow. "And who is going to make me?"

Eva growled. "Can I please just use my ax? Nobody ever lets me use my ax."

"No," Bloom answered, tightening his grip on her arm.

Annie couldn't let Eva use her ax either. But they had to do something. She knew Walden. He'd never move. Not for her. *He is a horrible, rotten rat of a boy—no offense to rats— and he hates me,* Annie thought. Frustration took over, and for a second her whole body shook as she suddenly imagined a nice, calming field of flowers.

"You other twerps can go. I just want Annie so she can pay for what she did," Walden insisted as he lunged toward her.

"No!" Bloom and Jamie shouted as Eva bellowed an unintelligible war cry.

But Annie barely heard them. A burst of purple light flew from her left fingers and slammed into Walden's hands. The light blinded all of them for a moment. And when it dimmed, Walden's hands had morphed into giant pink bouquets, with polka-dotted green stems where his fingers should be. Flower heads had replaced his fingernails.

Walden jumped backward, raising his flower-hands in front of him.

"Wh-what?" His face turned red. He shook a flower at Annie. "You did this! You—y-y-y-you f-f-freak! You crazy freak!"

Mouth wide open in shock, Annie stared at her hands. She had done that, hadn't she? Without drawing? That purple light had come from her and turned Walden's hands into flowers. *How?* But she didn't have time to think about it. They had a sputtering Walden to deal with and a gnome to return, and she was suddenly so terribly tired. It was hard even to stand up.

"Get out of here, Walden," Annie ordered. "Go back to your mother and never come here again. And please be nice to people from now on."

He gawped at her but didn't move.

For a moment, Annie thought her legs might be shaking.

"You don't want the rest of you to turn into a flower, do you?" she threatened, eyebrow arching.

That did the trick. Walden turned and ran up the road. Well, it was more of a fast walk really. Like Eva, Walden wasn't much of a runner.

They stood there in the dark night, watching him go. Finally, Eva broke the silence. She jumped around in a little circle, a dwarf version of a happy dance. "That was so cool! It was so freaking cool! Holy coolness, Annie. Didn't know you had it in you. Wish you'd done it to the trolls, though. Way to hold out."

Even Jamie was smiling. Annie blushed, suddenly embarrassed by all the attention. She was about to explain to them how she'd been imagining a flower field when something wicked howled in the distance. The sound echoed across the town, piercing their happiness.

"Do you still have the gnome?" Annie asked Jamie, an idea formulating in her head, an idea that involved not just breaking a rule, but committing an actual big-time crime.

Jamie pulled it out of his shirt just enough so that the others could see the red hat and two blue gnome eyes that seemed to be twinkling mischievously. Annie petted the gnome on the hat and Jamie tucked it back inside his shirt again, just as the howling continued. It sounded like a hundred hungry wolves, and it sounded much closer than it did before.

Annie turned to the others and said something she never imagined she would say in a million years, "Maybe we should steal a car."

33

And So a Life of Crime Begins

There has got to be a freaking car to steal around here somewhere," Eva grumped as they walked past house after house and empty driveway after empty driveway. Everything felt abandoned and spooky, clouded by snow.

It wasn't easy to find a car to steal in Mount Desert. Wealthy summer residents owned most of the houses and brought their cars back with them to their real homes for the winter. Cars were important to people. It was how they got to the grocery store or the doctor's or . . . well, wherever it was that adults always needed to go.

"How about there?" Eva pointed to a small green house with a crooked white porch that needed paint. A little red Subaru station wagon with a rusted-out bumper and a sticker that said GIVE PEAS A CHANCE sat in the middle of the driveway.

"No . . . That's the school nurse's. She's super old. She can't walk really well. She needs her car." Jamie shook his head.

Eva rolled her eyes and threw her ax up in the air with one hand and caught it with the other.

"He's just being nice, Eva." Annie put her arm through Jamie's as they trudged through the snow.

Her arm felt good and safe to him and made him almost forget how dangerous everything was.

Annie smiled. "It's nice to be nice."

"Oh . . . that's brilliant." Eva mimicked Annie's voice, "It's nice to be nice. I thought the Stopper was supposed to be smart."

Annie stopped midstep. Jamie opened his mouth, but he didn't know what to say. Annie pulled her arm away and sort of hugged herself, feelings hurt. He wanted to snatch her arm back and tuck it in his own. Instead he just stood there like a doofus.

"Eva!" Bloom scolded. He shook his head, apologizing. "I think Annie is brilliant. Jamie, too, and you're just being a jerk because you're scared. You always—"

"I am not scared!" Eva bellowed.

"—act like a troll when you're scared," Bloom finished.

"I do NOT act like a troll!" Eva's ax moved into a menacing position. Bloom stood there, completely unafraid.

The howling in the woods increased. They all paused and scanned the direction it came from. All they could make out was trees and darkness.

"That sounds closer," Annie whispered.

Jamie had an idea.

"Follow me . . . please . . ." He pulled in front of every-one and started running, feet kicking up the snow. The gnome bobbled up and down in his shirt. He checked to make sure the others were behind him and increased his pace, half running and half sliding down Sea Street, past the main entrance to the town office and then into the parking lot where the police cars were.

Three were parked in the lot. The others caught up to him. Eva took an extra bit of time and arrived panting.

"We can't go to the police," Bloom said. "Your father is one of them, sort of, and we have to protect the secret of Aurora and—"

"We're not," Jamie explained as they huddled by the street lamp. "We're going to steal a police cruiser."

Eva jumped straight up in the air, smacking her thigh with her hand. "Now you're talking!"

"Shh . . . ," Bloom urged her. "People will hear."

Jamie smiled at her reaction, and Bloom nodded his agreement.

"Brilliant!" Bloom clapped him so hard on the back it made him cough.

The three white police cars with their blue lights and big tires beckoned. The writing on the doors read MOUNT DESERT POLICE. They were sort of spiffy looking.

Jamie rubbed his hands together. They just needed keys, and he knew exactly where to get them.

"I like the whole cop car thing, but couldn't we take a fire truck?" Eva asked, finally breaking the silence. "They have hoses and ladders and all those gauges and . . ."

"No." Bloom glared at her. "What if there is a fire?"

"Well, what if there's a crime?" she countered.

"There are three cars and one police officer," Jamie explained. "But you always need all the fire trucks in case there's a fire. It's not the same with police cars."

"I don't know if that's any better," Annie murmured.

Eva threw her hands up in the air. "Stealing a car was your idea!"

Annie shivered in the cold. "I know . . . but . . . oh . . . The more I think about it, the more wrong it seems."

They stared at one another for a moment. Jamie didn't have a clue as to what was going on inside Annie's head. She had been so brave a second ago.

In fact, they all were chilled to the bone. Jamie needed to get them somewhere warm. And they needed to get the gnome back to Aurora before other monsters came and killed everyone. A car was warm and fast. Fast was important. Lives were at stake.

"We will just *borrow* the car," he announced. "We will

bring it back. Plus, we aren't stealing from a person. We're taking it from the whole town. That's who the police cars belong to: the whole town, all the taxpayers. And surely this qualifies as an emergency. The police cars are there to keep the town safe in case of emergency. So, we're really using it for that reason. That's not so wrong. Is it, Annie?"

"Brilliant!" Bloom said again.

"He likes that word," Eva grumped.

"It's a better word than 'freaking,'" Bloom said in an exasperated voice.

They all settled into silence, waiting for Annie's decision. Eva tossed her ax back and forth between her hands, sighing impatiently. Jamie stared at his footprints in the snow, and Bloom just stood there, eyes closed, face tilted toward the sky.

Finally, Annie gave a tiny nod, and once she did, Jamie set off to get the keys. As he hurried, Jamie worried he'd mess this up. And he didn't really want to because if he did, he'd go to jail. A jail for children. They had those. And he wasn't the sort of boy who wanted jail in his future. He wanted Aurora in his future.

There was just one entrance to the Mount Desert police station. The front door was right by the dispatcher's office, which was where Jamie's father worked the night shift. Jamie thought of his father, passed out on the lawn. He obviously wasn't working tonight. *Good.*

Creeping forward and hiding alongside a bush, Jamie peeked through the window into the dispatch office. Marie was working. He liked Marie. She had a pit bull that could pretend to be shot and then come back to life. Marie would always scowl at Jamie's father whenever she saw him. She also would sneak Jamie treats, pieces of crystallized ginger mostly. His mouth watered just thinking about it.

The problem with Marie was that she didn't fall asleep at work, not even on the night shift, not even when she was working with Frostie, which is what she called Officer Frost. The other problem was that all the keys to the police cruisers dangled from a hook board on the far wall behind her huge black swiveling chair.

"I can do this," Jamie whispered, teeth chattering.

Not only would a car get them to Aurora much more safely, it would also warm up Annie, and since her skin was turning blue, that seemed like a pretty big priority. Jamie glanced back at his friends. Bloom and Eva hunkered down by the cruisers. Bloom gave him a thumbs-up sign. Eva was trying to pick the lock on the door. Jamie had to hurry up and just do it.

He ran forward at a crouch, bounded up the stairs past the window, and smooshed his body against the white siding between the police station door and the window. Jamie pried open the door just enough to slide his thin body through, grabbed the handle, and closed it gently behind him.

He breathed in and held his breath.

He flattened himself against the wall, staring at a cork-board publicizing town meetings and harbor committees. He was in the short corridor before the locked door to the dispatch office. The dispatcher had to buzz people through to the rest of the police station.

The door was not an option.

However, Jamie spied the open countertop. The counter always reminded Jamie of a ticket booth. It was there so that dispatchers could give out overnight parking permits to people heading out to Swan's Island or Islesboro on the ferry. The space was big enough for him to climb over into the dispatch office, but he had to do it without Marie seeing him.

He breathed out.

He could do this. He had to.

Turning around, Jamie carefully peeked over the counter-top. Marie was sitting in her chair, staring at the computer, completely bored. Her hand was moving the mouse around and occasionally clicking. She probably was playing a video game. The room smelled of spaghetti sauce, the kind from a can. Jamie breathed the aroma in and stared at the keys on the wall behind Marie's head. They were dangling there, waiting for him. If only he could be invisible.

A sudden beeping startled Jamie so much that he jumped backward. It was the microwave in the back room. Marie hopped up out of the chair and trotted to the back room to retrieve her dinner. He didn't have much time before she'd be back.

Now! Jamie thought. He boosted himself up and over the counter, shimmying through the small opening, and then landed gracefully on the gray carpeting of the dispatch office. He bounded two steps across the room, snatched the keys, and bounced over the counter again.

The door of the microwave closed. Marie's footsteps sounded across the carpet. The chair squeaked as she sat back down. Jamie pressed himself against the wall beneath the counter and crawled to the front door.

"Marie!"

He heard the hearty rah-rah voice belonging to Officer Frost. It was a raspy, sort of soccer-player kind of voice. "Toss me the keys to the Charger."

Jamie froze.

"What for?" Marie asked.

"I'm going to cruise around."

No. No. No. No . . . Jamie closed his eyes. He'd taken the keys to the Charger. It was the smallest cruiser. It seemed like it would be the easiest to drive. Marie and Officer Frost would see them missing. They'd come looking and they'd find him . . . And they'd send him to jail, or worse, they would send him back home to his father and grandmother.

Please. Please. Please. He begged silently, opening his

eyes. The fluorescent light that hung from the ceiling had a hundred tiny dead bugs trapped inside it.

"Frostie. What are you thinking? *Police Women of Kennebec County* is on in five minutes," dispatcher Marie said. "Plus, it's snowing."

Officer Frost said a swear word. Another chair squeaked as he sat down. "Turn it on!"

Marie harrumphed. Once she'd told Jamie she thought Officer Frost was too bossy. Marie did not like to be bossed.

The television was turned on, and Jamie crawled toward the police station door, sliding it open enough to slip through again. Then, sticking to the bushes he ran down the granite steps and into the parking lot. The others met him by the cruiser.

"Did you get it?" Bloom asked.

Jamie didn't answer. His heart was beating so fast he thought it might break through his ribs.

"He didn't. I told you he was too much of a goody-goody. Pay up," Eva grumped.

Annie looked embarrassed for him, but Jamie smiled slowly and pulled the keys out from his pocket, dangling them in front of Eva's face.

"Ha!" Bloom yelped and then immediately whispered, "Pay up."

"Stop yelling. They'll hear us." Eva pulled a candy bar out of her coat pocket and handed it to the elf, who promptly broke it into four pieces and gave them each a share.

Annie nibbled hers and said to Jamie, "You drive, okay? I'll hold the gnome?"

Jamie hesitated. "Okay."

They climbed into the police car. Annie and Jamie went up front. Bloom and Eva clambered into the back. A wire cage divided the front seat from the rear passengers. It was meant to separate the officers from the criminals they were taking to jail. In between Jamie and Annie were all sorts of radio and computer equipment. Behind them, mounted to the metal bracket beneath the wire separator was a high-powered rifle.

"This car is so freaking cool," Eva whispered. "I totally want one."

Bloom groaned. Annie latched her seat belt. Then after a moment's hesitation, she reached over and latched Jamie's seat belt as well. His hands were shaking so much. He gave her a curious half smile.

"Just, um . . . helping," she explained.

Before he could respond, Eva leaned forward, rattling the cage with her fingers. "Start the car and let's go."

"Yes . . . Right . . . Um . . ." Jamie fumbled about with the keys. He attempted to stick them into the heating vent.

"Jamie?" Annie asked.

"Okay . . . Right . . . Yep. Sorry!" He stuck the keys into the steering wheel, honking the horn, which caused Eva to start saying naughty dwarf words. Annie unbuckled her seat belt, while keeping an eye on the police station. Marie and Officer Frost didn't turn their heads from the TV set.

Jamie threw his hands up in the air. "I don't know how to drive."

His face was a despondent mess.

"Well, yeah, obviously," Eva snorted.

Annie opened her door. "Let me."

He got out of the cruiser as well, and they met in the front. The wind blew snow all about their faces. Jamie squinted through it to have a good look at Annie. "Do you know how?"

She handed him the gnome. "Nope. But I've played video games. One of my foster moms was completely into video games. Okay . . . Keep this safe and buckle up. We can do this, Jamie, I promise. I promise we can."

She hopped into the driver's seat and shut the door behind her.

Jamie swallowed hard and tucked the gnome back inside of his shirt. He plopped down in the car's passenger seat, buckling his seat belt.

"I should drive," Eva grumbled. "Dwarfs are good at mechanical things."

"That's not the same as driving," Bloom countered as Annie started the engine.

She got the windshield wipers on and shifted the car into

reverse and slowly pulled it out of the parking spot. Her eyes were wide and huge.

Bloom kept talking. "We're all good at certain things. We all have skills. You, Eva, are good at bickering."

Eva punched him in the arm. *He didn't even say ouch,* Jamie realized. Elves were tough.

"Annie is good at magic, even though she doesn't know it yet," Bloom continued. "She's also highly caring, as is Jamie, it seems. They both basically just ooze kindness. Annie's a bit bossier, though, so she's probably good at being a leader. Eva is not good at being a follower, but she's good at hitting and having a temper and tinkering with things."

"And you are good at talking," Eva interrupted as Annie slowly pulled the cruiser out of the parking lot and turned onto Sea Street.

"You turned," Jamie said. "Good job."

He felt proud of her, oddly enough. He let out a big breath, relieved that he wasn't the one driving.

Annie's hands were tight on the wheel, and her eyes were focused. She was somewhat terrified. She still managed to quickly turn her head and flash Jamie a smile. Then as they drove up the hill she called over her shoulder, "What's Jamie good at, Bloom?"

"He's good at stealing the keys to police cars, and at being kind, which is a very helpful trait." Bloom paused for a second. "He's smart. He's encouraging. He notices things. He can tell how people are feeling, which is an important skill . . ."

Is that it? Jamie thought, crushed.

"I think he is good at being good," Bloom declared.

Eva snorted.

"What?" Bloom countered. "That's the most important thing of all."

Jamie thought he might have said more but the elf paused. Jamie turned his head so he could glance over his shoulder at the passengers in the backseat, but his attention was distracted by something behind the car, just down the hill, coming up from the harbor.

He tried to speak, but no voice came out. He cleared his throat with a squeak and tried again. "Um, Annie, there's a pack of wolves following us. I'm thinking that you might want to speed up."

34

Surrounded by Wolves

As they entered the main street of Mount Desert, the wind blew hard, scattering snowflakes every which way. Annie had to lean forward just to see if the cruiser was still driving on the actual road.

"Are the wolves still behind us?" she asked.

Jamie's knuckles were white from gripping the back of his seat so ferociously. "Yes."

"Okay . . . okay . . ." Annie's own hands clutched the steering wheel. She pushed a bit more on the gas pedal. They were going too fast on the snow already. She didn't want to have an accident. Not only would they lose a quick, relatively safe way back to Aurora, but they'd also be at the mercy of those wolves.

"Does anyone actually know how to get to Aurora?" she yelled over the roaring engine and the sirens. "Wait. Why are there sirens?" They were coming from the police cruiser. "Jamie? Can you stop the siren noise?"

Jamie gave her a frazzled groan and started randomly hitting buttons. Blue lights turned on from their position atop the roof, casting swirling blue rays around on the snow. The radio blared dance music.

She rounded the corner onto Route 198. "Am I at least going the right way?"

"Yes," said Bloom.

"No," said Eva.

They bounced around in the backseat, staring out at the wolves, which were still bounding after them.

"Guys!" Annie was exasperated. *They had to know where they lived, didn't they?* Annie groaned inside. She was stealing a police car, driving illegally, and putting all their lives in jeopardy. The least they could do was know how to get home. The moment she thought it, she felt guilty for thinking mean thoughts.

"It's okay, Annie," Jamie said next to her.

"What?"

"To get grumpy sometimes."

She wanted to see his expression but she didn't dare. "How do you know I'm grumpy?"

"I can sort of feel it," Jamie explained.

"You feel it?"

"Yeah, like I feel other people's emotions. Plus, you're making a grumpy face." He paused.

"I'm not a hundred percent grumpy. I'm just so stressed. We have to hurry back before things happen. Everyone's so defenseless, just frozen in feathers. We need to hurry." Annie peered at the straight stretch of two-lane state road ahead of her. There was a mountain to one side and a pond to the other. They were driving away from the ocean. That couldn't be right. "And I can't even tell if we're going in the right direction."

"We are definitely going the wrong way," Eva insisted, "and the wolves are catching up."

Jamie yelled back, still trying to get the siren to stop. "How can they catch up? We're speeding."

"I don't think they're regular wolves," Annie said in a low tone, slowing down.

"They're freaking magic, obviously," Eva shouted simultaneously. She pounded her tiny fist against the roof of the car. "It is so not fair that Jamie gets shotgun. I'm the dwarf. I should be playing with those gadgets. Annie! What are you doing? You're slowing down."

Annie bit her lip and eased the cruiser into a stop. She put the big stick lever into reverse again and started to turn around. "We're going the wrong way."

"The wolves!" All three of the others pretty much shouted it at the same time while Annie tried to turn the car around.

It wasn't easy. There were a lot of angles involved. Annie had never done anything like it before in real life. Just video games.

"Dude! The car is sideways! Let me drive!" Eva commanded, pulling on the metal cage to emphasize her demand.

"Which way are we going now?" Bloom asked. "Also . . . the wolves . . ."

"Annie!" Jamie didn't say anything else.

Annie breathed out a large breath as the wolves circled the cruiser. The blue lights cast wide beams along their fur, tinting it. They all stood with their ears back, teeth bared, tails raised, at full attention. Annie cut the engine. The siren stopped.

"Um . . . They've surrounded the car," Jamie said quietly.

"I know." Annie unbuckled her seat belt. She stared into the brown, dilated eyes of the wolf-dog closest to her.

"Drive, Annie!" Eva declared.

"I don't want to hit them." Annie opened the door before any of them could say anything else. Cold air burst inside the cruiser. She jumped outside, closing the door behind her. She could still hear her friends yelling for her to come back, screaming their questions about what she was doing, and Eva doubting her sanity.

"Trust me," she whispered, staring at the closest dog. "You know me."

The wolf-dog's ears moved forward just a bit, and his jowls relaxed so that his teeth were no longer showing.

"You remember me, don't you?" Annie said in a soothing dog-whisperer kind of tone. "From the trailer? We escaped together."

The animal cocked his head. His tail wagged one quick time as Annie squatted down. She slowly stretched out her arm toward him so that he could smell it. Behind her, Jamie had opened the passenger side door of the car. The others tried but couldn't get out. The cruiser's back doors were locked.

"Annie . . ." His voice was a terrified whisper.

"It's okay," Annie answered, not even sparing a glance back at him. "I know them. That's Big Mister Number Seven."

A wolf near Jamie growled, low and threatening.

Annie wiggled her fingers. The wolf-dog near her moved forward an inch, which was just enough for his nose to touch her fingertips. He sniffed. She tried not to move. The wolf-dog skulked closer another inch, moving his head so that Annie's digits grazed his muzzle. She scratched it, and cooed, "There . . . there . . . everything is okay now."

His tail began to wag happily in a circular motion. Eva and Bloom stopped shouting and banging on the windows. Jamie uttered some sort of exclamation under his breath.

Annie petted Big Mister Number Seven's head. He made a happy dog noise and sauntered closer, pressing his side into her knees. She thought of Tala, that magical white dog that she missed so much, trapped at Aurora. She had to save him. Maybe these wolf-dogs could help. She stood up slowly, quickly counting to see how many there were. She hadn't gotten a really good chance to notice because she'd been so focused on driving and now . . . Now? She gasped.

The cruiser was completely surrounded by a pack of wolves or wolf-dogs. Annie wasn't sure what the difference was between them. It didn't matter. There were twelve of them, including Big Mister Numbers Seven and Nine, all staring at her. The good news was none of them seemed to want to bite her or rip her head off. Actually, none of them even growled at her.

"Thank you," Annie said to Big Mister Number Seven, "for trusting me and for calming them down."

The lead wolf-dog nuzzled her hand for more petting.

"They like you," Jamie said quietly, almost reverently.

"We have some history together," Annie said. "Two of them were prisoners with me."

"At Walden's?"

"Yeah."

She briskly shook the memory away and addressed the wolf that was now leaning against her legs and making a noise that sounded almost like purring.

Turning to the wolf, she asked, "Do you know how to get to Aurora?"

The wolf wagged his tail and stood up again. His eyes met hers.

"Will you lead us there?" Annie asked. "Be warned. I am a horrible driver. So, you'll probably just want us to follow you."

For a second the wolf-dog didn't respond. Then he backed up several paces and lifted his head to the sky. He howled once, long and sad, then marched around the cruiser, prancing and nudging the other wolves, yipping at them. Eventually all the canines lined up in front of the car, except for Big Mister Number Seven. He leaped over Jamie and sat in the passenger's seat.

"We aren't going to both fit," Jamie explained.

The wolf growled.

"Okay . . . Okay . . . I'll just sit in the back." Jamie unlocked the back door and hurried into the seat. Eva grumbled and moved aside so that there would be room.

"Afraid of a dog," she muttered.

The wolf turned around and snarled at her. She stopped muttering.

Bloom snorted and leaned forward despite the wolf-dog's huge teeth hovering just beyond the cage that separated the seats. "Annie? Are you ready?"

Annie turned around, smiling at him. She petted the wolf-dog. His tongue lolled out of the side of his mouth, and then he remembered to give the children in the back another menacing stare.

"Cross your fingers," Annie said. "We are on our way."

Turning back around, she switched the ignition on. Nothing happened. She stepped on the gas. The engine did not roar to life. She switched the ignition on again and stepped on the gas at the same time.

Nothing.

The cruiser wouldn't start.

35

Sleigh Wolves

It was Eva's idea. Of course it was. Nobody else would have had the audacity to hook up eleven wolf-dogs with harnesses made of belts and rope and police tape and then attach the entire contraption to a car, turning the police cruiser into a bobsled.

But it worked.

Eva sat on the top of the squad car with her feet hooked beneath the blue lights. She held the makeshift reins in her hands. She squealed with delight. Jamie figured out the heating system and from his position in the backseat explained to Annie how to turn the heat on. She rolled down the windows so Bloom could keep an eye on Eva and make sure she didn't fall off during all the lurching and curving angles of the road.

Still, even as they got closer and closer to Aurora, Jamie had a niggling feeling inside his chest that something was going to go horribly wrong. Eva barked at him not to be a negative naiad, but he could tell from the expression on everyone's face that they had the same lurking feeling. And, no, it didn't have anything to do with the wolf in the passenger seat. It was something bigger than that.

"Almost there!" Bloom chirped from where he was hanging out the window. "Almost . . .

The elf's blond hair swept back from his face. Horror rewrote his features. "Eva!!!"

Jamie jumped to his own window and glimpsed out, terrified that Eva had fallen off the top of the cruiser, but she was still there holding the reins.

"What now, elf?" She snorted. "You jealous 'cause I get all the fun?"

She was smiling so broadly that her whole face beamed.

"No! The crow!"

Bloom pointed to the left. Black swirling wings beat at the air. The monster was coming straight for them. They must have crossed back over the stream and not even noticed.

"Eva!" Annie screamed. "Get in! Get in the car!"

"I can't." The dwarf shook her head. "If we stop, the crow will get us." She cracked the reins. "Hurry, wolves! Hurry!"

The monster was getting closer. They rounded a corner and moved up a hill.

"How much farther is it?" Jamie asked.

Bloom didn't even turn to glance at him. He just kept staring at the crow. His voice came out dazed. "What?"

"How much longer till we get to Aurora?" Jamie asked.

Bloom shook his head. "A half mile . . . Maybe less . . . I think."

Jamie began calculating the speed of the car, the speed of the crow, and the distance between the two. There wasn't enough time.

"We won't make it, will we?" Annie asked.

"No." Jamie shook his head, heart plummeting. This was it. They were done for.

"Ideas? Anyone?" Annie gripped the steering wheel as if it would help her somehow.

"You two run," Bloom said. "Eva and I will hold it off and distract it so you two can run into town. It's just up the road. Hide in the woods. Go fast. Just get the gnome inside the town line. There'll be a sign." He took a small crystal out of his pocket and began murmuring.

"The crow will freeze you," Annie argued. She hiccupped with emotion. "We can't . . ."

Jamie touched her shoulder. "Bloom's right. We have to. There's no other choice. We'll get the gnome inside Aurora, and it will unfreeze everyone."

Bloom sat up even taller. "It'll be okay, Annie."

The crow was so close. Annie put the car in park. Jamie pushed on the cruiser door. He was locked inside.

"Annie, unlock the doors!" he urged frantically.

Annie began pressing buttons. The siren blasted back on. The blue lights swirled. The radio blared. And finally, finally, the doors unlocked.

Jamie pushed the door open with his feet, double-checked the security of the gnome tucked into his shirt, and peered back at Bloom. The elf was too busy mumbling and creating a ball of light between his palms to pay any attention.

"Annie?" Jamie yelled.

"On three, Jamie. Jump on three." She held on to the door frame, ready to leap out of the cruiser. It reminded Jamie of parachuters about to leap out of military planes. He took the same position. The cold wind rippled at his clothes.

"Please do not let me die," he mumbled.

"One!" Annie yelled. "Two!"

The beast was closer than ever. Jamie could feel it just behind them, ready to attack. His whole body screamed with fear.

"Three!"

They jumped. The ground rushed up to meet them. Annie landed almost catlike on two feet in the snow, but Jamie's body curled into a tiny ball and hit the snow with a bouncing sort of plop. He rolled through it and down toward the ditch at the side of the road.

"Jamie!" Annie yelled.

Snow flew up and all around as he tumbled down along

the side of the road. He could hear Annie running behind him, trying to catch up.

"Flatten out!" she hollered after him. "You're like a bowling ball. You're rolling, Jamie! Oh my gosh. Oh my . . ."

Jamie rolled past twigs, snapping them. He bumped over rocks. Bruises started forming. Annie was right. He had to flatten out. He flung his arms and legs away from his body and came to a stop by a boulder twice his size.

Frantic, Jamie tugged on his jacket zipper. *What if the gnome had broken? What if he'd ruined it?*

"Jamie!" Annie ran to his side. Worry etched her features into something sad, almost like a cartoon. She got down on her knees next to him and peered at him. "Are you okay?"

In one motion, he pulled out the gnome. There were no broken pieces, no scratches, nothing. Relief flooded his heart as Jamie tucked it back inside his shirt. He stood up warily, muscles and skin protesting the movement.

"I'm okay," he told her, grabbing her hand. "Let's go . . ."

They kept to the shadows, skulking low among the bushes, stopping only for the briefest of seconds to determine what was happening in the battle behind them.

The wolves had come free from their tethers and reins. They leaped up at the crow, growling and with teeth bared, only to become quickly surrounded by feathers. Bloom's light balls had little effect on the monster, and he'd yanked Eva inside the cruiser with him, rolling up the window. Jamie didn't know how long that would protect them.

"We have to hurry, Annie," he whispered.

They both knew that as soon as the crow was done with Eva and Bloom, it would come searching for them.

"Can you run?" she asked.

He nodded.

They stood and raced forward. No longer hidden by the shadows, they were much more vulnerable. Behind them, Eva opened the window and hollered, "IT SEES YOU! GO! GO! GO!"

If I open the window, that means that the beast could get inside the police cruiser, Annie thought. It meant that Bloom and Eva were frozen now. It meant that Jamie and Annie were the only hope left.

Jamie ran as hard as he possibly could. Annie grabbed his hand and he pulled her along.

"Almost there," he said. He was trying to be encouraging but his voice was so full of fear that the words came out in terrified squeaks.

"I can hear giant things marching, Jamie." Annie clutched his hand with all her might.

"It's the trolls. The book said the trolls would come." They were running so hard that it took all of Jamie's effort to speak. Images from the book burned into his mind. The trolls would kill everyone, destroy everything. Mr. Nate, Miss Cornelia, Helena, and the rest of them would be helpless.

Wings flapped behind them. As cold as it was, Jamie could feel the heat of the crow monster on the back of his neck, so close behind them and moving closer. He pushed them faster. The muscles in his legs burned. He and Annie slipped and slid in the snow, but kept moving forward, one stride after another.

"Got you!" the thing croaked. "I've got you."

The sign WELCOME TO AURORA was half-covered with snow, but Jamie could still make out the words. It loomed in front of them and seemed to twinkle as they raced toward it. If they could just get there, they would be safe. Jamie nearly screamed from frustration. Just a few more feet . . . just a few . . . more . . . It was so close. They had to make it.

"It's right . . . It's right behind us, Jamie . . . ," Annie panted.

Jamie tripped. Arms outstretched, he let go of Annie's hand and fell into the snow. The coldness of it bit against his face and sputtered into his mouth. He flipped around as quickly as he could. The crow was merely a couple of feet behind him. Wings filled the air, flapping wickedly. Scrambling, he stood again, moving up and forward, blindly, batting his way through the feathers. Annie was right behind him, he thought. He could feel her hand on his back.

Then the sky exploded with darkness.

36

Gnome Home

The darkness surrounded them. Jamie had let go of Annie's hand. He screamed and tried to stumble forward, but Annie couldn't make a sound. She batted at the feathers with her hand, knowing in one second both of them would be frozen if she didn't figure out what to do.

The book had said to nail the monster down and kill it inside the town. Once again she felt for the phurba, and this time she knew. She did the only thing she could think of doing. She pushed Jamie with all the strength she had, watching as he broke through the feathers and disappeared, hopefully all the way across the town line. She yanked out the dagger Miss Cornelia had given her. Clenching it, she scooted forward, then scooted forward again, praying that she was inside the town line, and then when she felt as if she could almost no longer move, she swung down hard, driving a mass of feathers to the ground.

For a second there was nothing but a swarm of blackness. Then the feathers all began to pop, one after another, after another. Annie covered her ears and peered in front of her as the feathers exploded into black dust and disappeared.

Annie forgot how to breathe. Had she killed it? Was it really gone? And Jamie? Was he okay? She scurried forward, inching along the snow, not strong enough to get up yet, and spotted him.

Jamie lay stretched out, facedown in the snow. His arms were extended in front of him. He clutched the gnome in his hands. He was well past the town line. And the phurba? She had made it by inches.

Annie staggered up to him.

"Jamie." She grabbed him by the wrists and tugged him forward away from the town line. She didn't know why. It just felt safer. She shook him by the shoulder. "Jamie?"

He lifted up his head. Snow covered his face. "You pushed me?"

She squinted at his face. "I'm so sorry. I had to get you across the town line . . . and we had no time . . . I didn't hurt you, did I? Oh my gosh . . . I would hate it if—"

"No . . . No . . ." He shook his head. "Did we make it?"

Annie reached forward and brushed some snow off his face.

"The crow monster is gone," she said, smiling. "I think we made it. See? The town line is right there."

A line of gold and silver zigzagged through the snow. In repeating words it spelled out TOWN LINE.

"So we did it?"

"Yeah, I think we did it."

Jamie broke into a grin. "So it's over?"

"I think so." She laughed with relief and started to say something more, but her attention was diverted by a dwarf, an elf, and several wolf-dogs running in their direction.

Eva bounded right into Annie, knocking her down. "You two did it! You flimsy human things! I thought for sure you wouldn't be able to, but hoo . . . boy . . . Man, being frozen stunk. Those feathers smelled nasty. It's all done now, though, huh? We're safe, right?"

"Calm down, Eva," Bloom said, but he laughed as he said it. He noticed the phurba in the snow, yanked it out, and handed it to Annie. He lifted an eyebrow in acknowledgment. "Well done."

"Well done, you," Annie whispered back.

The wolves circled them all, and then most of them ran ahead toward the main street of Aurora, a street that was coming to life with murmuring noises and shocked exclamations.

"We did it, didn't we?" Eva asked again. "I mean, we're heroes! We saved the freaking day! That's heroic, right? They'll probably make statues of us."

She let go of Annie and began to make muscle poses, flexing her arms and staring off into the distance, her face frozen into a triumphant yet serious expression.

"Eva," Annie said, laughing. "There are no cameras here."

Eva broke the pose for a second. "You never know when there will be cameras."

She began posing again. Bloom positioned himself closer to Annie, Jamie, and the dogs. His smile filled his face, and his green eyes widened with joy.

"We really did do it. You two did it," he said.

Jamie shook his head and hit the elf awkwardly on the arm. "Nope. It was a team effort. You and Eva sacrificed for us."

"We did, didn't we?" Bloom said. His eyes glinted with happiness.

Annie hadn't thought it was possible for the elf to look prouder, but he did. "You were really brave. You and Jamie and Eva. And the wolf-dogs."

Missing Tala, she bent down and scratched behind one of the wolf-dog's ears. He wagged his tail only once, but was then distracted by something in the distance. His muscles went rigid with attention. A low, deep growl left his throat and mingled with the cold air. Annie followed his gaze down the hill, along the road, and then just to the right.

"Bloom . . . ," she said, but Bloom was still talking to Jamie about how brave they'd all been. He was preening and smiling and talking about how proud Canin and Miss Cornelia would be. He didn't hear Annie at all. She kept staring toward the woods, but reached out and tugged his pants for attention. "Bloom . . ."

"Sorry. What is it, Annie?" Bloom shook himself out of his reverie.

"The gnome is in Aurora, right?" she asked.

"Yes . . ."

"So that means that the town is hidden, right?"

"Yes."

Annie didn't take her eyes off the large pack of trolls approaching Aurora. "Does that mean that it has a bubble around it like a force field so things that try to come in just bounce off or something?"

"No. It means that they are deflected away by a glamour. Whoever or whatever's trying to find us will decide to look elsewhere." His voice lost its happiness as he saw the trolls.

"Trolls," Bloom said, voice lowered with worry and fear. "Trolls are coming."

Eva stopped posing and roared. "What? That's not possible. We brought the gnome back. THE GNOME IS RIGHT HERE!"

Annie stood up and put an arm around her. "Eva. Calm down."

"Don't tell me to calm down!" she roared. "There's freaking trolls coming up the hill. We led them here! Oh my gosh! They will eat EVERYONE and—oh my freaking—"

Jamie caught her as she passed out, wondering how she could be so brave sometimes and so frightened others. Bloom and Annie quickly came over, and they dragged her to a spot beneath a maple tree and settled her into a half-sitting position against the tree's massive trunk.

"She's right," Annie said. "We must have led them here. Maybe they smelled us or something. I bet those are the others the crow warned us about, remember?"

"We should hide," Jamie suggested.

Annie shook her head, watching as the wolves paced just inside the town's boundary line. "No. If they come through, we have to stand our ground and fight."

"With what?" Jamie asked. "Your dagger? Eva's passed out. Bloom's dagger or bow or light balls? Can you make that purple-light magic thing happen again?"

"I don't know . . . Maybe I can stop time again. Maybe—" Annie broke off midsentence. The trolls were stomping forward, up the hill, not even trying to be sneaky. The ground thudded with their heavy footsteps. Their skin glinted in the night.

"They have such large teeth," Annie added quietly. "Such very large teeth."

"And there are so many," Bloom added, stepping forward.

"You two hide or run for help. I will hold them off. I wish I had my bow . . ."

He unsheathed his dagger and took another step forward almost beyond the town line, but Annie reached forward and grabbed him back. The trolls were hurrying toward them. They carried large clubs made of tree limbs. One carried a pizza box and was eating out of it as he ran.

The troll in the front sniffed the air. "I can smell 'em. Elf and Stopper. Not far. Not far."

"I ain't had elf in years," the one with the pizza said as they thundered closer.

"Ain't none of us have, doofus," said another, " 'cause they're all dead."

A disgusting smell overwhelmed the children as the trolls marched forward. They were maybe two hundred feet away at the most. Repulsed by the stench, Annie clutched Bloom's arm. Jamie's teeth chattered. She used her free hand to grab his fingers and began frantically trying to remember how to stop time. She'd have to focus. She'd have to think really hard. She'd have to say the word, right? Or maybe just draw it on the snow?

A hundred feet.

Troll smell made her gag, but Annie refused to make a sound.

"Be ready," Bloom whispered.

An injured Mr. Alexander was there. So was his mother.

Jamie's knees shook. The trolls' eyes were a sickly green, the color of boogers.

Fifty feet.

Eva snored by the tree.

Twenty-five feet . . . twenty . . . fifteeen . . .

And then just before the town line, the trolls took a sudden right turn. They marched off the road and into the woods as if it were the most normal thing in the world. Tree trunks snapped as they pushed them out of the way. Branches cracked down onto the ground. The trolls tromped through the snow and the underbrush. Nothing stopped them.

"They're heading away," Annie whispered, heart thumping wildly with relief. "They just turned."

"The gnome worked!" Bloom yelled. He whooped and grabbed Annie, spinning her around in the air, ripping her hand free of Jamie's hand as Jamie watched. Bloom noticed and grabbed him in a happy, bouncy hug that seemed very elfish to Annie. "We did it! We really did! I thought we did when the crow vanished but this proves it. The town is safe! It's safe!"

A voice came from behind them.

"For now."

Annie, Jamie, Bloom, and Eva whirled around. Miss Cornelia smiled and opened her arms, and they ran into them, everyone, even Jamie. She hugged them all.

"I told you that you would have to be brave, didn't I?" she asked.

More townspeople were streaming toward their little group. They shook their heads, and bundled their coats around them. A few stared anxiously at the sky, but they were all safe, each and every one of them. Annie wanted to explode from happiness.

"We sort of broke into the mayor's house and stole a police car, and I killed a living creature even if it was a monster, but we *were* brave," she said, focusing on Miss Cornelia's kind, wrinkled face. She'd never seen a face more beautiful or more safe.

"You were very brave, indeed." The old woman released them and waved the rest of the town toward them. "This calls for a celebration! Actually, a double celebration. We have a birthday boy in our midst."

People began cheering their agreement and by the tree, Eva shook herself awake.

"What? What? Did I miss something?" she demanded, adjusting her pigtails and standing up.

"Nothing," Annie said. "Nothing at all, hero dwarf girl."

Eva smiled, picking up her ax.

"Hero dwarf girl," she repeated. "I like the sound of that."

37

A Celebration

The townspeople hoisted Jamie, Bloom, and Annie onto their shoulders and carried them down the road into town. Eva insisted dwarfs were never hoisted nor carried despite the fact that she had just been carried a mere hour or so earlier. Instead, she walked proudly beside her father, who kept punching her in the arm and telling her that she had done a good job and asking her how the skis worked. She beamed.

So did Annie. Her face was lit by torchlight, and she sat up straight and smiling, not at all bothered by the height or even by the attention.

Jamie wondered if he looked the same way. He struggled to find a word to describe how he felt. *Proud? Settled? Happy? Safe?* It was probably a mixture of all four words.

Miss Cornelia insisted that the children change out of their cold, wet clothes and then come back outside for the celebration.

Jamie and Annie rushed up the stairs. The mermen and mermaids in the fountain flapped their tails (even Farkey's pink one) in a salute to their bravery. Several pixies flew about the children's heads shouting "thank you" and trying to plant kisses on their cheeks. Gramma Doris shooed the pixies away and took each child's arm at the top of the winding staircase.

"That's enough. That's enough. Thank you very much. We need to get them out of their wet clothes. You can kiss them at the celebration," she shouted, rolling her eyes and giving Jamie and Annie a conspiratorial wink before muttering, "Pixies. Always kissing."

Annie's room was first, and Gramma Doris hurried her inside. She snapped her fingers, and a pair of polka-dot pants, shirt, and wool sweater with matching polka-dot socks materialized in the air.

"Wow . . . ," Annie stammered at Jamie. "Did you see that? Just . . . wow . . ."

Gramma Doris snapped her fingers again, and the door shut behind Annie, who was still gawking.

"Hurry up out of those wet things!" Gramma Doris called out. "We'll not be losing you to cold after all this."

Then she turned to Jamie and waggled her finger at him,

smiling, "And that goes for you, too. Off you go, young man. To your room."

Jamie trotted after Gramma Doris's rotund form. She was wearing bunny slippers beneath her skirt. They stopped outside his doorway, which had a new flashing sign above it. It said JAMIE'S ROOM!!! in huge fluorescent red letters.

"You like?" she asked, putting her hands on her hips. "I thought your room needed a little more pizzazz."

"Uh-huh," Jamie answered, dumbfounded.

"A little pizzazz works wonders," she added.

Jamie gazed forlornly at the flashing sign. Now that the threat of death was over, the idea that he could still turn into a troll came flooding back. He examined himself in the hallway mirror. *No visible nose hairs. No green skin. No troll signs, so far.*

"Young man?" Gramma Doris gently took him by the shoulders. Her voice was soft. She smelled of cookies. "Jamie? What is it?"

"It's just—ah . . . What if . . . What if I become one of them?"

"A troll, you mean?"

"Y-y-yes."

Her eyes closed a bit as she scanned him up and down. "James Hephaistion Alexander, it is our actions that determine who we are. Not our genes. Not who our parents may or may not be, but our own choices."

She pulled him into a soft hug and then kissed the top of his head. Jamie's hand reached up to touch his hair. Before Aurora, nobody had ever kissed him there before. Actually, his father and grandmother had never kissed him at all. It felt . . . good.

But he had to make sure. "So, I won't be—a-a—"

"A troll?" she finished for him. "We won't know that for sure for a year, Jamie, but I'd say that there is no troll in your heart." She loosened the hug and waved a hand over his chest. "No, no troll in your heart at all. In fact, I'd say you're the least trollish boy I've ever met. Trolls are about greed. They are about taking—not about giving—and you, Jamie Alexander, are the opposite. You understand me?"

Jamie said that he understood even though he wasn't exactly sure he really did.

It was enough to satisfy Gramma Doris. She sent him into his room with a pat on his back and a bunch of warm clothes floating in behind him.

"Get dressed, sweet Jamie. We are in need of a celebration, and you, my dear boy, are one of the guests of honor."

Jamie and Annie met by the fountain, warmly dressed in dry clothes. Annie's heart lifted to see him. Her wispy hair was tied back in a braid. He hadn't been able to do anything with his wet hair. He'd shaken it out in the bathroom, but water still clung to it. So, he took the wool hat that had been floating by his bed, pulled it on, and tried not to worry about looking ridiculous.

"I like your hat," Annie said shyly.

The mermen started singing:

I like your hat
Your hat is phat
Your hat is stylin'
It keeps me smilin'

"Is this the best song you have?" Bloom asked, striding out from the kitchen. He wore a dry dark-green cloak that went down to the knees of his deep-brown pants. He had three buns in his hands, two of which he tossed to Annie and Jamie. "Fresh out of the oven. Try to ignore the mermen. They sing when they are happy. It's ridiculous."

The mermen switched positions in the pool, lined up like chorus girls, and started harmonizing again:

It's ridicu-lous
It's ridicu-wonderous
It's ridicu-glorious
And so . . . ridiculously . . .
Say you'll love me.

"Hurry. The singing will ruin your good mood," Bloom said, shooing them toward the entrance.

The door blew open, and the mayor and Tala hustled inside. "There you are!" The mayor spread his arms wide open, welcoming the children. "Hurry! The entire town is waiting to celebrate our heroes."

The mayor's voice was large and matched his body. Jamie figured only someone as confident as the mayor could live with a monster book in his home. For a second he wondered if the book had calmed down yet. He hoped so.

Despite the fact that Tala had tackled Annie and covered her face with doggy kisses, the mayor managed to hurry them out of Aquarius House and into the garden. It was full of creatures, both human and nonhuman looking. Orbs of light hung from all the trees, which had somehow blossomed into purple and white flowers. Flags depicting moving scenes from the children's adventures floated midair. Small bonfires were set up throughout the yard, and fairies danced around them. Tables lined up in rows. Flowers were strewn on top of the linen, and candelabras lit the table settings. The chairs all moved backward and forward by themselves, and several joined a good ten or so cats that were dancing on their hind legs to fiddling music produced by Mr. Nate and an assorted group of werewolves and owls. Dwarfs and vampires, shifters and hags all laughed together. Several younger vampires morphed into bats and swooped above the tables in a game of tag.

"Oh . . . wow . . . ," Annie breathed out.

"Yes, exactly!" The mayor slapped her on the back so hard that she stumbled forward and Bloom had to catch her by the arm so she didn't fall over. "Wow."

Everyone seemed to notice the children at the same time and turn to stare at them with mouths wide open. An owl hooted. A wolf howled. Applause began to ripple through the crowd until it was suddenly thunderous.

"Our heroes!" a witch cried.

"Brilliant job!" called Ned the Doctor. He dropped his glasses in his excitement. A pixie scooped them up and flew off with them.

"Wait!" Ned yelled. "I need those. Oh, dear . . ."

SalGoud raced after the pixies, trying to retrieve Ned's glasses. It was chaotic and awesome and beautiful. All of it. It was everything Annie had ever dreamed of.

"Hooray for Annie!" a small gray cat yelled. It was definitely the cat that had helped Jamie in the house. It gave him a paw wave. He waved back.

Annie startled. "Cats can talk?"

"Everything can talk inside Aurora," Bloom explained. "Sort of . . . Well, sometimes . . . I guess that's not completely true . . . Um . . . yeah . . . It's complicated."

People had started to chant her name. Annie shook her head and cupped her hands. "Hooray for Jamie!" she corrected. "And Bloom and Eva!"

Megan, the cranky blond hag with the questionable predictions, sauntered closer to them, arms crossed over her chest. "That's too many to yell."

"Well, I'm not the only hero," Annie said.

Megan stuck up her chin. "Obviously."

The tension was eased by several pixies hovering over the mayor's head and rapidly blinking their eyelashes. "Mayor! Mayor! Speech!"

Bloom motioned for Annie and Jamie, and they sat at a table beneath a weeping willow tree. Huge light orbs swirled and lit the silverware. Annie's seat moved her closer to the table, which was heaped with all sorts of food and treats. She still had the roll from Bloom. She bit into it and gave a piece to Tala, who wagged his whole body in a happy wiggling motion.

The mayor hopped up onto a table, which made him even taller than normal. The hags sitting there had to adjust their hats and crane their heads to see him.

"We are saved!" he yelled happily. "And it is because of our youth that we are here tonight, and the fine magic of Miss Cornelia. Please, Corny, take a bow."

Miss Cornelia moved out from the shadows under a tree and bowed somewhat stiffly. She caught Annie's gaze and then Jamie's, giving them both a sweet smile.

"And I must say, Gramma Doris and Helena have outdone themselves with the fine pies of happiness and tarts of joy. Hopefully, you have all availed yourself of the deliciousness before the main course . . ."

Bloom and Jamie were digging in. Annie hadn't finished her roll. A pixie whizzed by her ear and settled on her shoulder. "Annie, the mayor goes on and on. You should eat."

Jamie gave her a thumbs-up. "It's super good."

"Now," the mayor continued as Miss Cornelia made her way to Jamie's table. "This town has been under a threat the likes of which we haven't seen for a good ten years, and the theft of the gnome and the invasion by the crow monster is likely to be only the first attempt to end us."

The crowd moaned.

"But the Raiff and his forces of darkness shall not prevail. Not now. Not ever. For we have not one but two Stoppers!"

The massive noise of cheers shook the trees and tables. Hooves and paws and feet stomped on the ground. Glasses clinked and forks rattled against plates.

"Not like Miss Cornelia is getting any stronger or Annie has any clue what she's doing, but oh yes, let's cheer," Megan snarked.

Eva growled at her.

The mayor's chest puffed up and his face turned red. "Aurora shall never fall. Never."

"Never!" a dwarf yelled.

The crowd began to chant it. "Nev-er. Nev-er. Nev-er."

Jamie joined in. Everyone did except Annie, who seemed to be turning whiter than normal.

"Annie?" he whispered. "What is it?"

She leaned toward him. "It's nothing. It's just . . . It's a lot of responsibility, isn't it? Being a Stopper."

"I'm not sure," he said after a moment, "but I think so."

Her mouth tucked itself into a thin line. "Yeah, that's what I thought."

He could feel her worry that she wouldn't be good enough, that she'd fail them. He knew how that felt. He nudged her. "You'll be amazing."

She slowly glanced up at him. "You think so?"

"I know it."

A smile spread across her face. "You know, you were so worried before . . . about your life being pointless. Do you still feel that now? Like you don't have a purpose? Because I think you do."

"You do?" His hip bumped into hers. She bumped back.

"Yeah. I think one of them is to be the best person you can possibly be. That's sort of everyone's purpose in life. But another is to be here, to have saved Aurora."

"How about being your friend?" he asked.

"That, too." She laced her fingers between his. "Definitely. And part of my purpose is to be *your* friend and help find you sugar when you get hungry."

He laughed. "Best friend ever."

The magical sky seemed to bounce with lights and flags and pixies. Jamie relaxed into his chair. The mayor finally got the crowd to calm down.

"My own special personal thanks go out to Miss Eva, whose dwarfy resourcefulness and willingness to steal her father's skis was instrumental in our rescue," the mayor nodded toward Eva, who promptly raised her arms above her head and did a victory lap around the garden.

Once she settled back in her seat and the cheers died down, the mayor continued, "And thanks go to Bloom, the last elf, whose bravery and willingness to sacrifice his own life for the success of the mission proves that he is an elf to the core."

People hooted and screamed their praise. Bloom turned a bit red and gave a jaunty wave.

"To Annie, our Time Stopper . . ." The mayor blew a kiss at her.

Annie sunk so low in the chair that she almost slid out of it. The chair bounced her back up. She gave up trying to hide and covered her head with her hands.

"Your magic is our future, our promise, and our salvation. May your heart always want to see the good in even the most evil of souls."

The crowd went wild. Streamers fell from the sky. Balloons popped and reinflated. The trees seemed to sing out their praises. The mayor hopped off the table, his speech finished.

Annie leaned over to Bloom. "What about Jamie?"

Jamie sat there, smiling and applauding and chewing.

Bloom made big eyes. The mayor hadn't mentioned Jamie.

Miss Cornelia glided to the center of the room, lifting up into the air just slightly. She seemed to glow as her rainbow skirts swirled about her ankles.

The crowd silenced.

"And last and never least," she said, shooting the mayor a stern frown, "to Jamie, who faced his biggest fears to save us, and faced them well. Using his wits and bravery, he brought us all our gnome."

She gently motioned for Jamie to stand up. He swallowed hard and did so. There was a smudge of cinnamon sugar on his cheek.

"To James Hephaistion Alexander, who proves without a doubt that worth does not come from the magic in your blood, but from the kindness in your heart. HAPPY BIRTHDAY!" She coughed and checked the position of the moon high in the sky. "Or Happy Twelve Minutes after Your Birthday to be exact!"

The crowd exploded with applause once again, and Bloom playfully reached over Annie to punch Jamie in the shoulder. Annie clapped and beamed at him. Jamie turned a deep shade of red, much worse than Bloom's. A gang of vampires swooped in and bounced him up onto their shoulders, lofting him into the air and swirling around the garden with him as people cheered and threw the confetti that magically appeared in their hands. Fireworks spelling out *HAPPY BIRTHDAY, JAMIE!* filled the sky with golden sparks.

"Ja-mie!" people shouted. "Ja-mie!"

Annie and Bloom and Eva were the loudest shouters of all. Mr. Nate gave him two huge thumbs-up, and Jamie forgot for a moment what it had been like to have been scared, hungry, and unloved. Instead, he finally knew what it was like to belong.

"This is our home now, Annie," he said as Eva caught them up in a bouncing group hug. "You finally have a home."

She laughed, joyous finally. Her face glowed with happiness.

"Yes," she said as Eva accidentally stomped on her foot, "we finally do!"

Much later, when the children were all tucked into bed, after Eva was grounded again (this time for dunking Megan's face into a vat of Happy-Birthday-Hero juice) and Bloom was safely perched inside his tree home, after Jamie's stomach was finally full, and Annie's heart was finally feeling like she had a home, was when they came for Miss Cornelia.

As silent as the pause between heartbeats, someone stepped from behind the front door of Aquarius House into the darkness of the foyer as she passed by, grabbing her by the hands and lifting her into the air before tossing a Sleep-Till-I-Say-So potion into her startled eyes. She slumped against him as he kicked open the front door, hoisting her still body atop the horse, the same horse the children had seen earlier that day, riding through the barrens. The Each Uisge huffed, and the rider hopped on behind Cornelia.

He spoke into the darkness of the night, "I bring her to you, sir." Then he held on as the horse broke into a run.

And from a mirror, and then a window, the Raiff's image watched as Miss Cornelia was whisked away. Sometimes even a demon can't help but smile. The glass of the window cracked. The mirror clouded. But only Annie Nobody stirred in her bed. The rest of Aurora slept on, oblivious to the fact that the woman who had spent the last few decades keeping them safe had been taken from them and it would be almost impossible for any of them to ever be safe again.

Acknowledgments

To Emily Ciciotte, the coolest daughter ever. Without Emily's insistence on "five more pages," this story would never have been thought of (or written) during our long car rides and boring afternoons. Thank you, glorious Emily the Greatest, for making me a grown-up writer for children, instead of a newspaper person forever. **Caution: do not try to write and drive at the same time.**

I know that there is a belief that acknowledgments are rather "uncool," but I can't think of how not to publicly thank some of the kind and lovely people who got me through this book process. *Time Stoppers* is not my first published book, but it's the one that I wrote first and revised a million times. It means a lot to me—and the people who supported me as

I wrote it? Well, they mean a lot to me, too. **Warning: revising a book a million times is dangerous work and hard on your typing fingers, but your teachers at Vermont College of Fine Arts will expect it of you.**

So, here is everyone's much-deserved public thank-you!

Thank you to my Agent of Awesome, Edward Necarsulmer IV, who works so hard for other people's glory and recognition while expecting so little in return. Everyone should have an agent of awesome who is full of kindness and humor and goodness. **Caution: not all agents are agents of awesome.**

There is no greater editor than Cindy Loh. She makes okay books into great books, and she is brilliant and funny and everything good. It seems unfair that one human being can be so exquisitely talented. **Warning: amazing editors make you spoiled.**

Many thanks to the amazing team at Bloomsbury for all their passion and intelligence. I have never met so many people who try so hard to make amazing books for kids. Many thanks to Donna Mark, John Candell, and Owen Richardson, who made this into such a beautiful book. Hali Baumstein and Brett Wright, Linda Minton, Patricia McHugh, Ilana Worrell, and Melissa Kavonic, the managing editor. They all are unsung heroes. As are Cristina Gilbert, Lizzy Mason, Courtney Griffin in publicity as well as Erica Barmash, Emily Ritter, Eshani Agrawal, Shae McDaniel, Beth Eller, Linette Kim, Ashley Poston, and Alona Fryman in marketing. **Caution: Do not get spoiled if you have an astonishing publishing team. Not all teams are this awesome or have sock puppets.**

Many thanks to the real Mount Desert Police Department and their chief, Jim Willis, for allowing me to be a dispatcher and help them save people, as well as inspiring portions of this story. They are much better police officers and dispatchers than the ones in this book! **Caution: um . . . don't be a criminal on Mount Desert Island.**

Many thanks to the People of Mike and Lynne and Grayson Staggs' house, who inspired joy and story in me almost every Wednesday night, with special thanks to Samantha Spellacy and Nate Light, Jon and Sarah Day Levesque, Joe Pagan, Nicole Ouellette, John Bench, and Stuart West. It is always good to have friends to make you laugh, and therefore many thanks to Steve and Jenna Boucher, Lori Bartlett, Sherri Dyer, Susy Davis, Richard Cleary, Elsie Flemings, Annette Higgins, Dwight Swanson, and the marvelous Marie Overlock. **Warning: when you think about how lucky you are to have such awesome friends, you may cry.**

Many thanks to my brother, Bruce, who somehow always manages to be proud of me. It's good to have someone like that. **Caution: My brother is amazing, and a long hugger. Be prepared if you hug him.**

So much thanks for the lovely people who read my books! I don't want to call you guys "fans," because it doesn't really fit. I think of you more as super-cool friends who I don't usually see in real life. But thank you to the readers, librarians, teachers, writers, kids, and other humans. I still can't quite believe how awesome you are and that you read my books and support them. It means everything to me. **Warning: Sometimes other people's kindness can make you cry. Not that I'm crying right now or anything . . . cough . . . cough . . . ahem.**

And finally, many thanks to Shaun Farrar, who somehow always manages to love me. It's good to have someone like that, too. I am terribly, terribly lucky to have him to slay all my dragons and demons. **Warning: Six-foot-six warrior-knights are pretty awesome and will spoil you and make you feel loved. Also, they are hard to pick up and carry. Believe me, I've tried.**